THE

MYSTERY

BOX

Eva Pohler

Green Press

This book is a work of fiction. The characters, happenings, and dialogue came from the author's imagination and are not real.

FIRST EDITION

Library of Congress Cataloging-in-Publication has been applied for

ISBN -13: 978-0615686479
ISBN-10: 0615686478

Chapter One: A Box

Yvette pulls into the driveway to find her husband standing in the front yard in the rain, in his t-shirt and shorts, soaked. She parks in the garage and rushes through the house and out the front door, popping open her umbrella. "Devin?"

"What in the hell is that?" he asks, pointing.

She follows his finger. Where the lawn is usually flat, there's a hill. It swells, as though some living thing beneath gestates, about to be born.

Having just returned from frantically herding her children off to school with their loose papers flapping, she should be alarmed by the swelling mound, but she's giddy. She touches her husband's arm. The strong muscles surprise her. They've always been there, of course.

Of course.

She's wanted to get out of this rut, this monotonous loading and unloading of dishes and laundry and kids and groceries. Like a hamster in its wheel, she's gone round and round, teaching the same class each semester online, washing the same dishes over and over, forever and ever without end. Wasn't she made for more than this? And now, her front yard mysteriously bulges, as if in answer to her prayers. Her yard is giving birth to what? Some monstrosity, most likely. Be careful what you wish for, they say with good reason. She's wanted a change, a shift in her universe, and here it is, ready or not.

Before Yvette says a word, the hill explodes, and water shoots up from the ground. It reaches twenty feet in the air against the pouring rain and turns the yard into a swampland.

"Great," says Devin. "We have a geyser in our yard."

"What do we do?" The air feels fresh as she breathes it in. She wants to drop her umbrella and turn a cartwheel.

Woo-hoo-hoo!

Devin says, "If you need any water, better get it."

Yvette runs inside, giggling, slipping in her wet flip-flops, and fills two pitchers with water, one for hand washing and the other for drinking. She peers out the kitchen window to see Devin falling in the mud and is overcome with laughter. Devin is cursing. He kneels at the cut-off and twists, but nothing changes. The geyser continues to spray.

She covers her mouth and wonders. This is it. She can feel it. Her life is about to change, and there's nothing she can do to stop it.

Yvette meets the workers in front, no longer delirious. It didn't take long to stifle the giggles: a load of laundry, a load of dishes, and solving the problem of what to cook for dinner without having to go to the store buried them. Plus, there was that sobering omen that something else was about to happen.

The rain pounds against the roof, the trees, and the sidewalk, beating out a rock concert.

Ta-ta-ta-ta-ta-ta-ta-ta-ta-ta-ta-ta-ta.

She has to shout hello to be heard from beneath her umbrella.

"We got to dig up the pipe, weld in a replacement part," the foreman says.

"Is our tree in danger?"

"It's planted on city easement, so there's no guarantee."

Yvette frowns. She and Devin planted the young live oak together last year. "I understand. But you'll do your best?"

He nods. "We'll come back next week and lay new sod."

She cringes as a worker drives a bobcat onto the yard and digs its teeth through the turf. The machine creaks and moans, like a monster lamenting its dead child. It scratches at the ground and digs a hole the size of a human grave.

Yvette sits at her computer, slumped like a semicolon, grading compositions for her online class, correcting the same errors she has been correcting for centuries, when the city workers leave. She knows they have left because Mr. Frodo Baggins, her beloved Jack Russell, stops whining and pacing like an expectant father and settles at her feet beneath the desk. The rock concert has ended, so she steps out the door with Frodo to inspect the gaping hole and to mourn what was once a beautiful yard.

She walks past a UPS box left on her front porch—probably fishing or golf supplies for Devin—to inspect the young live oak, perched on the edge of the grave, its roots exposed. Beside the tree and also exposed is Tommy's hamster skeleton in its shoe box. She recalls the way it used to spin in its wheel, round and round, going nowhere.

Tizzle-tizzle-tizzle-tizzle-tizzle.

She steps out of her flip-flops and into the squishy mud for the lid. She picks up clumps, like a child making mud pies, to reinter the tomb so the kids won't see it. Then she squats beside the tree and covers its roots, tucking them in beneath a blanket, hoping, like a new mother, it will thrive.

While she washes off at the hose, a neighbor drives up to ask what happened, and Yvette tells the story about the pipe bursting and the sod coming next week, and ten minutes later, returns inside with the UPS box from the porch.

She sets it on the counter and studies it. It isn't heavy—about two feet wide, a foot deep, and a foot high.

She finds her own address on the mailing label, but above it is a name she doesn't recognize: Mona Smith.

Her mind searches, like a computer data base. Mona Smith?

Nothing comes up. There's no match.

She calls UPS, and the man on the phone says it's been delivered to the correct address.

"But there's no Mona Smith at this residence."

"Sorry, ma'am. I'll call the sender and get back with you."

The red light on her answering machine blinks like a broken traffic light. Someone must have called while she was out front.

She presses the button: "What do I have to do to get you to shut up your dog? Make him stop or I will!"

Her again.

Yvette fights the urge to run to the backyard and scream over the fence. She can't return the call, because the caller ID is blocked, and she doesn't know the woman's name to look her up. Good thing too, because Yvette wants to let her know exactly what she thinks of her. She'll write her a letter, that's what she'll do. She'll say quit screaming at my kids over the fence and leaving threatening messages on the phone. She'll say we made Frodo an indoor dog because of you, even though Devin never wanted an indoor dog.

She'll ask why she moved into a house surrounded by yard dogs if she hates them so much.

Never to her face, Yvette and the kids call her Cruella, and sometimes Witchy Woman, but in her letter, Yvette addresses her as "Dear Neighbor."

Despite her best efforts to write what's on her mind, Yvette writes her apologies. She will try harder to keep Frodo inside and quiet. Today was more difficult than usual because of the city workers. Blah, blah, blah, and grovel, grovel, grovel. Yvette sighs. She has no backbone.

No backbone.

Her mother would have stood up to Cruella, her petite frame and hands no indication of the fire she carried around in her belly, able to burst through her mouth in flames at a moment's notice. Yvette remembers her mother making homemade cookies for the whole block of kids that always came to Yvette's to play because her mother was the only one who'd allow it. But Yvette also remembers the sharp tongue and quick-temper that kept the neighborhood kids in line and the adults in reverence of her mother's authority. Surrounded by neighborhood kids and her mother's book club and pinochle group, Yvette still felt disconnected from the machine that was her mother.

Before Yvette drives the letter around the block, the phone rings, and UPS tells her the sender confirmed the box has been sent to the correct address.

She hangs up the phone, bewildered. It is time to open the box.

Inside, she finds an infant's dress, a pacifier, and shoes and socks. She wonders if the items were meant for a new mother, and her mind wanders to her own children and their infancies. Matt became a teenager last May, and, next October, Casey, her youngest, will be double digits, too. It's gone by so fast.

She runs a hand through her hair, aware again of the gray roots.

Too fast. I'm forty-five. Soon I'll be an old woman.

She blinks back tears as she holds up the yellow dress. What a sweet thing. Some poor mother must be expecting this gift, and here it is, at the wrong house. Maybe Gloria or Heidi knows of a Mona Smith in the neighborhood. Rummaging through the Styrofoam pills, she finds a card, and on this card is the correct address. It's the street right behind hers.

Relieved, Yvette packs the baby items into a gift bag to make them easier to carry, goes to the van, and drives around the block. Maybe she'll get to hold the new baby over tea. She loves holding those sweet, precious little bodies. How she misses the way her own babies would snuggle in the curve of her neck.

Mamama, they called me. Even Casey.

She squints to read the numbers on the mailboxes. Suzanne Kelley waves from her driveway on the corner where she washes her third new vehicle in two years. Yvette waves back, wishing she looked as good as her neighbor. Summer's around the corner. Her daily walks aren't enough anymore.

Time to get back to the gym. And to the hair salon.

A few of the mailboxes don't display the addresses, and shrubs and mature trees block some of the numbers mounted on the homes. No, this is the even side; here are the odds. How is an ambulance supposed to find an address if she can't? Ooh, she notices a new fountain at a two-story ranch, where the slanted siding from the eighties has been replaced with horizontal cedar. Maybe she should consider a fountain in front. Now that they have the huge hole, why lay sod? Just hook up one of those long, flowing waterfalls and fill it in with river rock.

Yeah, right. Devin would never go for that. Too much maintenance.

She stops at the house with the address from the card and blinks. This can't be right. It's the house right behind hers. She points an air conditioning vent at her face as she breaks out in a sweat.

The box belongs to Cruella? To the Witchy Woman? The Wicked Witch of the West?

She drives away, a coward, to practice what she'll say.

Mr. Baggins waits for her, tail wagging, at the door from the garage to the laundry room.

"Now what am I going to do?" she asks him.

Why she should feel guilty for having a box that belongs to someone else is beyond her comprehension. It's not like she's stolen it. She called UPS. Maybe she should keep it. Boxes get lost in the mail all the time.

Frodo brushes his front paws against her shins as she makes her way into the house. "Okay, boy. I know what you want. Just a minute." She finds her Ipod from where it has been charging on her bookshelf, gets his leash from the hook, and grabs three plastic grocery bags and wads them up in her left fist. "Let's go, Frodo Baggins."

While they walk around the block, Yvette listens to *The Girl with the Dragon Tattoo*, by Stieg Larsson, which, once she got past the tedious descriptions of the Swedish financial scene, became so compelling that she has put off grading papers until the last minute, as usual. She's near the end. Almost there.

Listening to audiobooks is a relatively new experience for Yvette. What started as a habit meant only for walks and her exercise bike has become an obsession. Had she not been grading online essays today, Yvette would have been listening to the audiobook as the workers fixed the geyser, as she washed and loaded dishes into the dishwasher, and while she folded the unending piles of laundry. Her switch to audiobooks was meant to elicit more physical activity—she could do two things at once, read and exercise—but it quickly infiltrated her everyday activities so that soon she was driving her kids to and from school, making trips to the bank and the grocery store, and falling asleep at night with at least one earbud stuffed into the side of her head. Once a story took possession of her, all she could do was listen. She had no choice.

So enthralled is Yvette by the narrator of *The Girl with the Dragon Tattoo* that she forgets the reason she has taken this route in the first place: to scope out Cruella's house. If Frodo Baggins hadn't chosen the corner of Cruella's patchy lawn to drop his business, she would have walked on by. After she bends over with her plastic bag cupped around her hand like a mitten to clean up, she glances at the front windows. A curtain moves, but she cannot tell if she's been noticed. Even though she has left no trace behind, she worries Cruella will be upset if she knows a dog has done his deed here. But how can she be upset? It's not like she has any grass to speak of. Yvette flicks away the guilt and worry, glad her little Frodo has shit in the devil's yard.

Ah, hell. She should deliver the box. And she will, after the kids are home.

After picking up the kids from school and feeding them a snack, Yvette steps up to the Witchy Woman's house and rings the bell, her nerves twitching. A woman opens the grimy front door and pokes her head out.

Her red frizzy hair dances in all directions, as if it hasn't seen a brush in days. She's shorter than Yvette, even as she slouches on the stoop of her doorstep, and thin—too thin. Her ratty pink robe is secured at the waist, her hands hiding in the front pockets. Her dingy socks hang loose around bony legs and ankles.

"Mona?" asks Yvette.

The door slams in her face. She hears a rustle as the woman latches the chain. The door cracks open and two beady eyes peer out. "How did you find me?"

Yvette steps back, startled.

"How did you find me?" Mona repeats. "Who you are you?"

"I'm your neighbor from behind the fence," Yvette stammers, holding up the hot pink gift bag. "I think this is yours."

"Leave it on the porch and go away."

Well, damn.

Yvette puts down the bag, gently, as if it were a baby, and stumbles from the porch to her van. Before she turns the ignition, she sits for a minute to catch her breath.

She glances at the crazy woman, who is stooped over the bag with a look of utter shock. Yvette freezes as she meets her eyes, her neighbor's eyebrows disappearing in the mat of frizz surrounding her face.

In her dingy socks with her hair flying, she dashes across her front lawn to peer at Yvette through her van window. "Where did you get these?"

Yvette doesn't know whether to answer or drive away.

"It was you, then!" Mona cries.

Through the window pane, Yvette calls, "UPS dropped them off. I have no idea what you're talking about."

Mona narrows her eyes.

"I can bring you the box," Yvette adds. "For proof."

"Do that. And hurry back."

Like hell.

Yvette hopes to never see the witch again. She probably practices black magic and kills small dogs for her evil spells. The poor kids haven't been able to play in their own backyard with Frodo Baggins since Cruella moved in a year ago.

It's the fear she will do something to Mr. Baggins that makes Yvette return with the box.

But first she finds Devin, who's out front adding dirt with a shovel to the base of their tree. "I'm not sure it's going to make it."

She tells him what's happened. "Please come with me."

Devin holds up his dirty hands. "I'm not getting in the car with all this crap on me."

"Please," says Yvette. "She's deranged. We could walk around the block."

"It can't be that bad." Devin wipes the palms of his hands against his pockets. "What is it you always tell Casey? You're a strong, independent woman."

"Young woman," Yvette corrects. "I say strong, independent *young* woman."

Young! She runs her fingers through her gray roots.

He winks and returns to the dirt.

Obviously Yvette wasn't able to convey the extent of this woman's craziness. She expected her to be grateful, not this. She plays it over in her head as she returns to the house for the box full of Styrofoam. Yvette will remind Mona she didn't have to bring the things over. She called UPS. It's not her job to deliver their damn packages.

With slow strides like a mud wrestler, she steps over mounds of dirty laundry in the washroom on her way to the garage, loads the box into the van, and drives around the block. She can always use her cell to call 9-1-1 if things get out of hand.

Quit being so melodramatic, Yvette.

When she pulls up to the curb, Mona isn't waiting for her in the yard. Yvette grabs the box and tip-toes to the door thinking she'll leave the box and ding-dong-ditch her neighbor. But Mona answers too quickly for Yvette to make her escape, and she appears entirely different.

Shee-iiit. How did she do that so fast?

Mona's hair is wet and pulled back in a tight knot at the back of her head. Her face has been washed and powdered, and she's dressed in a cream button-down blouse with a collar and baggy tan pants. Brown flats barely show beneath the hem.

"Forgive me for snapping at you," Mona says. "You can't imagine what a shock that was."

Yvette can think of nothing to say.

"Yvette, is it?"

She nods.

"I'm so sorry. I was sound asleep when you rang and was having the strangest dream. I don't sleep well at night."

"I'm sorry I woke you."

"No. I'm sorry. Truly." She clears her throat. "And tell me, how is it you came to learn my name?"

"It's on the box." Yvette holds the label in Mona's direction. "With my address. UPS told me there was no mistake, so I opened it. That's when I found the card inside with your address along with the baby dress and shoes and things. Are they for your baby?"

Yvette hears a shuffle behind the woman, but when she peeks inside, Mona steps onto the porch and pulls the door shut.

"Excuse me for not inviting you in. The house is a mess."

"Don't worry about it." Yvette glances at a front window in time to see a curtain move. "Do you live alone?"

"Yes. It's just me."

I saw someone, you liar.

No baby? "Oh, I thought I saw—"

"May I have the box?"

"Um, of course." Yvette hands it over.

Before Yvette lets go of the box, Mona covers her hands firmly with her own. "Yvette, I need to ask you a favor. Please don't tell another soul the name you found on this box or the items you discovered inside."

What the?

"I—" Yvette stammers, frozen like the squirrels Mr. Baggins teases. "Is Mona not your name?"

"Come again tomorrow and I'll tell you the story. Are you free around four?" The woman's cold hands chill Yvette.

"I suppose—"

"Tomorrow then," Mona says, turning away. "I'm looking forward to it."

As she walks to her van, Yvette wonders why she didn't tell Mona not to worry, her secret was safe, even without explanation. Why didn't she say no thanks, it's okay, have a good life? She couldn't afford to go and listen to this woman's story with piles of laundry waiting to be washed and an inbox full of ungraded papers. One thing's for sure, she won't be going back.

Yvette takes Frodo Baggins with her to the backyard to water her vines while the spaghetti boils. Her vines have a way of calming her nerves and cheering her up.

You're so lovely.

She weaves a new branch of Confederate Star Jasmine around trellis she has staked near the fence when Mr. Baggins barks in the direction of Mona's house.

She peers through the slits of the fence and sees someone staring at her between the slats. She pops back.

Shit!

Once her nerves settle, she peeks through the slits again and sees the person, who looks nothing like Mona with cropped dark hair and a baseball cap pulled over dark eyes, rush into the house.

You liar.

Hired help to mow the dead grass? A boyfriend? Whoever he or she is has been staring at Yvette, for how long?

Casey opens the back door. "Don't we have Girl Scouts tonight?"

"Not 'til after spring break." Yvette walks inside and gives Casey a kiss. "Homework done?"

"I told Erica tonight."

"Better call her, then, sweetie pie. Inside, Frodo!"

Yvette drains the noodles as Matt comes in, dropped off by a friend.

"How was robotics?" Yvette asks.

Matt heaps his backpack on the kitchen table. "Good, but I need a battery cell, copper wire, and reflector tape for a project due tomorrow."

Not again. Why do her kids always wait till the last minute?

"Doesn't Tommy have a pack meeting tonight?" Casey asks.

"What time is it?" Yvette has forgotten the meeting was moved up a week because of spring break.

"Six o'clock."

Yvette hustles to Tommy's room. "Throw on your Cub Scout uniform. We've got to go!"

Tommy looks up from his video game. "I'm starving."

"Eat a piece of bread and cheese on the way. We're already late."

Matt puts his hands on Yvette's shoulders. "Mom. This is important. I need—"

"Tell Dad. I've gotta go. The whole pack's depending on me for the Webelos report."

"Tell Dad what?" Devin asks from the laundry room, where he strips out of his dirty clothes.

"Matt needs stuff from Home Depot." Yvette rushes into the garage with Tommy in tow.

Tizzle-tizzle-tizzle-tizzle.

Devin wraps himself in a dirty towel from the pile and follows Yvette to the garage. "I've got a conference call in twenty minutes. I can't go to Home Depot."

"I'll call Matt from the pack meeting."

Casey pokes her head into the garage to say something as Devin disappears into the house, but Yvette is already backing out and waving goodbye. Then she stops, rolls down the window, and shouts, "Tell Daddy to turn off the broccoli! It's probably burned!"

Casey shouts something back, maybe that the kitchen cabinets are on fire, but Yvette backs out onto the road and drives off.

The next day, after she picks up the kids from school, feeds them a snack, and gets them started on their homework, Yvette is watering her vines, having just finished *The Girl with the Dragon Tattoo*, and feeling bereft of the company of characters who had become like family to her, when, once again, Frodo barks toward the fence. She peeks through the slats to see Mona standing on the opposite side with her face pressed against the wood.

"Hi Yvette," she says.

Holy shit. "Frodo, stop that!"

"He sure is rambunctious."

"Inside, Frodo!" Yvette opens the back door and closes it behind him. "Sorry about that."

"He's protecting his family."

"That's right. He doesn't know you."

"You should bring him over one day."

Yvette resists a chuckle. Cruella and Mr. Frodo Baggins in the same house? "Maybe so."

"I've brewed fresh tea and baked a batch of cookies for our visit. Been looking forward to it all day."

Hell. Yvette doesn't know what to say.

"Still coming at four, aren't you?" asks Mona.

"I'll be there."

No backbone.

Yvette decides to walk around the block to Mona's. Their homes are both in the middle of a long block, so when she rounds the corner she still has six houses to go. She admires the homes as she passes them, even though she has walked this route with Frodo many times. She appreciates how each home is unique—unlike the newer tract homes these days—and each garden well cared for, until she reaches the patch of dirt sprinkled with dead grass that belongs to Mona.

Mona waits on the porch of one of the smaller one-story homes on the block, the front door propped open against the peeling wooden siding with a box. More boxes are stacked behind it in the living room, where Mona leads Yvette to a grouping of two wooden chairs. The musty odor of dust, dirty dishwater, and mold lingers in the air. Yvette fights off pinching her nose.

She hears a clap in one of the back rooms down the hall.

"Babs, my cat," Mona explains with a forced, suspicious smile. She scoots the box away from the door and closes it, latching the chain. "Please sit down. May I get you iced tea and a plate of cookies?"

"Sure. Thanks."

"Sweet or unsweet?"

"Unsweet, please."

Mona leaves the room.

Cat hair on the stained carpeting confirms Mona does own a cat even if it isn't responsible for the sound in the back bedroom. The brick fireplace on the wall toward Yvette's house is barely visible behind two stacks of cardboard boxes sealed with packing tape. A window and a

French door on either side of the fireplace are blocked by tightly closed and dusty mini-blinds. Otherwise the room is empty.

Like an old, haunted house.

"Moving?" Yvette asks when Mona returns with the glass and plate. She takes them and realizes there is no place to put them down, so she balances the plate on her lap. "Thanks."

Mona sits in the other chair and soon a gray cat with one eye hops in from out of nowhere and onto Mona's lap. Mona strokes it tenderly. "Yes, though, I must admit, these particular boxes were never unpacked."

Thought so.

Layers of dust have collected on them, but it seems odd a person would live in a house for a year and have unopened boxes.

"When do you leave?" She is pleased about the impending move. Frodo Baggins can finally reclaim his yard.

"In a week or two." Mona strokes the cat but studies Yvette. "How's the tea?"

It's obvious she hasn't tasted it, for the glass is still full, but under the pressure of Mona's gaze, she puts it to her lips and takes the smallest sip so the poison won't kill her, if it is poisoned, or, just as bad, full of filthy bacteria from a dirty sink. "Good. Thanks."

"Try my cookies."

She takes a tiny bite. "Mm. Delicious. Thank you."

Stale, store-bought.

"I'm glad you like them. It's the least I can do after asking you to come and hear a lonely woman tell her sad story."

"I don't mind."

No backbone.

"But you have to promise not to tell a soul, not even your husband, until the time is right."

"I promise."

"I need you to take this seriously," Mona warns. "You can't talk about this until after I've gone."

"Not even then."

"Thank you, Yvette. This means so much to me. I will forever be in your debt."

"I'm glad to help."

Mona looks down at Babs. "I started school late. My parents held me back twice because I was small and sick as a child, so by the time I entered college, I was twenty. That doesn't mean I was any more mature than the other students, though. Stupid, stupid girl, I was. Most are, you know. You better watch out for your daughter. Casey, isn't it?"

Yvette wonders how Mona knows her daughter's name. It freaks her out.

22

"I hear your children in the yard," Mona explains. "You have three or four, don't you?"

"Three."

"Three. That's what I thought. Well, my story starts in college. Ten years ago."

Yvette studies Mona's sallow face. The deep lines around her beady eyes and thin mouth make her seem so much older than thirty years.

Liar.

"I know I haven't aged gracefully, but are you really shocked?"

"No. I—"

"Once you hear my story, you'll understand. My fiancé, Bijan, and I were at the Christmas Ball at the University of Texas at Brownsville, where we were both students, when my life changed."

Before Yvette says anything, Mona adds, "No, this is not a love story, though that's how it starts." She puts her face in her hands above Babs's back, like she is going to cry but doesn't. "Oh, if only we could turn back the clock. It's stupid to waste time on regret, so let me move on. I need to tell you all the details, because only after you've heard them will you be able to understand why I had to do what I did."

Chapter Two: The Taliban Spy's Lover

Bijan and I were dancing, he in a tux and I in my only formal gown, pale blue chiffon, when I sensed the Taliban Spy's Lover watching me from the balcony above us, a solo and intimidating dark figure in a black tux against a backdrop of white ornate walls and marble columns.

The Taliban Spy's Lover. That's what Bijan called him. Apparently, that's what everyone called him. He stood on the balcony above us gazing down, and his piercing dark eyes unnerved me. He was too far away for me to make out their color, but close enough for me to see they were trained on me. I led Bijan back to our table and begged him to tell me what he knew of the man.

"I'll get us drinks first," he said. "Dancing dehydrates me." He gave me his irresistible wink, and before I could stop him, he left our table.

I glanced at the man on the balcony. To my astonishment, he saluted me, like an American soldier. I scanned the room to see if the gesture was meant for someone else, but no one turned in his direction. When I glanced back up, he was gone.

After Bijan returned with our drinks and took his seat across from me, the Taliban Spy's Lover appeared out of nowhere beside our table, causing Bijan to spill a drop of

24

his red wine on the white table cloth. I saw then the man's eyes were hazel, his mouth thin and his jaw square. He was taller than I initially thought and built across the chest.

"Excuse me," said the man to Bijan. "I didn't mean to startle you, but I couldn't help admiring your companion and wished to introduce myself." He held his hand out to Bijan. "I am Professor Ahmed Jaffar." He spoke with an accent in a way that was stiff and formal and awkward, unlike his body, which was smooth and sexy.

Bijan introduced us, and when I gave the professor my hand, he held on to it for a moment, like a jeweler inspecting the stone on my engagement ring, except I had given him my right hand, and it bore no ring. I pulled away, blushing, because I had bitten my cuticles down to raw skin during final exams.

Plus, his hand was warm and had given me an unexpected thrill.

Unlike Bijan, who was beautiful with his short thick hair, full lips, and boyish grin, the professor was strikingly serious with a sharp nose and high cheek bones, serious in spite of his tight tux and hair feathered back like they did in the seventies. He was young, early thirties. I was relieved when he left us.

Bijan was born in Iran, and I suppose I had a thing for Middle Eastern men, their dark eyes and sexy accents and thick, black hair.

I begged Bijan to tell me what he knew of the professor.

"Well, he's Pakistani, I think. A philosophy professor. He disappeared last year after nine-eleven. This is the first I've seen of him in over a year."

"He hasn't been teaching?"

"No. And they say he was dating a student, a woman from Afghanistan, believed to be a Taliban spy." He took a sip of wine.

I rolled my eyes, disappointed. "The Taliban doesn't use women. The school in Kabul was only recently reopened after the Taliban closed it. They wouldn't have a woman spy."

"But he disappeared in October right after nine-eleven. Everyone said he'd been detained for questioning. The Afghan disappeared at the same time. Her name was Fatima, but that's all anyone knew of her."

"Hardly enough to accuse someone of being a spy."

"So you see? Just silly rumors. Everyone's suspicious of us these days." I knew by "us" he meant people from the Middle East. He leaned over and touched his sweet lips to mine.

Petulantly, I frowned. "Is there nothing else?"

"Forget about him." He kissed me again. "He's nothing to us."

But thoughts of Professor Jaffar haunted me.

26

A few days before the spring semester, the professor found me among the stacks in the campus library. I sat on the third floor facing a window overlooking downtown.

"Miss Smith?"

I turned. "Oh, you scared me. I didn't hear you."

He looked ravishing in his t-shirt and stonewashed jeans, so different from the formal tux, and so, well, sexy. "It's nice to see you again. I didn't expect to find students in the library before term."

"I like this spot. I hang out here a lot. I haven't seen many professors around."

"I just returned from a philosophy conference. I came to find an article a colleague recommended."

"Philosophy?" I sat up. "I love philosophy. In fact, I wrote a paper last semester on philosophy about the author John Fowles. Have you heard of him?"

"Of course."

"Well, the scholars say he's an existentialist, but, in my paper, I argue he's a Darwinist. He doesn't believe in freedom."

"Then Fowles and I have something in common." He took a step closer, and my breath caught. "And you, Miss Smith? What do you believe?"

"I believe in freedom. I consider myself an existentialist."

He didn't hide the smirk that crossed his face. I wanted more than ever to prove I was smart, but I could think of nothing else to say.

A week later we saw each other again. The spring classes had started, and to my surprise, he was my Philosophy of Literature professor. It seemed too strange to be a coincidence, but I couldn't imagine why he would go to such lengths—to literally change his teaching schedule—to be near me. I could hardly look at him without blushing.

On the back of his syllabus was a map to his house. He was throwing a party and our attendance was required. We were to bring our favorite poem and be prepared to discuss why it appealed to us. He dismissed us early. I rushed from the room.

I worried over what I should wear and what poem I should choose. At the time, my real favorite was a short lyric by Robert Frost, but because I didn't think I could explain why I liked it, I decided to pick something more philosophical and logical. I chose "Hap" by Thomas Hardy.

I printed out a copy on my roommate Letty's computer and walked to the party in my favorite cardigan and leggings. Letty had gone ahead of me in her car, not wanting to be late. His house was a block from campus, though it was quite a distance from my dorm, but I liked to walk and needed to clear my head.

I was disappointed when a classmate—and not the professor—answered the door. He offered me a glass of ruby wine. The professor stood across the room talking to a group of girls, I jealous of them and enamored of him in his clingy turtle-neck and faded jeans. Those jeans, the sexy ones he had worn to the library. I found Letty and stuck to her like sweaty sleeves as I sipped the wine. I was on my third glass when he invited us to join him in the living room so he could begin his lecture.

"Please, make yourselves comfortable," he called.

The brown leather furniture and four dining chairs weren't enough for the twenty or so people present, so, in a brave and daring moment, I drank down my third glass of wine, left it on the kitchen bar, and slipped past the sofa to sit on the floor near the hearth directly at his feet. Above the mantel was a portrait of a Muslim woman, the mysterious eyes with nothing but veil around them. She dared me to do what I might never do.

For the first time that night, the professor met my eyes, and my cheeks stretch of their own accord into a nervous smile. "Teach me," my eyes must have said, aglow with the freedom from inhibitions because of the wine. "Show me what you know."

The professor cleared his throat and asked for a volunteer to share a poem, but the room was silent. "Hmm. This is not a good sign."

A girl raised a tentative hand. "I'll go."

She recited *my* Hardy poem, but as I watched the professor's lips twitch down into a frown, I was relieved I hadn't been the first to volunteer. He didn't like Hardy. I folded my poem over and over until it made a tiny square, which I hid inside my fist.

If the professor had trouble soliciting volunteers before, he couldn't expect an easier time now. He continued his lecture on the relationship between narrators and readers, saying, "It's the job of a narrator to seduce us. How does the speaker in Hardy's poem use language to draw us in?"

I surprised myself by raising my hand. "Maybe it's not the language. Maybe it's the rhythm or the form of the poem." The innuendo in my own words became apparent to me only after I uttered them. Rhythm and form, precisely what attracted me to Ahmed Jaffar.

"Hmm. Interesting. Why don't you share your poem with us, Mona?"

What in the world could I possibly say? Before my mind caught up with my lips, I recited "The Pasture" with my eyes closed. The poem invites the listener to join him in the pasture.

When I opened my eyes, the professor was smiling at me. "An excellent example of how readers are drawn in by speakers. What is it about words that lures us in, like fish to the hook, like children to their abductors? How does Frost seduce us?"

"I don't know!" I blurted out, elated he liked it. "It's my favorite, and I don't know why."

Another student raised his hand. "It's an invitation from the speaker to the listener to join him in his humble work in a pastoral setting. The spring, the leaves, the calf, and its mother are part of God's creation. The speaker's inviting the listener to join him in caring for God's world."

I glanced at Letty, and she rolled her eyes. I giggled.

The professor sought my attention, like the Muslim woman in the painting above him. "Is it an invitation?"

I raised my chin and met his eyes, though I was afraid. "Yes. It is."

I think he might have blushed.

Several others read their poems, and the group discussed their speakers and their seduction strategies. Professor Jaffar talked about the original "Beauty and the Beast" tale and "Bluebeard" and their themes of seduction and captivity as a metaphor for the relationship between readers and narrators. As the session ended, I slipped through the gatherers to the back of the room. When Professor Jaffar gave me a quizzical look, I mouthed in the form of a question, "Bathroom?" He nodded and pointed to the hallway on the left side of the house.

There was something unexpectedly intimate about being in his bathroom. Touching the plush taupe towel on the rod, damp from when he must have showered earlier, I imagined the places the towel would have touched him. I hovered by the door between the bathroom and his bedroom and wanted to peek but feared detection.

I ditched the folded poem into the wastebasket.

My thumb was bleeding again. I bit off the corner of skin, and, as I did, some of the students called out their goodbyes. I wondered what would happen if I didn't come out until the others had left.

Chapter Three: Friday the Thirteenth

The gray cat hops from Mona's lap and scratches at the back door to be let out. The ice in Yvette's nearly empty glass has melted, so she drinks it, too enraptured by the tale to think of the possibility of poison. Her plate is empty. Outside dusk stretches across Mona's dead shrubs like a tired cat.

It's getting dark?

"Oh, my Gosh." Yvette pulls her cell phone from her pocket to check the time. "Seven, already? The kids must be starving. I'm surprised no one's called."

Mona frowns. "I haven't gotten very far, I'm afraid. I haven't even told you what happened to the baby."

So there was a baby.

Where is it?

"I can come back tonight, after supper, if it's convenient."

"No, it's not. Why don't you come over tomorrow around four? I'll bake a cake for you."

Both of their heads turn toward the hall at the sound of a loud whack.

"My other cat," says Mona.

Liar.

"Can you come tomorrow?"

33

Yvette agrees.

Yvette's family sits around the kitchen table eating bowls of chili.

"Where were you?" asks Tommy.

"With er, the neighbor lady. She needs someone to talk to. She's a sad and lonely woman, I think."

Crazy's more like it.

"But *we* needed you," says Casey. "I have a spelling test tomorrow."

"And I'm doing the announcements in the morning for the entire school!" Tommy says. "Did you forget? I need to practice."

"My spelling test is more important."

"Did I mention this is for the *entire* school?"

"Why didn't you guys call me?"

"Dad said we couldn't," says Matt. "And no, I didn't finish my homework. I can't figure out the answer to this last question about ancient China. Dad doesn't know it either."

"What about Google?" She leans over the pot of chili on the stove, inhaling the spices as her mouth waters. "Thanks, Honey. The chili smells good." Then she adds, "I'm sorry, sweetie. Show me your words."

"How did China's geographical landscape affect its culture and social development?"

"Type that into Google." Yvette sits at the table and slurps up a spoonful of chili. "Let's hear Tommy's announcements while Casey studies her words. Then I'll give you a test, Casey."

"Dad already did," Casey says. "So never mind."

Devin smiles and winks at Yvette.

"Nothing's coming up on Google, Mom."

"Good morning, Encino Park faculty, staff, and students."

"Are the kids' clothes washed?" Devin asks. "I want them to pack tomorrow so we can leave early in the morning on Saturday."

"Dad!" Tommy objects.

Choke Canyon! In her haste to hear Mona's story, she has forgotten about the trip to Choke Canyon they planned for spring break.

"I'll wash them tomorrow. Don't worry. I'll have us ready by tomorrow night. Matt, get the encyclopedia, volume 'c-h,' bottom shelf, and bring it here. Go ahead, Tommy. I'm listening."

Tizzle-tizzle-tizzle-tizzle.

She finishes her bowl of chili as Tommy discusses the lost-and-found items, the upcoming spelling bee, and the menu for tomorrow's lunch. She has him repeat the announcements as she reads about ancient China and underlines areas Matt needs to put into his own words. Then she loads the dishwasher while Tommy practices again.

"Good work. Now get ready for bed."

As she squats in front of the washer stuffing in a load of the kids' clothes, Devin puts his hands on her shoulders and squeezes.

"You startled me."

"Sorry." He rubs her shoulders. "You coming to bed soon?" A question which really means, "Are we having sex tonight?"

Oh, Devin. I'm so tired.

"I told Casey I'd sleep in her room again and swap back scratches."

"When do I get my turn?"

"Soon, Honey. I promise."

Yvette lies beside Casey, scratching her back as her mother once scratched hers when they cuddled together like this, before Yvette's father died. After his death at age forty, when Yvette was twelve years old, where others would collapse and crumble, Yvette's mother hardened into a solid mass of rigid spine. Yvette misses the soft side of her mother, the nurturing part that made Yvette feel safe and loved. She doesn't miss the other side, the fierce side, though she could use a bit of it herself.

When Yvette's father died young of colon cancer, her mother, after a few weeks of floating white-faced like a zombie of few words, regained her composure, and her back became straighter, her tongue sharper, solidifying her reign over the neighborhood. Soon her mother was the one people went to for advice for everything from nursing a sprain to treating a bee sting, from making pecan pie to the proper way to bury a loved one. And Yvette, an only child, bore the brunt of her mother's anger and anxiety—anger over losing her husband early in life and leaving her a single parent, anxiety over how she would make ends meet. Anger and anxiety proved a deadly combination, and within twelve years of her father's death, her mother was struck down by a heart attack.

Yvette was twenty-four, teaching college composition, alone in the world until she met Devin a few months later. She supposes she never had to grow a backbone, because she went from living in the stark shadow of her mother's tyranny to the easy, pampered wife of a successful businessman—that is, until they had children and her life became a whirlwind, a spinning hamster wheel.

Having been an only child, she wanted a big family, but she had no idea what she was getting herself into, and every day she felt she was floundering. Devin warned her to stop volunteering to lead cub scouts, girl scouts, and PTA, but her mother had done all these things, and Yvette felt that's what mothers were supposed to do. Of course, her mother had only one child.

Yvette washes and folds clothes for most of the day on Friday, makes chicken and rice, and cleans the house so no one can complain when she abandons them for Mona. More than once she shakes her head, laughing at herself as she gets into the van to pick up the kids from school. She thought she'd never want to speak to Mona again, and here she is anxious to see her, drawn in to the tale like a child by its abductor. It's the baby. She wants to know what happened to the baby.

She thinks back to the items packed in the UPS box and recalls a detail she missed before: the dress had no tags, wasn't actually new. They might have been hand-me-downs from a relative, but there doesn't seem to be a baby anymore.

Once at home, she makes the kids start their spring break homework and tells them to fill their plates from the pan on the stove when they're hungry. Daddy will be home soon.

"Mom, what's wrong with Mr. Baggins?" Casey shouts from the kitchen as Yvette crosses into the washroom toward the garage. "Come look! He's trying to eat himself!"

"Oh no!" Tommy cries "Mom! Look how red he is!"

"Look at his leg," Matt says.

When Yvette enters the kitchen, all three kids are squatting on the tiled floor around Frodo with tears brimming in their eyes.

"What's wrong with him?" asks Casey.

Yvette stoops down to inspect Frodo. Fur has come off on his back foot where he obsessively licks and gnaws.

"It's a skin condition." Yvette finds the phone and calls the vet, who can squeeze her in right away. "Wash your hands, kiddos," she says when she hangs up the phone. "It could be contagious."

"Mom, help him," Casey says.

"Come on, Frodo. Looks like we're going to the vet."

Matt hands her the leash. "What if they have to amputate?"

"They won't have to amputate."

"How do you know?" Tommy asks.

"They won't have to amputate."

"I want to come, too," Matt says.

They all want to come. And so they pack themselves into the van, Frodo's stubby tail wagging and his tongue hanging to one side, ready for a ride, his favorite thing. The vet says it's ringworm and gives them an ointment, antibiotic, and a medicated shampoo, and three hundred dollars later, they are on their way back home, itchy and suspicious of every red bump on their own skin.

Yvette is an hour late to Mona's house.

When she opens the door, Mona appears harried, but not as wild as the first day. Her frizzy hair is loosed from its knot and her face is not made up, but at least her hair smells clean and is combed across her shoulders, and she wears clothes and not the ratty pink robe.

Thank God.

"I'm sorry I'm late," says Yvette. "Frodo, well, it doesn't matter."

"Come in. I didn't think you were coming." They cross the room. "You'll have to excuse me, but I didn't sleep well last night. So many memories, you know."

Yvette sits in the same chair as the day before. Two new boxes have been added to the stacks in front of the fireplace.

"Iced tea and cake?" Mona offers.

"If it's no trouble." Yvette hears a plop and a creak down the hall, but Mona doesn't explain.

Liar.

"No trouble. I baked a lemon cake for you." Mona pads in her socks to the kitchen.

While she's gone, Yvette slips a few paces down the hall, determined to see if it is really cats making those sounds. "Do you mind if I use your bathroom?" she calls.

Like a ghost, Mona appears at her side. "Wait!" Then she collects herself and says, "It's such a mess. I haven't changed the kitty litter. I'd be so embarrassed. Run home and come back when you're ready."

"No, that's okay. I can wait." Yvette returns to the chair, flabbergasted.

No backbone.

Mona brings the tea and cake and sits opposite Yvette. The cake does not look homemade. In fact, Yvette has bought this same lemon cake from the grocery store. It comes pre-sliced. Mona waits while Yvette takes a bite.

"It's good. Thanks."

"How are you today?"

"I'm okay. The kids started their spring break, so hopefully things will slow down around our house for a while. How 'bout you?"

"Oh, not well. Drudging up these memories, well, I know it's good for me. Scrubbing the wounds so they heal, isn't that how it goes?"

"Something like that. It has to hurt before it can get better?"

"Yes. That's it. Where was I? Ah, yes, standing in the professor's bathroom waiting for my fellow students to leave."

"So you went through with it?"

"Unfortunately, yes."

Chapter Four: A Fish Upon the Hook

Letty came to the door and asked if I was okay.

"I'm fine. Thanks," I said through the door.

"Do you want a ride back?"

"No, thank you. I want to walk."

"It's cold out. A cold front came in."

"That's okay. I like the cold."

"I'm leaving then."

"Good night."

I held my breath, counted slowly to twenty, and then, with a new rush of adrenaline, opened the bathroom door and returned to the living room. It was abandoned. I glanced around, confused. Where had the professor gone? I clutched my fuzzy pink key chain, crept to the front door, and put my hand to the cold knob.

"Are you leaving?" He stood in hall in the shadows, so I couldn't see his face.

"Hasn't everyone else gone?"

"Yes."

"Then, I suppose I ought to get going, too." I reached again for the knob. "Thank you for having us here. It was nice."

"You enjoyed the evening?" He moved closer.

The nearer he stood to me, the more my belly fluttered. "Yes."

"Good. Let me get your coat."

"I didn't bring one."

"But it's below freezing. Let me help you to your car." He took a blanket from the back of the couch and wrapped me in it, his arms momentarily around me. "You can cover yourself with this."

My knees weakened. "I didn't drive."

"It's much too cold to walk across campus."

"I'll be alright," I said, though my knees were in no condition for walking. I removed the blanket and handed it to him.

He bit his bottom lip, drawing my eyes to his mouth. "Why don't you sit and have a glass of wine and then I'll drive you back? I'd take you now, but I'm exhausted from the lecture. I need to sit and relax a few minutes."

"Are you sure it wouldn't be too much trouble? I don't mind the walk. Or I could call my roommate to come get me."

"Please, come sit by the fire while I get us each a glass."

When he returned from the kitchen, I took the glass of wine and sipped, even though I knew I had already had too much.

The professor fed a new log to the fire and sat down on the hearth. I sat on the loveseat an arm's length away. He drank his wine. I avoided his gaze and stared past him at the dancing fire.

When I got the nerve, I said, "Don't look at me like that."

"Like what?"

"You looked at me that way at the ball. It makes me nervous. What are you thinking?"

He lifted his eyebrows. "You want to know?"

My mouth fell open. "No." I shifted in my chair and drank more of the wine.

He smiled.

"That's better," I said.

"Yes? Good. Then I'll look at you like this. It should be easy since I find you very beautiful."

I was speechless.

"The fire feels good on my back. Come see how nice it feels." He patted the brick hearth.

I sat beside him. "I didn't know it was going to get so cold tonight." The adrenaline pounded through me. Our shoulders touched as we warmed our backs at the licking flames. I took another drink, the pink, fluffy key chain dangling from my finger.

"It's nice, yes?" I didn't think he meant the fire.

"A little too warm," I whispered, about to get up.

He took my hand and made me stay. "Give it a minute. You must get used to it first. Then, it's nice."

He continued to hold my hand in his, resting them both on his thigh. His hand was hot, and mine began to sweat.

"We need to warm up before we go out in the cold," the professor said. "I'll take you home in a minute." He hadn't let go of my hand. "How did you do on your paper last semester, the one about existentialism?"

"I made an A, but it was about Darwinism, remember?"

"Do you still consider yourself an existentialist?"

"I believe in freedom."

"It's a nice thing to believe in," he said sadly. "Are you comfortable, Mona?"

I nodded, though I was far from comfortable. My hand was sweaty, and it literally pained me to be touching him. "Not pure freedom," I said. "We are dealt a certain hand, but then it's up to us."

The doorbell rang and made me jump. I laughed.

"Excuse me. I'm not expecting anyone."

He crossed the room in a few strides and opened the door. "Yes?"

It was Bijan! I heard his voice before I turned around and saw him. "I'm sorry to disturb you," he said. "But I was worried about my fiancée, Mona, walking back to her dorm in this weather. She hasn't gotten back yet. Is she here?"

I hopped up from the hearth quickly, dropping my glass on the dark tile. It shattered across Professor Jaffar's living room. I stooped over the twenty or so shards and quickly collected them.

"Please, don't worry. I can get it with the broom," the professor snapped as he walked over to me. When I didn't stop, he touched my shoulder. "Mona. I insist."

Bijan came over and helped me up, and as we dodged the shards of glass on the way to the door, he whispered sarcastically, "Sorry I startled you."

The professor followed, crushing glass beneath his shoes. He possessed an odd coolness unlike his demeanor from moments before. He thanked me for coming and said he would see me in class.

I took the professor's hand and passed him the shards I had collected. We both looked down and saw I was bleeding. His hand was streaked with my blood. He pulled a handkerchief from his pants' pocket and dabbed it up. I expected him to give me the handkerchief, but he folded it and put it back into his pocket. I told him I was sorry about the mess, and he ushered us through the door without another word. It closed with a soft click behind us.

On the way to the car, I asked Bijan how he found me, since I hadn't given him the map.

"Letty."

I nodded, ignoring the anger in his voice.

"Disappointed?" he asked.

"Disappointed? No, what do you mean? We had a good class."

"I noticed you were the only pupil left." He clicked open the automatic locks on the car and we climbed in.

"He was going to drive me back, but he wanted to sit down for a few minutes. He felt tired from the lecture."

"I bet he felt tired."

"Are you calling me a liar?"

"I'm calling your professor a liar."

I relaxed as he drove to my dorm. "I'm glad you came. He was giving me the creeps."

He shook his head. "Why don't you ever use your cell phone?"

"I'm not used to it."

"Is your thumb bleeding again?"

"I cut myself on the broken glass."

He asked to see my hand, and he kissed it. "It can fit in your pocket, you know."

"What? Oh, the phone." I lifted my cardigan to expose my hips. "No pockets."

"Ooh, do that again," he said.

I laughed. "This?"

"Higher."

I flashed him a quick view of my bra, and we laughed.

For a while, I tried to ignore the professor's attention. I rarely met his eyes in class, and I left as soon as it ended to avoid talking to him. But one day when I was feeling down and dumpy while Bijan was out of town, I decided to join Letty for a workout at the campus gym.

She drove, and I followed her into the weight room—a square, musty, mirrored room with a nineteen-inch television mounted up high in the far corner broadcasting a basketball game. Half a dozen men and one other woman worked out on the machines, dumbbells, and free weights.

"What's good for thighs?" I asked Letty.

"Over there. It works both abductors and adductors." Her twin braids swung with her head as she pointed to a machine resembling something you'd see in a gynecologist's office.

"Will you show me how to do it? I'm more of an aerobics person."

She agreed, and I climbed onto the machine. I tried to push my legs open, but the weight was too heavy. Letty showed me how to move the pin to decrease the weight to forty pounds. This time my legs sprung wide open.

"Whoa. That's too easy." I moved the pin to fifty pounds.

Letty left to lift free weights on the other side of the gym. Then I recognized Professor Jaffar staring at me in the mirror across the wide room, so I clamped my legs closed. I pretended not to see him. I hadn't done a full set of ten, but I jumped from the machine to find something else.

I saw a classmate, so I skipped over to him to say hello, feeling safe by his side. We spoke for a few minutes, and then he showed me how to use a machine on his way out. I lay on my stomach, hooked my ankles beneath the weights, and curled my legs from the knees.

My arms were folded on the bench beneath my chin and my bottom stuck up in the air as I forced the hamstring curl under the weight. Suddenly warm hands pressed my hips against the bench. I opened my eyes to sexy, sweaty Professor Jaffar.

"You'll engage too many other muscles in this position," he said. "Keep your body on the bench. Try less weight." He moved the pin for me. "There, try that."

I lifted the weight as he held the small of my back down on the bench, electrifying my spine.

"That's the correct form." As fast as he appeared, he left for another machine.

My hips burned where Ahmed Jaffar's hands had held them. I couldn't believe he had the audacity to touch me. Who did he think he was? I finished the set of ten and then marched over to the free weights to speak with Letty.

"I think I'm going to head back," I told her.

"So soon?"

"I guess I'm not used to this. Thanks for letting me come along."

"Are you okay, Mona?" She let the weights hang limp at her sides.

"I'm tired."

"What did Professor Jaffar say to you?" She narrowed her brown eyes at me.

"Nothing." I glanced across the room, but the professor had already disappeared.

"I can't believe he touched you like that."

"I'll see you back at the dorm."

I took my jacket and my fluffy pink key chain, which lay on top of Letty's bag in a corner, and left the gym. Folding my arms across my chest, I bore the wind as I made my way across the campus to my dorm, biting the inside corners of my lips. I kept thinking, "How dare he?" yet I felt light in my shoes.

Once in my dorm room, I changed from the workout clothes, put a few books in my backpack, and headed for the library on foot.

I hadn't been there long when I heard a familiar voice.

"Hi, Mona."

"Professor Jaffar!" I tried to sound casual. "What are you doing here?"

"I was hoping I'd find you." The corner of his mouth twitched into an enigmatic smile.

I shivered at his following me, which seemed hard to believe. Nervous and flattered, I wondered if I had willed him to come. I wanted to spend time with him. "Bijan is out of town with the geology club," I told him in what I hoped was a steady voice. "They traveled to San Saba to study an unusual rock formation, so it's just me this weekend."

"I see."

"It's strange. I don't know what to do with myself."

"Perhaps you wouldn't mind doing me a favor, then, since you have found yourself with idle time."

"What is it?"

He sat on the end table beside my chair. "The department recently informed me my application for a research assistant has been approved. They were waiting to see if there would be enough funding. I was hoping you would accept the position."

I was flattered.

"You don't have to give me an answer right away. You'll want to talk to your parents, and perhaps your fiancé."

I knew if I did accept, I could not tell Bijan.

"I normally ask a senior, but I've been away from teaching for a while and haven't had an opportunity to get to know anyone I can trust. Well, I asked one young man, but he declined. He's taking eighteen hours this semester to graduate on time, and he didn't think he could handle the job."

"So I'm second choice?"

"To be honest, you're the third, but who's counting? Had you been a senior, I would have asked you first."

"Well, I'd be delighted to accept the position. Thank you for offering it." My heart contracted at this bold submersion into a role of duplicity.

"Thank you for accepting it. And listen, I want to apologize for my behavior back at the gym. I used to be a personal trainer. I hope I didn't make you feel uncomfortable."

"It's okay," I said, deciding not to make an issue of it, appalled at myself and simultaneously triumphant. To this day, I wish I could go back in time and tell my younger self, Say it! Say no! But, I was thinking this position would be good for my career.

"Here's the catch," he said, and I braced myself. "Since we're getting a late start in the semester, I have a lot of work built up for you, and so I was hoping you'd have time this weekend to help me, say tomorrow afternoon at my office?"

"Tomorrow?"

"Is it too soon?"

"No, but I'm free tonight if you'd like me to start right away." I couldn't believe my own words.

"The work's at my house, but you're welcome to come by. I could load you up with a few projects."

"Sure. I'll go back to my dorm to get my car."

"Or you could ride with me."

"I don't want to trouble you." But I wanted to go with him. I told myself going with him would save time, accepting the position would help my career, this was a rare opportunity for a sophomore, and I could learn from this man. I told myself everything but the truth.

He said, "Are you kidding? You're doing me a favor, remember?"

"Well, it helps me, too. I'm hoping to go to graduate school, and I this will look good on my application."

"Indeed. It will. Come, then. My car is outside."

I loved the opportunity to ride in his shiny red corvette. In the car, I asked about the Islamic art in his home and whether he was Muslim, but he said no, though his parents had been, and the pieces had come from them. He seemed sad to think of it, so I told him I hadn't meant to intrude.

"It's okay," he said in a voice softer than usual. "I'm not used to people showing me sympathy, especially these days." The soft bend in his brows made him appear vulnerable.

We were quiet in the car and again as we walked into his house, but once in his study, I asked, "Why especially these days?"

"It's a long story."

"I have time."

He took two books from a shelf and handed them to me. Then he wrote notes on a piece of paper. He clenched his jaw and frowned.

"Professor?"

He stepped past me and headed to the door. "Come, I won't bore you with my sad stories."

"It's okay," I said, not budging. "You won't bore me."

But if he heard me, he didn't stop to listen. So I stood up and followed him to the door.

"I have here a few journal articles I'd like for you to copy in the library." He kept his eyes on the pile in his arms. "Here's a card for you to use in the Xerox machine. I'm giving you two journals here in which I have written notes, and I'd like you to compile them into a single document. Keep track of your hours so you can be properly compensated."

"I'm a good listener, I've been told."

"Yes. I believe it."

I followed him to his car and he took me home. I should have realized his sudden indifference to me was part of his game. It made me eager to please, eager to win his attention again. And, after weeks of having me look up and copy articles, he one day unexpectedly gave it.

During those weeks, Bijan had no knowledge of my new position. When I needed to do research in the library, I told him I was working on a paper. When I needed to meet Ahmed at his office, I was attending a study group. It had become thrilling to me, this life of duplicity.

I still blame the nuns who raised Bijan for the first fourteen years of his life for my growing obsession with Ahmed. His parents had been diplomats to the Shah of Iran and fled to France during the Khomeini revolution. They were followed and killed outside of Notre Dame Cathedral. The sisters heard the shots and found Bijan, a baby in the arms of a dead woman. They raised him until his uncle tracked him down. Had the nuns not so completely indoctrinated Bijan into the Catholic faith, including the part of staying chaste until marriage, I might not have been tempted. The alluring eyes and smile of my professor and the implicit promises behind them were too irresistible for my aching body to ignore.

A week before spring break, Ahmed dropped his bomb. We were in his office sitting on opposite sides of his desk leaning over an article I had copied for him. Unlike his home, his office had little in the way of art or decoration. A few books and stacks of papers, nothing personal. He gazed at me for a moment without saying anything. I thought he was going to kiss me, and the air rushed from my body. I didn't know what I would do. But instead, he asked, "You know what they call me around here, don't you?"

I pretended to be ignorant. "What do you mean, Ahmed?" We were on a first-name basis by then, and it thrilled me every time I had an opportunity to say his name.

"Come on, I think everyone on campus has heard of the Taliban Spy's Lover. Surely you have as well."

I shrugged. "They're just rumors."

"But behind most rumors lives some truth. Aren't you curious? You've never asked."

"Do you mean there is something to those rumors about you?"

"I've never spoken of it, not to anyone, but I think I need to."

I smiled.

He asked if I was going away for spring break, and I told him I had no definite plans, but this was a lie. Bijan and I were supposed to go to Los Angeles to visit his aunt and uncle, who were like parents to him. Ahmed asked me to have dinner on the first Friday of the break. I should have told him I wasn't free. I should have said I could come the

Friday after—Bijan and I would be home by then, but I was dying to know his story. So I said yes, I would come.

That night in my dorm, I pretended to be sick to get out of going to Los Angeles with Bijan.

He begged me to go. "Maman and Baba will take good care of you, and seeing new places might lift your spirits and help you get better."

I lay in my bed beneath the covers clutching my head. "I've taken two Advil, and the migraine hasn't gotten any better," I told him. "My throat's on fire, I feel irritable as hell, and I don't want your family to see me this way."

"I'll stay then." He leaned over and kissed my forehead. "I'll stay and take care of you."

"That wouldn't be right," I said quickly. "She'd hate me. Don't make me the bad guy." Until moments before, I thought I would call the professor and reschedule for the following Friday. "Besides," I said. "I bet Maman would enjoy having you to herself for once."

This new strategy worked. "Will you stay with your parents while I'm gone? Your mother can help you."

"Being around Leroy will make me worse." Leroy was my pothead brother. He was thirty and still living at home in Brownsville, a drain to my parents' feeble income. "I'll be fine here. Letty will be around. She's not going anywhere."

He wasn't so convinced. "Are you sure? Have you talked to her?"

"No, but come on. We're talking about Letty. Where would she possibly have to go without me? I'm her only friend."

Friday afternoon, after I kissed Bijan goodbye, I took a hot shower and then rummaged through my wardrobe for something to wear to the professor's house, settling on a white blouse and straight black skirt.

I pressed a tube of lipstick to my mouth, smacked my lips to rub in the color, and whispered, "There's nothing to feel guilty about. I'm helping him."

Chapter Five: Lies and Goodbyes

Mona's story is interrupted by a moan coming from a bedroom down the hall. She and Yvette turn like soldiers taken by surprise.

"Babs is in heat," says Mona, rising to her feet. She hurries down the hall and says in the voice of a kindergarten teacher, "Stay in here, dear, and no more noise." Then she pads back into the living room, running her skinny fingers through her hair. "I put Boots in a room separate from Babs, but don't be surprised if we hear him moaning for her again. She's old and she doesn't want him forcing himself on her."

Liar.

That moan did not sound like a cat's mating call. It sounded like a person waking from a bad dream. She couldn't tell if the voice was male or female, adult or child, but it was definitely human.

"Perhaps this is a good place to stop," Mona says. "I can't tell you how this helps me. I'll have to do something special for you when I'm done."

"Oh, no. That's okay. Like I said, I'm glad to help."

I want to know what happened to the baby.

"Can you come back tomorrow at four?"

Devin has loaded the supper dishes into the dishwasher and is watching TV in the den when Yvette returns home after nine o'clock. She tucks in each kid and gives out hugs kisses before quietly stepping into the den. Mona's story of getting out of her spring break trip with Bijan has given her an idea.

"Honey, I don't feel well," she says, approaching him from behind and resting one hand on his shoulder. "My stomach is queasy."

Devin turns around. "You mean from dinner?"

"I don't think so."

Liar.

Yvette sits down beside him on the couch. "I think I might be coming down with a bug. I shouldn't sit so close." She scoots a few inches away from him.

"You might as well," he says. "We'll be in close quarters on the drive to Choke Canyon tomorrow."

"That's the thing." Yvette folds her arms. "I don't know if I'm up for it. Maybe y'all should drive up tomorrow without me, and I'll join you in a couple of days."

Devin's eyes widen. "Is it that bad?"

Yvette nods, looking anywhere except her husband's eyes. She wishes she can tell him the truth: this woman's story is important to her. Plus, she has gone on many trips with the kids without him, could she please have a turn to stay behind; instead, she rubs her stomach.

No backbone.

She's becoming her father. He was forty when he died but by his thirties had withdrawn from social gatherings and kept to his room, reading, watching television, doing crossword puzzles and Sudoku or sometimes working out in the garden—everything solitary, the opposite of her mother. While her mother was wanted at every social gathering in the neighborhood, she went alone, her father finding it too tiresome to put on a show of interest in other people's lives and preferring his own company. So whenever Yvette displayed the slightest introverted tendencies—she shared her father's love of books and puzzles and plants—her mother warned her not to turn out like her father. She needed to embrace opportunities to spend time with her family and friends because life was too short to spend it alone.

Yet Yvette felt alone in spite of her mother's social competence. Surrounded by a dozen girl scouts in grammar school, Yvette felt lost in the crowd and the least noticed, as though her troop-leader mother were intentionally putting up barriers between them and finding ways to avoid being alone with Yvette.

So here Yvette is, passing on an opportunity to share time with her family, not to read alone in her room like her father, not even to listen to an audiobook as she walks Mr. Frodo Baggins, but to discover the secrets of an eccentric character, nonetheless—a kind of heroine of her own novel, and to possess the story herself. Mona is a book, and Yvette wishes to stay behind to read it.

He frowns. "The kids will flip out."

"I don't want to get them sick."

"Why don't you see how you're feeling in the morning?"

Yvette sighs and stands up. "Alright. I'll sleep on it."

"Yvette?" Devin turns down the volume of the television with the remote.

She stops and turns in the doorway.

"Are we ever going to sleep in the same bed again?"

Yvette's mouth falls open. "You snore so God-awful loud, Honey. What's the big deal? We still have sex."

"Yeah? Can you remember the last time?" Devin's blue eyes glow with the reflection from the television.

Yvette crosses her arms and leans against the door frame. "A few weeks ago?"

"More like a few months ago."

Yvette recalls the morning the yard exploded, when she was dying for him, but usually she didn't have the energy. "You're exaggerating. Besides, tell me when you're in the mood. We can still have our fun. Then I can move to Casey's trundle bed and get good sleep."

"That's not exactly romantic, having to make an appointment."

Well, damn. I can't do everything for everybody all the time.

"Then do something about your snoring. Hell, Devin, I told you I don't feel well. This isn't the best time to throw on the guilt."

"There's *no* good time." He sighs and turns to the TV. "Never mind. Go to bed."

Oh, Devin. She hesitates, not sure what to do. If she made a move tonight, he would see it as charity sex. Besides, she really is too damn tired. "Good night," she says softly before leaving the room.

Yvette lies beside Casey, rubbing her fingertips along her daughter's baby-soft skin, dwelling on her recent thoughts of her father's anti-social behavior. Her mother told Yvette for years she was turning into him and to fight it. At the time, Yvette agreed she didn't want to spend her time shut up alone. Now, although she loved her family, she longed for moments when she could be in her own company with her own thoughts without the constant interruptions.

But when left with her thoughts, usually at night while scratching Casey's back, they horrify her. She thinks of her parents' short and dissatisfied lives, feels her deep longing for their company, and realizes her sense of loss together with a feeling she serves no purpose other than to wash clothes and dishes and floors.

"Goodnight, Mom," Casey mutters, turning onto her side.

"Goodnight, sweet girl. I'm so glad God gave you to me." This is a saying Yvette has whispered to Casey since she was a baby, and it has become a tradition. She doesn't say it every night, because she doesn't want it to lose its meaning, but she says it often, and tonight she needs to say it.

"I'm glad he gave you to me," Casey says.

In the morning, Yvette's stomach really does feel queasy. She doesn't have to pretend to be sick, but that doesn't make telling the kids any easier.

"Frodo Baggins is coming with us," Matt insists.

The kids know Yvette will be scared without her guard dog, and they think this will change her mind. "Fine," she says. "I won't be up to taking care of him anyway."

Liar.

"Mom!" says Casey. "Are you sure? Don't you want to be with us?"

"Of course I want to be with you, precious girl." Guilt churns in Yvette's stomach, and she wonders if that's what's making her sick.

No backbone.

"I want to be with all of y'all," she assures them. "And I will. When I'm feeling better. Promise."

Yvette helps them load their bags into the pickup and gives them each a kiss on the cheek, even Devin, who hasn't softened. He's mad—they all are.

"I'll come up in a few days. I'm sure this stomach ache will be gone by then."

Casey wraps her arms around Yvette. "I'm not going without you."

"Come on, Snookie." Devin peels Casey's arms from Yvette's waist.

Casey fights against him, tears streaming down her cheeks. "I want Mama to go with us. I don't want to go without her."

"I'll come in a few days." Yvette strokes Casey's long brown hair, fighting tears.

Tommy comes up for another hug. "We'll miss you."

"Come on, kids," says Devin. "Get in the truck."

"It's just a few days," Yvette says again.

"Keep your eye on the tree," Devin says. "Since you're home, maybe you could water it."

"Of course, Honey."

"Bye, Mom," says Matt, holding Mr. Baggins. "I wish you were coming with us."

Once they back from the driveway and turn down the street, she runs into the house, collapses onto the couch, and cries. What kind of mother is she, lying to her kids, disappointing them like this? And what kind of wife?

I'm a liar and I have no backbone.

She knows exactly what she'll be missing at Choke Canyon: the children's squeals of excitement when they hook a fish, their silly jokes and skits at their evening campfire, more roasted marshmallows than she can eat, and Devin's spooky stories in the tent as they go to sleep.

But she also wants to know how the professor ruined Mona's life. She wants to know who is living with Mona and why she is lying about it. She wants to know why Mona freaked out over the baby items. Above all, she wants to know why she is telling her story to Yvette.

What happened to the baby? Is it living with her? Is there something wrong with it?

In the end, she decides her family can make it without her for a couple of days. Hasn't she sacrificed for them? Doesn't she live her life for everyone else most of the time? She has to stay to hear the rest of the story. She has no choice.

Four o'clock arrives, so Yvette drives around the block. Mona doesn't answer her door right away, and suddenly Yvette worries she has stayed behind for no reason. Panicked, she pounds on the door.

Bam bam bam.

66

Fortunately, Mona greets her a moment later with swollen, red eyes. "Hello, Yvette."

"I thought you weren't home. What's wrong? Have you been crying?"

"Too many memories," she explains.

She brings a glass of iced tea and another slice of store-bought cake without asking this time, and they take their seats in the two wooden chairs. Three more boxes have been stacked with the others in front of the fireplace.

"We left off as I was on my way to Ahmed's for dinner. Right?"

Yvette nods. "You okay? We don't have to do this today." Common courtesy comes automatically, though she hopes Mona won't take her up on the offer.

Liar.

"No. I have to finish. I have to tell you my story."

Chapter Six: The Seduction

When I arrived at Ahmed's Friday night, the food had already been laid out on the table. Ahmed said hello and took my leather blazer and hung it in the front closet.

"Come in and have a seat." With black trousers, he wore a snug gray turtleneck.

The table glistened, and the food looked and smelled tantalizing, like my host.

I asked, "Did you cook this?"

"Oh, no. I had a restaurant deliver proper Indian food. I hope you like it. My father's grandmother, who was Hindu, used to cook this."

He pulled a chair for me to sit, and then he poured me a glass of wine before taking the seat across the table from me. He told me about the food—flat bread called naan, chutney, vegetable curry, and tandoori chicken.

"No beef, you understand," Ahmed said.

"I thought pork was the taboo food of choice." Bijan's aunt and uncle were atheists and Bijan was Catholic, so I wasn't sure.

"You've got the Hindus and Muslims confused— something that could get you killed if you were living in other parts of the world."

"Oops."

"I would have taken you to the restaurant, but what I have to tell you I cannot speak of in public. I hope you understand."

"Of course."

As we ate, we spoke first of school—how I was doing in my other classes and whether I was enjoying his.

"Yours is my favorite," I told him truthfully. "I love philosophy as much as literature. I'm thinking about doing a double major."

"Yes? Well you have the mind for it. You are an analytical thinker."

He poured me another glass of cabernet, and I thanked him again as I returned the glass to my lips.

He said, "You look beautiful tonight, as always."

"That's nice of you to say." My face got warm.

"I am a mere observer who speaks the truth."

Afterwards, he led me to the living area, where we sat for a few long and awkward minutes before Ahmed stood up and said, "Now that you are here, it's not so easy to tell you what I've wanted to say. Please be patient. This is difficult for me."

"I understand."

He sank back into the leather chair and crossed one ankle over his knee. He held his wine glass in both hands, his elbows supported by the arms of the chair, the glass leaning against his chest. I found him so alluring, because of both his physical magnetism and the enigma that shrouded it. He took a drink of the wine, cleared his throat, and began.

"I was twelve when my parents died while trying to help our relatives in Kabul during the Soviet invasion of Afghanistan. We lived in Pakistan. My parents were devoted to the Islamic faith and they gave their lives for it. My relatives in Kabul disagreed with Russia's influence on the government. Communism and Islam don't mix well. My Pakistani relatives could not take me, so I had to go to Afghanistan to live with my grandmother, who was so stricken with grief over the death of her daughter, that she barely noticed me. I no longer prayed to Allah. She could not see the hatred rising inside of me.

"I understood then what a waste the death of my parents and of our friends and relatives had been. These people were dying for nothing, for stupid lies, but the Russian forces were even worse, because although they pretended they wanted to help, they wanted power. As a boy I wondered why nations and people within them couldn't live and let live. Now I understand such a thing is impossible. One must always be in a state of war just to survive. We are like wolves in a pack. Sometimes we fight together for the same cause, but, at any moment, we may turn on one another and kill.

"I decided to fight with the guerillas against the Russians, not because I cared for Islam and its cause, but because I wished to avenge the death of my parents and loved ones, and because I had accepted war as a way of life.

"When I was eighteen, my grandmother used every bit of money she had scraped together and saved at her own extreme sacrifice to send me to Canada to attend the University of Manitoba, where I learned to speak English and French. I was drawn to philosophy, for I was able to find fraternity among scholars who thought like me. After I took my degree, I came here to the U.S. for graduate studies. I attended the University of California at Berkeley, and then, when I finished my Ph.D., I accepted a position here. I taught here four years when the Afghani student, Fatima, came into my life."

He took another drink of his wine and then quietly stared at the empty fireplace, as though in a daze.

I asked, "Are you okay?"

"She reminded me of my mother. She was beautiful—small like a bird—and devoted to her Islamic faith. She wore the required veil and never looked me in the eyes. I wondered how such a woman would find herself educated and at a university. She said her parents had smuggled her out of Afghanistan and wished her to learn nursing so she could return and care for the casualties of war.

"I should have been suspicious of this young woman, but I fell in love with her. She tried to discourage me, but she entranced me further."

I reminded myself I was engaged to Bijan and should be happy this poor man, who had been through so much, had found happiness at one time. But I found myself wishing I looked more Middle-Eastern.

As he stood to light two candles on the mantle above the empty fireplace, I watched his back, the way he filled out his trousers, the way the muscles tightened in his shoulders as he reached up to put the flame to wick. He blew out the flame on the match and tossed it into the fireplace. He continued his story with his back to me, his hands up on the mantle, leaning against it.

"She moved in with me. We made love every day and night. She transformed from this quiet, shy, submissive girl into a carefree and fabulous lover. She was such a mystery to me, so complex. I felt each day as though I were in love with a different woman. I wanted to take care of her. But truly, she took care of me." He stood for a moment, clenching his fists as though he might break something. I covered my mouth with my hands as I listened, my eyes drawn to the dancing flames of the two candles on the mantle.

"I was captured once by Soviet soldiers when I was sixteen. I cannot tell you of the horrors. I barely escaped, but not without having experienced the worst kinds of violation." I caught a glance of his profile, of the clenched jaw and tightly shut eyes. At last, he sat on the brick hearth with his back to the fireplace, his elbows resting on his knees, his back slouched, his eyes cast to the floor. "I miss her, even after all she put me through."

I hadn't meant to speak when I asked, "Do you still love her?"

He looked up at me, as though he had forgotten my presence. "I don't know. It's possible."

"What happened, Ahmed? What did she do to you?"

"She used me. She never loved me. She was spying for the Taliban, and, when the FBI came searching for her after nine-eleven, she fed them me."

"You mean she got away?"

"I don't know. I was in police custody for nearly two months."

"Police custody!"

"Supposedly I was a material witness, but I was never brought before a grand jury and never charged with a crime. I lied to you when I told you I was on a sabbatical. I am writing a book, that part was true, but I was on leave and I nearly lost my position."

"How terrible!"

"But I didn't care. I could only think of her and what she had done to me. It was like being betrayed all over again."

"Again?" I was confused. "Who betrayed you before?"

He met my eyes and then looked away.

"I'm sorry," I said. "It's not my place to ask such things."

"Yes it is." He fell to his knees on the floor in front of me and took my hands. "Yes, Mona. I thought I could never feel again, and then I saw you. Please forgive me, but I cannot help myself. I find myself in great need of your help."

"I don't understand." I leaned back on the couch to put more space between us, though I was, at the same time, drawn to his troubled hazel eyes. I did not pull my hands from his. "How can I help?" But I knew the answer.

He kissed my hands.

I felt myself falling. His brilliant hazel eyes and strong hands made me weak. And yet, he was the one in need of me. He was the fragile one who needed to be cared for. I was moved with great pity and desire. He glanced at my mouth and I unconsciously moved it nearer to his.

We kissed. I closed my eyes to the final objection of my conscience and submerged completely into the thrilling fires of passion, unwilling to think, unwilling to fight against the desires of my body. He took my face in his hands and

74

moved his luscious lips over mine as though he had never tasted such sweetness, as though he had been starving for these very lips, this very tongue that belonged to me. And I felt dizzy, so dizzy, and breathless.

And with the dizziness came an awful image swirling behind my closed eyes: Bijan. I saw him with Maman and Baba and his cousins sitting together in Los Angeles. Then I saw his face, hovering above my own on the first night he told me he loved me, his black eyes soft with affection. My spine stiffened at the thought. Slowly, I opened my eyes and pushed Ahmed away. "What am I doing?" I whispered, more to myself than him. "What have I done?"

"Mona?" He touched my cheek, and I pushed him away, unable to meet his eyes. Then I rose slowly to my feet, dazed.

"I can't do this."

He knelt, dumbfounded, his arms across the cushion where I had sat moments before. I brought my hand to my mouth as though covering my lips would erase the pleasure they had just taken from his. "I'm so sorry," I said. "I don't mean to hurt you, Ahmed. I like you so much. But I'm engaged. You know I'm engaged!"

He stood in front of the hearth and squinted at me. "You can't have kissed me like that and be in love with him. It's not possible."

"I've got to go." Panic was rising in my throat like bile, and I turned around, desperately looking for my shoes. "I'm so sorry I can't help you. I wanted to, I really did. But not like this!" I ran to the front closet to get my blazer, I slipped into my shoes, and opened the front door. "I'm so sorry! Please understand!"

He stood before the hearth as I ran through the door. He did not try to stop me.

I tore off my clothes, crawled into bed, and cried. My tears were mostly for myself and the mistake I had made, but they were also for poor Bijan, who did not deserve my preoccupation with the professor, and for poor Ahmed, who at the time I thought did. I cried until I fell asleep, which was well after midnight and long before Letty returned. When I awoke late in the morning, I was alone again.

Later that evening, when Letty came home, I nearly pounced on her.

"Where have you been?" I demanded.

"Downtown. Why?"

"Downtown? Why downtown?" She looked prettier than usual with her brown hair loosed from it braids.

"Farmers' Market," she said, setting a paper sack on my desk. "Here. I brought you fresh cantaloupe. Oh, and Bijan called last night, by the way. I almost forgot."

I sat up. "What time?"

"Six or six-thirty. I left at seven, so I know it was before then."

"What did you say?"

"That I didn't know where you were. I thought you grabbed a bite at the dining hall. I left a message for you on your desk. It's here by the bag of cantaloupe. Are you feeling any better?"

I walked over to my desk. "I guess I didn't see it. Yes, a little."

I spoke to Bijan Saturday night, and told him I had been out eating Friday when he had called—which was not a lie—and I spoke to him twice on Sunday, three times on Monday, and once or twice on Tuesday, reassuring him I was staying in bed and getting plenty of rest, which was true. I rarely left my room. If I had not been sick before, I certainly was then.

A single memory kept surfacing in my mind as I lay in bed each evening after hanging up the phone. A year before, Bijan and I had driven to South Padre Island, when we were still new to one another and awkward and afraid. I had gone for a walk on a boardwalk outside our hotel room and had overheard an old woman telling a younger one about her future. They sat at a table outside a café and, by the light of a candle, were looking over a kind of diagram, which the older woman explained to the younger. I stopped a few feet away with my back to the women, leaning against a rail, gazing out at the sea, to listen.

The old woman said, "And finally, because we are moving into the year of the orbit of Pisces, the Aquarian must be particularly careful when making voyages. I wouldn't make the trip this year, if I were you. Wait two more years, when the Pisces orbit is on the Gemini side."

The younger woman thanked the older, put money on the table, and left. The older sat alone, staring past me at the water.

I leaned over the railing and asked, "Excuse me, I couldn't help overhearing a little of your conversation, and I was wondering if you could tell me about my future, too."

The older woman eyed me suspiciously. "I worked two weeks on that customer's zodiac chart. I can't possibly do for you in a few minutes what I did for her in many days."

"I understand," I said. "But maybe you can offer advice? You see, I think I'm in love. I have money with me."

The woman motioned to the chair where the younger one sat moments before. I walked along the railing and through a gate onto the patio of the café.

As I sat down, the woman asked, "When is your birthday? I need month, day, and year. If you know the hour and minute, that would help, too."

I told her what I knew.

"Aries. And the man you think you love?"

"September 20, 1979."

"Virgo. Oh, dear."

"What?" I asked, leaning forward on the table.

"You are a fire sign and he is an earth."

"What does that mean?"

"Well, what happens when you put earth on fire?"

"The fire goes out?"

"Exactly."

"No, it can't be. We get along so wonderfully. Are you sure?"

"These next two years will be especially bad for fire and earth relationships because we are in the orbit of a water sign. Water on fire does what?"

"The water extinguishes the fire, like the earth."

"And water on earth?"

"Makes mud."

"So you see, you have no chance. It's in the stars."

I should never have given the old woman's words a second thought, should never have sat down and invited the future to be told. A part of me scoffed at the unfavorable prediction, even as I put the ten-dollar bill down on the table and left. But a less confident and less secure part of me grasped on to the words in horror lest they might be true.

So here I was, a year later, thinking on them again and of all the ways Bijan smothered my flame.

I spent Tuesday night memorizing Ahmed's phone number. I would call to apologize, I told myself over and over as I dialed and then turned off the phone before it had begun to ring.

On Wednesday, I accepted an invitation from my suitemates to go out for drinks. I told Bijan on the phone I was feeling better and was going out with the girls, and he had warned me to be careful, to have a designated driver, and so on.

"Are you sure you want to go out with those girls?" he asked.

He didn't like my suitemates, and I took this criticism as further proof he was earth to my flames.

I asked from the backseat which bar we were going to.

"Gordito's," they answered.

"Isn't that a titty bar?" I asked.

"Yes, but it's got male dancers, too."

My mouth went dry. They offered me a cold wine cooler from the iced chest up front.

"Thanks." I sucked down the drink.

I stared at the maroon carpet to avoid the naked woman on the table we had to pass on our way to the bar.

I did what my suitemates did—first we threw burning shots of tequila down our throats and then slurped up Jello shots. We sipped on rum and coke while we searched for a spot near the dancers. But as we weaved through the crowd to get to the other side of the building, I was overcome with the giggles.

I had read female apes bend over and show off their backsides to the males when they are in the mood for love, and male birds of paradise show off their colored wings. As one girl bent over and shook her ass at me, I howled with laughter, because, in a way, she did resemble a thin baboon.

My suitemates and I sat at a table on the side of the bar where the men danced. As I leaned over to grab a handful of peanuts from a bowl in the middle of our table, I was surprised by the appearance of a dancer right in front of my chair. He gyrated and then turned to show me his ass, and I simply could not hold back the laughter.

The dancer rubbed his bare ass against my thigh. This seemed hilarious, especially as I reflected on the female ape. I fell out of my chair and almost peed in my pants. I shrieked as I lay on my back and begged the dancer to go away. My suitemates glared at me and then quickly offered dollar bills to the dancer.

They left me on the floor and moved to another table. When I found them and apologized, they told me to bug off.

I was drunk and at a loss. I got in line at a pay phone, cursing myself for forgetting my cell, which was probably dead. When it was my turn to use the phone, I tried to reach Letty, but she wasn't home. I should have asked a bartender for the number to a cab service, but the line of people at the bar was so long, and I didn't want to waste more time waiting again to use the pay phone, so, instead, I dialed the number I had recently memorized. A part of me had been searching for an excuse to call Ahmed all week, and now I was too drunk to seriously consider the consequences.

When he answered, I nearly hung up, but an impulse and numbed inhibitions spurred me on. "Ahmed?"

"Mona?" he sounded surprised and glad to hear my voice.

"I'm so sorry to call this late." I had no idea what time it was.

"Don't apologize. You didn't wake me."

"I'm drunk and abandoned."

"Where are you?"

"Gordito's."

"I'm on my way. Wait for me out front."

I climbed into his corvette. I thanked him for saving me and was disappointed when he asked if he should take me to my dorm.

"Or maybe you should drink coffee first?"

"Yes," I said. "I definitely could use coffee."

He could have suggested a restaurant, which is what I expected, but instead, he took advantage of the situation, as he was typically inclined to do, as he had trained himself to do, and said, "Then it's off to my place, for I have in my cupboard the best coffee you have ever tasted."

As we drove, I rambled on and on, droning as only drunk, naïve young women do best. "I can't believe that place! And those people! It's so crazy, so absurd. Gosh, am I glad to be out of that mess! Whew! Thank you so much for saving me. I had no one else to call. I could have called a cab, but the line at the bar was so long, I couldn't find a phone book, and there was this ugly old woman talking on the payphone by the ladies' room forever. I was so relieved when you answered. Everyone else I know was out. Gosh, I'm so tipsy!"

Before I knew it, we had reached his place. He helped me inside and we went straight to the kitchen. He started the coffee.

He asked, "Are you hungry?"

"Famished."

"Would a sandwich do?"

"Just the bread, if you don't mind. Whenever I drink too much, I get this craving for bread."

He watched me with amusement as I mashed two slices together and ate them, like an eager communicant, moving closer when I licked my lips. I thought he might kiss me.

After I finished the bread, he led me to the living room to wait for the coffee. "Make yourself comfortable."

Sitting on the couch, I recalled what had taken place the last time I sat in the very spot, and a shiver worked itself down my back. For the first time since I had called him from the bar, I wondered what in the world I had gotten myself into, and what I would possibly do now I was so irreversibly in the middle of it. I could leave. I could walk across the campus and find myself safely home. I could apologize for the inconvenience, thank him for the bread, and go while I still could—none of which I did.

Whether the bread had absorbed the alcohol, or whether the strangeness of the situation affected a level of sobriety in me, I knew I had to make a choice and make it quickly. I wondered about the professor's zodiac sign.

"When is your birthday?" I asked.

"February fifteenth. Why?"

I dared not say, fully aware of how ridiculous I was being. Aquarius. Air. And what does air do to fire? It feeds it! Air feeds fire! Of course! Aha! How simple it suddenly seemed! "Ahmed," I sat forward on the couch.

He had gone to get the blanket from the other couch, and as he handed it over to me, our eyes locked. I gazed up at him with unambiguous desire and invitation.

Full of the most intense passion, I reached my lips to his, and he took my head in his hands and met my lips with his own.

I shut my eyes, and, in so doing, I shut out reason, justice, and morality. I shut out all memory of Bijan and the pain this choice would inevitably cause him. I shut out all speculation about what this choice would mean for my own future. I shut out all thought of tomorrow. I would think only of today, tonight, this moment, and how wonderful it felt to be in the arms of this sensuous, strong, intelligent, sad man who needed me.

He lifted me in his arms and carried me to his bedroom.

With his eyes closed, and his lips near my ear, he whispered, "Are you on the pill?"

I didn't want to interrupt this thrilling moment, this most sensual of moments, so I nodded, not knowing what to say. He ravished me beneath the bedcovers and I cried out in pain. He mistook my cries for pleasure and relentlessly kept at it. I shrieked, screamed, cried, pressed my hands against his chest. From the moment he entered me, I felt nothing but pain.

He pulled himself from me and left for the bathroom. Flinging my face into the pillow, I realized I had been deceived by every film and television show and song that had made sex seem like the most romantic and beautiful of human encounters. It had not been romantic. It had not been beautiful. It had been brutal and painful and ugly.

He came to me from the bathroom and lay beside me. "Here's a clean towel," he whispered, wiping my tears. "Is it that time of the month?"

"What? No. Why?"

"I'm sorry. I didn't know."

"Didn't know what?"

He smiled at my ignorance. "That you had never, that," he dropped off.

"Oh."

"Are you okay?"

I nodded and closed my eyes.

I was the first to awake in the morning, aware of my back pressed against his beneath the covers. A dull ache filled my temples, and I put my hand to my head and sighed. A more acute pain clenched between my legs. I thought of Bijan and our engagement, and panic gripped me.

I climbed from the covers, found my clothes, and went to the bathroom. As I washed my hands, I could not meet my own eyes in the mirror. I covered my face and sobbed.

I could pretend this thing had never happened. I could drop Ahmed's class, quit the research assistant position, and never see him again. I could transfer to another university in another town. Bijan would be graduating in May. He would never have to know what I'd done. This was a mistake, but it need not sabotage my dreams for the future.

Yet, if we were still to marry, he would discover my secret. Even if I could come up with an excuse for the lack of blood on our wedding night, he was morally stained by what I'd done to him. I could not marry Bijan. I no longer deserved him.

My hands and knees trembled as I entered the bedroom. Ahmed's back was turned away from me, but I could see his profile nudged against the pillow, and again I was struck by his childlike need for a mother. He was a fallen angel in need of wings. He could not be faulted for my mistake. I needed to be gentle and sympathetic. After all, I did have feelings for him. There had been a chemistry, a meeting of the minds, even the zodiac favored us.

He stirred before I moved to the bed and looked up at me with sleepy, sexy eyes.

"Good morning," he said.

"Good morning." I sat on the bed beside him, afraid.

He lay back on the pillow with one arm across his forehead, his eyes closed.

"I've been thinking," I said.

He did not open his eyes.

"For a long time, I have wanted to break off my engagement." I couldn't believe the words that had come from my mouth.

"I can't let you do that."

I was flabbergasted. "Why not?"

He quickly sat up and took my face in his hands and stared intently in my eyes. "I cannot let you ruin your life over me. You understand? You forget this ever happened, you marry your boyfriend, and you go on happily ever after, okay?"

"But I thought you said—"

"I made a mistake."

"You mean you don't . . ."

"No." He went to the bathroom.

Chapter Seven: Surprise Visit

"Oh, Mona. Are you okay?" Yvette stands and lays a hand on her bony shoulder.

"I can't go on," Mona says through thick sobs. "Please come back tomorrow. Same time."

"You sure you're going to be okay?"

"*None* of us is sure."

Yvette unlatches the chain and lets herself out.

Yvette makes herself a plate of crackers and a mug of hot green tea to calm her nerves and stomach. The way Mona said, "None of us is sure," rang with an air of artificiality. Again she wonders why the woman chose to tell her this strange story.

Maybe I should forget this. She's crazy. Spooky. Weird.

She is so distracted by this thought that she almost misses the light beeping on her answering machine.

The message is barely audible as all three kids excitedly relate the story of Matt's big catch—a twenty-six-pounder, the hook getting stuck in his leg, and the trip to the nearest emergency room to get the hook out. Apparently all was well and worth the injury, and they'd have enough fish to last forever.

I should be with them. God.

After she calls to talk to the kids and Devin, Yvette watches television before going to bed but doesn't sleep most of the night. Too many questions itch her skin and crawl beneath the covers, poking her. All night long, noises around the house—in the yard and in the attic—add to the morose game the questions are playing with Yvette's head.

She hugs Devin's pillow, inhaling his scent, then realizes he has forgotten it. She imagines him lying in the tent with the children, telling them the stories they beg to hear over and over—about the man with the peg leg, or the rat in the attic, or the haunted boat driven by the little girl ghost—and his having to wad up a towel or a pair of sweats to support his head. She feels a sudden urge to drive down to the lake to deliver his pillow.

But instead, she holds it close and recalls the first time she met him.

Her mother died as the honeysuckle bloomed in mid-March. The redbuds and mountain laurels had performed their brief but spectacular explosions of hot pink and purple, the white scallops of the yucca had emerged, and the honeysuckle, their buds out and waiting for many days, had opened the day her mother died.

As though they knew it was a day of mourning, the bees hadn't come. Yvette sat out on her mother's back porch gazing at the garden, wondering what she would do with her mother's belongings, the little house, the rest of her life, when she noticed the bees were missing.

The bees had always come when the honeysuckle bloomed, her whole life they'd come. It was an exceptional year when she didn't get stung at least once as she played in the yard growing up. She had come to expect and not fear them. After years of stings, they no longer hurt. They had become one of those constants in her life, as few as they were, and so she noticed, in spite of her stupor, the day her mother passed, the bees had not come.

Thankfully, her mother was an organized person, so fierce in will even the spices wouldn't dare exist on any spot in the cupboard other than their designated one. Her mother would weekly pull out the items in the freezer, the refrigerator, the pantry, and lay them all out, purge the undesirables, and put what remained back, like the stacking and unstacking of cups in a pyramid, a whirlwind of will and organization. Yvette couldn't stand to be in the house during this weekly ritual, so exhausting was it to watch, so guilt-ridden would she feel for not wanting to help. When her mother died, she left no mess, no loose ends, no unfinished business for Yvette. Her funeral had been saved for, her casket and plot purchased, her bills paid, her laundry washed, her floors swept clean.

But Yvette inherited none of this efficiency, none of the ferocity of will, not a smidgen of confidence. She couldn't sell the house, nor could she live in it, and so she floated in a haze of indecision, the haze becoming a sea that would drown her.

In early June, she drove to Enchanted Rock, a four-hundred foot high slab of pink granite an hour away in Fredericksburg, where someone had recently jumped to his death. Curious to see the place where he took the leap, the crevices his body must have hit, the boulders where his bones would have cracked, she hiked up the rock alongside families and dogs and girl scouts, alone in the crowd, up and up in the heat of the summer, without sunscreen or a hat, to the summit.

She gazed out across the Texas hill country, the wild flowers still in bloom, the sun reflecting a diamond-like sparkle on the pink granite spread smooth like clay all about. She wondered what the man who jumped had been thinking. The paper had said he was a successful rancher, married, in his thirties with two daughters. Why had he jumped?

As Yvette peered down to where his body must have hit, someone asked, "Beautiful, isn't it?"

She almost fell, so surprised was she by another person there, speaking to her no less, just as she had been contemplating her end. The man grabbed her arm and saved her life.

Devin.

She hugs his pillow closer, wishing he was there to save her now from the scary thoughts and creepy sounds keeping her awake. She imagines Mona running through her backyard with a butcher's knife. It is nearly ten when she climbs out of bed, exhausted, Sunday.

She puts on the coffee and dresses when the doorbell rings, which is odd, because her friend Gloria isn't due to arrive until after lunch. Through the window of the door, Yvette recognizes Mona beneath a wide-brimmed straw hat and dark sunglasses.

"Oh, hello," says Yvette, opening the door.

Spooky.

"I came to apologize."

"Apologize? Why?"

"I don't mean to be rude to you, Yvette. I've become a cold and bitter person, angry at the world, angry at everyone, and, well, I'm sorry I take it out on you."

I've been too harsh. She's just lonely.

"Would you like to come inside?"

"I don't want to intrude."

"You're not intruding. Come on in. Would you like coffee?"

"If it's not too much trouble. But I can't stay long."

"Of course not, come in."

She leads Mona to the kitchen table and offers her a chair. She pours them each a cup and then sits across from her visitor.

"I'm in such a state," says Mona, taking off her sunglasses to reveal red-rimmed eyes. "My landlord is going to evict me."

"What? Evict you?"

"I'm several months behind on the rent."

"Do you have a place to stay? Have you found another place to move to?"

Please say yes, please say yes.

"I'll be alright. He gave us a week."

"Us?"

"Me and the cats."

Liar.

"You don't look well," Yvette says. "Can I get you anything else? Something to eat?"

"What a saint. Yes. I could use something to eat."

"Bacon and eggs?"

"Lovely. I'll tell you more of my story while you cook. That sound alright?"

"Of course."

"What a lovely home you have. It must be twice the size of mine."

"Thank you."

"Where did I leave off?"

"You and Ahmed had just—"

"Right."

Chapter Eight: Abandonment

I could have walked to my dorm from Ahmed's house the morning after we slept together, but I let him drive me. I was not yet ready to be out of his presence.

In the car, I asked, "What's going on?"

"You were drunk. I took advantage of you. End of story."

"But Friday you said—"

"I was wrong."

"I don't understand."

"Not everything is meant to be understood."

"This isn't a philosophy lecture."

We were silent until we reached my dorm.

"Thanks for the ride." Too hard, I slammed the car door shut and marched away.

"Where have you been?" Letty turned around in her chair from her desk where she had been working at the computer.

"They abandoned me at Gordito's."

"Why in the world did you go there in the first place? And they told me they wouldn't have left you."

"Yeah, right. And I didn't know where we were going." Slumped down on my bed, the floodgates opened. I couldn't hold up under this interrogation, so how would I face Bijan? "Oh, Letty! What am I going to do?"

"Why? What happened? Where were you?"

I took a deep breath and shuddered before I released my confession. "With Professor Jaffar!"

"What?" Letty looked horrified, both hands at her mouth.

"Don't tell a soul! I will tell Bijan myself. You must swear you won't tell a soul! We didn't actually sleep together!"

"Bijan will die! This will kill him!"

"Keep your voice down. We didn't actually sleep together!"

"Doesn't matter."

I felt more alone than ever as I buried my face in my pillow and wept.

Letty asked softly, "Why did you do it?"

I couldn't answer.

"Do you want me to read your cards?" Letty was already getting out the Tarot cards and flipping them over on her desk.

"Don't tell me," I said, but I wanted to know.

"Oh no."

"What?"

The phone rang.

"Hello?" Letty answered. "Oh, hi Bijan." She shot me a look as I jumped from the bed anxiously. "Um, is Mona here?" I shook my head, backing away. "Yes, she's right here." Then Letty cupped her hands around the phone. "I'm sorry, but I think you have to do this. It's in the cards."

I took it. "Hi." I felt nauseous and was literally shaking from my head to my toes.

"Hi. How are you feeling?"

"Worse."

"You sound like you've been crying. Are you okay?"

"I'm feeling lousy, and I'm sick of it."

"You didn't have a good night out with the girls?"

"No, and I don't even want to talk about it. Come home as soon as you can, okay? I miss you. And I need you." I avoided Letty's eyes.

"That's good to hear. To tell you the truth, Babe, I'm glad you had a miserable time. I was worried all night last night. It's stupid, never mind, but I'm glad you miss me, because I miss you, and I've decided to fly back tonight instead of in the morning."

"Tonight?"

"I leave around four, and I'm due to arrive around seven. I have a layover in Dallas. I'll come get you as soon as I land. I won't even drop off my luggage first. Let's go out to eat and then back to my place. José is in Mexico City visiting his girlfriend."

José was his roommate. They shared an apartment not too far from campus. "Sounds good. I'll see you after seven."

Sitting across from Bijan at the seafood restaurant, I had no idea what I would do. I started down one path, only to change my mind again and again. I had been clinging to him all night, and I could tell he mistook my swollen eyes, pale face, and solemn mood as symptoms of a worn out girl at the tail end of the flu.

"How is it?" he asked about the food.

"Wonderful." Any food was good food, for I had eaten nothing but junk in Bijan's absence—except for the Indian meal with my professor. "Don't you think so?"

"It's okay. I've had better." He was always pickier than I about everything.

"Tell me more about Maman and Baba and everyone. How was the beach?" As I listened to his tale about the fishing, the restaurants, and the family visits, I knew he would be all right without me, he would get on with his life and still find happiness and success, and, if I stayed with him, I would be miserable, because I would always know, every day of my life, I would be betraying him— unless I confessed the truth, but then he would surely despise me forever. "Oh, Bijan!" I interrupted one of his spring break stories.

"What is it?" he asked. "What's the matter?"

Out of the blue, as Bijan stared at me expectantly, I recalled an uncle I barely knew who was in a hurry to get home to his wife and five children when he decided to drive past two cars stopped at a railroad crossing, through the barricade and flashing red lights, and then, boom, the train hit, and his life was over in a matter of seconds. Some decisions are irrevocable.

I said, "I missed you so much!" I leaned over the table to kiss him, taking in his smell, like fresh peppermint. I loved his smell.

"My sweet, sweet Mona." He took my hand, which flinched at his touch, lest he sense some remnant, some indication of the man who had held it the previous night. Then he put it to his mouth and kissed it.

"Look at your thumb!"

I pulled my hand away. "I've been nervous lately."

"I thought you were going to quit."

"I don't always know I'm doing it."

"It looks ghastly. You might need to put ointment on it. Let me see the other one."

"Forget it. Okay?" I put my hands beneath the table.

After our meal, as we drove to his apartment, my mind reeled as I imagined how things would be if I stayed with Bijan. There had been something between me and Ahmed, a kind of connection I didn't always feel with Bijan. There was also the mystery of Ahmed's troubled past, of his complex personality, of his hopes and dreams. He seemed to need me more than Bijan needed me.

I knew all about Bijan. His life, his thoughts, his feelings were an open book to me, and this, of late, had dulled our relationship. I didn't want to make a mistake by accepting the first proposal offered to me.

I glanced at Bijan as he drove onto the exit ramp and recalled our problem with the zodiac and how he was critical of me when it came to cooking and cleaning and modern art. I decided to recite "The Pasture," as a kind of test.

He said, "Yes, I remember. You've told it to me before. It's beautiful."

"You think so?"

"Absolutely. So much nicer than others you have recited."

"Like the E.E. Cummings one?"

"Which one?"

"You know, the one about the balloonman?"

"Oh, yes. The goat-footed balloonman. That one didn't do much for me." I gave him a hurt look. "Come on. It's okay if we don't like the same things."

"But a good marriage is based on commonalities."

"Oh, brother. Just because I don't like one poem, now we don't have commonalities? We have a lot in common."

"I hate to fish and you love it."

"But, you like the beach."

"I like to go to operas and plays and musicals, and you can barely tolerate them."

"*Barely tolerate* is the operative phrase. At least I try to tolerate them for you."

"You separate your laundry and I throw everything together."

"We'll do our own laundry."

"You think homosexuality is sinful and I don't."

"If you ever bring home any gay friends, I promise to be nice. What's going on, Mona? Why are you saying these things?"

"Oh, I don't know."

"You're scaring me. Are you having second thoughts?"

I couldn't look at him. "No, no, of course not. I don't think so. Oh, I don't know!"

We fell silent. He drove into the parking lot of his apartment and parked the car, and then, together, like two sullen children, we entered his place.

Bijan closed the door and took me in his arms. "Don't do this, Babe. I love you. I love you with all my heart."

"I know." I loved him, too, but I didn't want to admit it as I was about to say good-bye.

He stepped back from the embrace, his eyes wide. "It's your philosophy professor!"

I gaped and couldn't speak.

"I knew it!" he shouted. He turned away from me, rubbing his fingers through his hair.

I followed him. "Bijan! Has Letty said something to you?"

"Why, does she know?"

"Know what? Nothing. She wants you for herself, and so she lies to you about me."

"Ridiculous." I knew it was, but I was desperate. He crossed his arms in front of his chest. "Now tell me, what's going on?"

"Nothing is going on! I'm just getting cold feet. I'm sure it's nothing. I just, I just, I just need time to think."

"Why now, all of a sudden?"

"It's not all of a sudden. I've been questioning things this entire semester. I guess having a little time away from you has made me see things differently."

"Tell me, Mona. How do you see things?"

I named everything about him I considered a flaw. He wasn't passionate about anything, he didn't understand true art, he was always critical of me, he smothered my free spirit and rained on my ideas, he wanted to move to Los Angeles or stay in Brownsville, and I wanted to move around, maybe even go to graduate school abroad. I hated the way he gloated over me every time he won a bet. He rarely wanted to kiss me on the lips anymore. And on and on and on. I became cruel and heartless in order to protect myself from exposing the truth, the terrible truth of my betrayal.

He stood there, bearing it all.

When I had finished, I covered my mouth, shocked by the words that had rushed from my lips. It was finished. I had made my choice, and by the ache in Bijan's eyes, I could see the choice was irrevocable.

After we stood, silent, for several minutes, he said, "I can't believe it." He spoke softly. "I can't believe it. Someone wake me up from this nightmare and give me back my life."

"I'm so sorry." I couldn't believe it either.

"I don't want your apology. That's something you say when you've dumped beer on someone's shirt." That was how we met. I had spilled beer on him by accident at a party.

He sat on the sofa, stunned, tears running down his cheeks. We were both silent. I sat beside him and tried to embrace him, but he seemed not to feel it. He put his face in his hands and wept. I rambled on about how sorry I was, I hadn't meant what I'd said, it was the flu talking, not me, but it did no good.

After a few more minutes, he stood and muttered, "Come on. I'll take you home."

In the car he asked for his ring. I didn't expect him to take it, but he did. It was a family heirloom, he said, and he intended to keep it in the family.

"Can I call you?" I asked.

"Why?"

"Oh, Bijan! I didn't mean those things I said! I'm so sorry!"

"You meant them. It was crystal clear you meant them." He pulled into the lot in front of my dorm. "Good bye." He waited for me to get out of the car and leave.

"I'll always love you. Please, Bijan, look at me. You don't deserve me. I'm the one who is wrong for you. Forget all I said tonight. It's me. You have always been so perfect. You would have been miserable with me."

He glared at me. "Yes. You're right, Mona. I would have been miserable. Thanks a million for sparing me." He drove away, nearly knocking me onto the pavement. I watched him go as the gloomy night rained down on me.

Fortunately, Letty was out. I cried for an hour without stopping. Then, I sat up, blew my nose, went to the bathroom, and thought of Ahmed Jaffar. A surprisingly pleasant feeling overcame me. It was the feeling of liberty. I was free.

I telephoned Ahmed but thought the lines must have gone down because of the rain, for a recording said the number was no longer a working number. I dialed again, in case I had dialed the wrong number, and I got the same recording. I was desperate to see him. I had to prove to him, and to myself, we were meant to be together.

I put on my jacket, grabbed my umbrella, and headed toward his house on foot. I could have driven, but I thought the walk would clear my mind. Once I turned back. Bijan stood there, huddled in his leather jacket near his car in the parking lot of my dorm. How long had he been standing in the rain? I should have run to him; instead, I gripped the handle of my umbrella and sloshed through puddles toward Ahmed's house.

I rang his bell. When several minutes passed and he still had not come to the door, I knocked, in case he had fallen asleep. I walked over to the garage and peeked through the small, square windows. His corvette was out. I was struck, before I took my eyes away, by how perfectly clean the garage appeared by the light of the street lamppost. There wasn't a thing in it.

I walked around, through a wooden gate, to the back of the house, to his bedroom window, and tried to lift it, hoping I might find a way inside and wait for him, but it would not budge. I peered in through the window. The blinds were closed. I tried to reach the kitchen window on the other side of the house, but it was higher up. I found an old bucket in the corner of the yard and turned it over on the ground beneath the window and climbed on top. The window would not move. There were no lights on in the house, but by the dim light of the moon, which barely broke through the tumultuous clouds above, I saw, to my great surprise, his dining room table and chairs were missing. Before I could think of what this might mean, I lost my balance on the bucket and fell, backside first, right into the mud.

Chapter Nine: The Nursery

Yvette's phone rings a new crazy tune Casey must have reset it to.

Casey. I miss her. I miss them all.

"Ready?" Gloria asks over the phone.

"Let me call you right back." Yvette hangs up. She has finished her eggs and bacon, but Mona is just now eating.

"It's delicious," Mona says with food in her mouth. "Thank you."

"So where did Ahmed go?"

Mona sips her coffee. "Should I finish when you come later? You are coming, aren't you?"

"Yes. That would be better. I'm going to the nursery with a friend of mine in a little while."

"Oh? Which one?"

Yvette tells her.

"Sounds lovely. I enjoy walking around all those beautiful plants."

Yvette wonders if Mona is hinting for an invitation.

Mona finishes up her plate and thanks Yvette again. "I'll see you at four."

Yvette whistles as she cleans and puts away the breakfast dishes. She looks forward to shopping for plants with Gloria. Every spring, they take a dozen trips together, not always to buy, though today she will not leave without three pots of annuals for her back patio. These visits to the nursery with Gloria have given continuity to Yvette's life, because it once was a tradition she shared with her father.

Her favorite trip occurred one spring when she was ten, two short years before cancer would take him, and her plant-shopping would come to an abrupt halt until her late thirties. Her mother wasn't a gardener. Unlike Yvette's father, who could spend hours outside training vines to a trellis, pruning roses, fertilizing the hydrangeas, her mother found no joy in such solitary tasks. Yvette thinks now her mother likely could not tolerate a hobby that undermined her complete control. No matter how much one trained, pruned, and fertilized, one could not dominate nature, but only guide it to become what it willed itself to be. No, her mother preferred to spend her time organizing the inanimate objects of the household and left the living to Yvette's father.

When they went on these trips together, sometimes her father bought new pots of flowers, but sometimes they just looked around to learn the names of more plants and to ask questions of the employees, especially Ed, a sweet old man who knew everything about Texas plants.

The first time they met him, though, they thought he was dead.

They were walking past the hydrangeas toward the vines and trees on the outskirts of the nursery when they found him lying face down in the dirt off the path. His denim jeans and boots were covered in mud, and the green uniform shirt was soaked. His elbows were bent and his hands were pressed against the dirt beside his head.

"Oh my God," her father said.

"Is he dead?" Yvette whispered.

"I don't know." In a louder voice, he said, "Sir? Excuse me, sir?"

The man on the ground didn't move.

"What do we do?" Yvette whispered.

"Let's turn him over," her father said.

"Shouldn't we get help?"

"You go for help. I'll see if he's breathing, if he has a pulse. I know CPR."

Before Yvette ran off, the man on the ground said, "Don't move."

Yvette stopped, unsure of what to do. By now others had noticed and a woman shouted to call 9-1-1.

"What's wrong?" her father asked the man.

"You'll scare 'em."

"Who?"

The man was staring at the ground. Yvette thought he was senile or delusional.

"Let me help you up," her father said.

"I said don't move. You'll scare 'em. Look at 'em. I think he's from Nicaragua."

Yvette glanced around, expecting radical terrorists with guns to emerge from a shrub. Then a movement on the ground by the man's nose caught her attention. Whatever it was, it was beautiful. Its body was long and narrow, like the bracts of a shrimp plant, but green instead of salmon, with a blade of grass pointing back from its face, like a feather on the head of an American Indian. Two blue blades swept from the end of its body like the forked tail of a whale, and its four legs resembled green plastic ties. Yvette and her father knelt beside the man staring at the bug, she wondering if it could really be an insect with four legs, before they heard the sirens.

Yvette's father jumped to his feet. "He's okay. We don't need an ambulance. He was staring at a bug."

"He was what?" someone asked.

"He ran off," the old man said, getting up. "Wish I had a picture of 'em. That there was the four-legged grasshopper talked about in the good book."

A woman in the crowd said, "Call off the ambulance. Tell them it was a false alarm. Ed's fine.

111

Everybody back to work." The crowd behind Yvette dispersed. The sirens continued in the distance.

"What? You called for an ambulance?"

"We thought you were dead, old man." My father slapped Ed on the back.

"I'm old, but I ain't that old. Man, I wish I had a camera."

"I wonder what kind of bug that was," her father said. "It was beautiful. Did you see it, Yvette? I've never seen anything like it."

"He won't last long here," the man said. "All by hisself. I'm glad I got to look at 'em but sorry he's here. Must've come in on a shipment."

"We could send him to the insectorium in New Orleans," her father said. "Let's look for him."

At first Yvette thought they were nuts, two men crawling on the ground on all fours searching through the nearby variegated ginger and Chinese laurels.

"I don't think we'll see him again," the old man said.

"But we might," her father said. "It couldn't hurt to try."

Inspired by her father's optimism, Yvette decided to join them, dragging her jean-clad knees through the dirt, peering on leaves and stems. She became interested in saving the bug, even though she was the kind of person who killed bugs when she found them in the house rather than

112

capture and release them outside, unless they were interesting or beautiful. She crawled around thinking how unfair she was to the ugly, plain, regular bugs of the world. And just as she was condemning herself for being an elitist—a bug elitist (she had just learned that word in school)—she found the rare insect and swept him up in both hands.

And then, with a sinking feeling in her chest, she asked, "He's not poisonous, is he?"

"I don't think so. I read the kids in Nicaragua carry 'em around in their hands."

She sighed with relief. "Well, I got him. Now what?"

"Way to go, Yvette!" her father said.

The man laughed and patted her on the back. "Well I'll be. Let's put 'em in a jar. Then we'll call that insectorium and see what to do."

"I can't believe you found him," her father said to her on the drive home, again and again. "I can't believe it. One in a million, your chances, and you found him. You know what that means?"

"What?"

"You're special, that's what." He gave her a grin and patted her shoulder.

Yvette's eyes fill with tears as she dries her hand on a dish towel.

In the car, Gloria pulls on the shoulder harness, complaining how they dig into her full-figure, how a better design was needed for rounder people. She reminds Yvette of her mother, the way she demanded the world live up to her high expectations in all ways, leaving her disappointed. Yvette prefers not to expect anything.

As Gloria drives Yvette to the nursery on the outskirts of their neighborhood, she says, "Heidi asked me to put a bug in your ear."

"I'm listening."

"I can't believe you skipped out on your family."

"I wasn't feeling up to camping."

Liar.

"Think of the kids. This is the time for making family memories."

"Is that Heidi's bug?"

"No. Heidi wants us to go on a cruise together."

"She's been saying that for years. I thought we decided we can't afford it."

Gloria pulls into the parking lot and finds a space. "She found an early booking deal. It would be in June, but next year, and it would be half the regular price. You have to put down a deposit within the next few days, but you have until a year from now to get your deposit back if you change your mind. She had ideas for how we could raise money."

Yvette steps from the car. "We could always sell our bodies for sex."

"That's what I thought, too. We could advertise ourselves on Craigslist as a three-some."

An older couple gives them a funny look, and Yvette and Gloria giggle as they enter the grounds of the nursery.

"We could stand on the corner of our street with a sign asking for donations," Yvette says.

"I'm sure our neighbors want to support our vacation."

"So what were Heidi's ideas?"

"She thought we could offer a homemade meal delivery service."

"I think I'd rather sell my body for sex than do all that cooking. I barely cook for my own family."

"But your family doesn't pay you. You'd cook for paying customers. Think of the cruise."

They come to the ornamental trees, which are Yvette's most recent obsession. She has mapped out on graph paper where she wants to plant several specimens. "So this redbud would take center stage," she says, showing Gloria her sketch. "I'd have loquats in the far corners, and then a Japanese maple here and a crepe myrtle here."

"Which are the loquats?"

"These." She puts her hand on the thin trunk of a young tree to their right. "I like the dense foliage. Great privacy." She thinks of the face in Mona's yard staring at her between the slats of the fence.

"And then where does the water feature go?"

"Here, in this corner. But I'm talking years down the road."

"Especially if we go on this cruise."

Yvette stares up at the beautiful trees, their graceful branches swaying in the gentle breeze. She imagines her back garden, and asks, "Did Heidi have any other ideas, besides the cooking business?"

"Holiday gift baskets, tamales at Christmas, and a community cookbook, which I actually thought was a good idea."

"Really, Gloria? A cookbook?"

"Wait. This wouldn't be your everyday cookbook. I'm talking nude. Not nude, but suggestive. We'd get people in the community who are well known to pose in a cooking situation."

They move past the trees. "Hmm. I still think I'd rather sell my body for sex. I'd just have to lay there."

"You might not make much money," Gloria teases.

An attractive younger man, stooped over a plant, glances up at Yvette. She gives him a mischievous smile, and he smiles back.

When Yvette turns, she almost walks into Mona. She wears the same wide-brimmed hat and sunglasses.

Spooky.

"Oh, hello. I didn't expect to see you here," says Yvette, and inside her head, alarms are sounding. She can't believe Mona has followed her to the nursery.

"Yes, well, when you mentioned you were coming, I couldn't stop thinking how lovely it sounded. I'm trying to keep my mind off things, you know."

"Of course. I should have invited you along."

Except you're scaring the hell out of me.

"Oh, no. I wouldn't want to intrude on your plans with your friend."

Liar.

"This is Gloria. Gloria, this is the neighbor lady I've been visiting."

Mona frowns, as though worried Yvette hasn't kept her secret.

Yvette quickly adds, "She's the one who makes such delicious cookies and cakes. We chat about the kids and such."

"Does neighbor lady have a name?" Gloria asks.

"Mary," replies Mona, extending her hand. "Nice to meet you."

"Nice to meet you, too," Gloria says. "You chat about the kids? Does that mean you have some of your own, Mary?"

Mona shakes her head. "You?"

"Six," Gloria says. "Ranging in age from two to fifteen."

Mona frowns again. "Well, nice to meet you. I'll see you later, Yvette." Mona turns and disappears behind the mandevilla.

Strange. Spooky and strange.

"What was that all about?" asks Gloria. "She didn't seem happy to meet me."

"I think she might have lost a baby once, but I don't know."

"You mean a miscarriage, or the baby died?"

"I don't know." A chill works its way down Yvette's back as she walks with Gloria through the perennials.

After Gloria drops off Yvette from the nursery, Yvette takes her new plants to the backyard and replaces a few of the annuals she has in pots on her patio. She's still shaken from her encounter with Mona and has decided she shouldn't return this afternoon as she has promised. As much as she wants to hear the end of the woman's story, she's too unsettled by Mona's intrusions into her life. It was one thing to appear on Yvette's front doorstep, but another to show up during her outing with a friend.

She's just too strange.

"Hi, Yvette," comes the familiar voice through the slats of the fence. "Find anything at the nursery? Oh, those are lovely."

Yvette doesn't turn to the fence, not wanting to see the spooky image of Mona's pale face pressed against the wood.

"Thanks."

"Do you think you can come a little early today? Two- o'clock?"

Oh hell.

"About that. I'm afraid I'm worn out from the shopping. Maybe we should shoot for tomorrow instead."

Liar.

"What?" Mona's voice is an octave higher and ten decibels louder. "Are you serious? You can't be! I'm nearly finished. You must come. You can rest here while I talk."

Yvette rinses the soil from her hands at the spigot on the back of her house ready to make a run for the back door if Mona doesn't calm down. "I'm sorry. I may be coming down with the flu."

"My aunt was a nurse and taught me everything she knew. Come over and I'll examine you. Or I'll come there."

"No, that's not necessary."

"So you'll come at two?"

"I suppose."

No backbone.

Yvette decides she better show up or Mona will come knocking at her door. Hoping this will be her last visit, she walks around the block. Maybe once Mona finishes her story, she won't be so needy. Maybe she needs to get the horrible burden of whatever happened off her chest. Then Yvette can go back to her normal life without Mona in it.

Mona greets Yvette at the door. "Did you enjoy the nursery?"

"Yes. I always do. You?" Yvette follows her into the house.

"Yes. I don't get out much. It was nice."

Yvette sits down. "Good."

"We could go together sometime. To the nursery. Maybe this week?"

Spooky and strange.

"Maybe."

No backbone.

"Would you like tea and cake today?"

"No thank you. I just ate."

Mona sits opposite her. "I believe I left off at Ahmed's disappearance."

Chapter Ten: The Book in the Box

I tried in vain all weekend to reach Ahmed by telephone. On Sunday, I drove once more to his house, but found no evidence he was there.

I half-hoped Bijan would call, but he didn't. I couldn't wait for Ahmed's class, so I could ask him where he'd been, but was shocked to learn another professor would be taking over the course. The class was told the previous teacher had emergency family matters to attend to in Afghanistan and would not be returning to the university. I left early, rushing over to the philosophy department hoping to learn more about Ahmed's whereabouts.

"Is there a telephone number or address where he can be reached?" I asked the secretary.

"I'm sorry. I don't have any info on this professor. You might check back with me in a week or so. He'll let us know once he's settled again."

As the days passed, I became more and more determined to find Ahmed, but I sometimes felt helpless, and it was during these times I considered calling Bijan and begging for his forgiveness. Twice I picked up the phone to dial his number but knew he must despise me and there was nothing I could do. I had to find Ahmed. I had given up everything for him.

During the following week, I made several trips to Ahmed's house peering inside windows, unable to believe he could have moved completely out in the short time that had passed. At last I had the idea to check out his office on campus for clues. I told the secretary I was his research assistant and needed to get my things out of his office.

She looked at me suspiciously. "Research assistant? Professor Jaffar didn't have a research assistant to my knowledge."

The blood rushed from my face. "But he paid me to do work for him. He said I was in the employment of the university."

"That's odd." I could tell the woman didn't believe me, but she said, "Well, his office is empty."

"Please?"

"Since no one new has been assigned to it, I guess there's no harm in letting you take a peek."

The secretary took a set of keys from the side drawer of her desk and led me down the hall to what had once been Ahmed's office. My heart raced as the woman unlocked and opened the office door. "See? Empty."

I walked past the secretary and pulled open the top drawer of the clean desk. Nothing. Not even a rubber band or a paper clip. I inspected the empty shelves. Just a bunch of dust. I was about to turn and leave when I caught sight of a cardboard box beneath the desk.

"Here it is! See? He put it under the desk and forgot to return it to me." I pulled the box from beneath the desk. It was not too heavy. "Thank you for letting me inside to get my stuff."

The secretary first narrowed her eyes and then, probably because she did not want to bother with challenging me, shrugged and followed me back up the hall. I gave her one last backward glance and then headed down the adjoining hall in the opposite direction with the cardboard box in my arms.

Inside was a manuscript written in another language. Even though I couldn't understand the words, I knew I had found Ahmed's book, at least a copy of it.

As I sat on my bed in my dorm looking over the manuscript, the lock on the door turned, and Letty and her friend Jan entered.

"Hey, how'd it go with Bijan?"

"We broke up."

Letty sat beside me on the bed. "That's what the cards predicted. I'm so sorry. Then again, so did that astrologist on South Padre Island. You knew this was coming."

"It's for the best." I fought the tears welling in my eyes.

"I'm sorry, Mona." Letty hugged me, but I sat impassive. "What's that?"

"Ahmed's book. He left it behind. I'm trying to figure out what language it's in."

"Listen, about your professor," Letty said. "I've got a bad feeling, from the cards."

Jan sat beside me. "Can I see?"

"She speaks five languages," added Letty.

"Can you read it?" I rose to my feet.

"No."

"Oh," I slumped back down beside Letty. "Do you know anyone who might be able to?"

Jan said she had a history professor who was from Pakistan who might be able to help, so the next day, which was my birthday—I turned twenty-two, and Bijan didn't call, didn't send a card, nothing—Jan, Letty, and I walked across campus to the history department to see Jan's professor.

He sat behind his desk and welcomed us into his office, which smelled of salami and pickles. He had a friendly, round face. "I love visitors," he said. "Come in. Find a place to sit down. Move the stack of books from the chair to the floor. Yes, right over there is fine. Now, what can I do for you?"

Jan said, "I've brought a friend who needs a book translated."

"Not entirely translated. I just want an idea of the book."

"I think it is written in Pashto," said Jan. "Can you read it?"

"Let me see."

I handed him the first page from the pile of loose sheets in the cardboard box. The professor moved his lips and muttered the sounds of a language I had never heard before.

"What does it say?" I asked.

"It appears to be a philosophical discussion about free will or the lack of it. The author is introducing a series of experiments he says disproves the notion we are free. He cites modern studies of the impact of genetics on human behavior."

"Thank you, Professor."

"I would be happy to read it for you and tell you what I can."

"I don't want to be any trouble to you," I said. "I know you must be a busy man."

"True. But I happen to find this interesting, and I haven't read anything in Pashto for quite a while. The experience will sharpen my skills."

I didn't want to leave the entire book with this man I did not know. It was the only thing I had left of Ahmed. On the other hand, this professor might be able to reveal, through reading the book, what had led to Ahmed's disappearance. "Well, okay. It's very sentimental to me, though. I wouldn't mind leaving it for a few days, but can I come for it next week?"

It was settled. I offered to pay, but he refused. As I walked across campus with Letty and Jan, I had a strange feeling.

Chapter Eleven: New Suspicions

The hair rises on the back of Yvette's neck. She knows someone is standing behind her as sure as she knows Mona is sitting beside her. She hears a shuffle and the slam of a door and turns to the hall as the one-eyed cat leaps onto Mona's lap. Yvette scans the empty hallway and listens for the person she knows was standing there, but the house is as silent as a graveyard.

Shit. This is too spooky and strange.

"Babs's tail does that to the doors sometimes," Mona says stiffly. "It scares her to death, doesn't it girl?" She kisses the top of the cat's head.

Liar.

"I thought I heard someone," says Yvette, her heart beating fast.

"There's no one here but us. And the cats."

Yvette doesn't force the issue, but she does come up with an idea. "I might have a friend interested in renting this place. I could take a look around and see if I think it will suit her."

"Not today." She pushes Babs from her lap and rises from her chair. "I need to check on my other cat. I'll be right back."

Her bony frame in the ratty robe sweeps across the floor like a ghost. The cat follows her into one of the back rooms. Determined to find a clue about the person Yvette knows is living there, she hurries to the first door off the hallway. It's the bathroom. She closes the door and locks it, heart pounding against her ribs.

Ta-ta-ta-ta-ta-ta-ta-ta.

Although she finds a box of kitty litter beneath the pedestal sink, she also discovers men's deodorant and cologne behind the mirrored door of the medicine cabinet along with three bottles of pills, but before she can read the labels, Mona inserts a key into the knob.

Shit!

"Almost done!" Yvette flushes the toilet. She closes the medicine cabinet and turns on the faucet beneath it to wash her hands. The door flies open.

"Oh, it's you," says Mona. "I'm sorry. I thought Boots had accidentally locked himself in again. He does that sometimes. Are you finished then? Oh, good."

Spooky and strange.

She waits for Yvette as she dries her hands. Red-faced and trembling, Yvette returns to her chair wondering what the hell she is doing. For all Yvette knows, Mona's whole story is a lie. But why would she invent it day after day?

Yvette is ready to leave and be done with Mona, but before she can say anything, Mona sits across from her and continues her story as though nothing out of the ordinary has happened.

No backbone.

Chapter Twelve: A New Turn

After I dropped off Ahmed's manuscript with Professor Hussain, I spent the weekend with my parents. They wanted to do nothing but watch the war in Iraq on the various networks—except for the few minutes we celebrated my birthday over cake and ice cream. I watched, too, anxiously absorbing every piece of information, although I had rarely cared to listen to the news before this war. I wondered whether Ahmed was trapped in an international airport, a hostage or worse, as he tried desperately to get to his family emergency in Afghanistan, if such an emergency existed.

I doubted he had left the country, since others from the Middle East had been denied by U.S. authorities their requests to return home. I sometimes felt him watching me and often waited on the third floor in the library for the meeting I knew must come. I was convinced he had sacrificed his love for me because he thought I would be better off with Bijan.

I didn't tell my family about the break up. I told them Bijan was out of town again with the geology club, and they had no reason to doubt it. But late Saturday night, when I took a break from the war to go outside by the back shed where Leroy smoked his pot, I blurted the news to him.

"That's too bad. He was a good guy."

"I didn't think you liked him."

We sat in lawn chairs beneath a huge pecan tree. Leroy propped up his feet on the homemade barbecue pit he had helped my father make years ago. I could barely see the smoke he exhaled in the dusk, but the smell was more conspicuous.

He said, "No, I liked Bijan. We didn't see things the same way, but I liked him."

"How do you see things?"

He paused to exhale. "Why do you care?"

"I'm curious."

As I waited for his reply, I recalled one Christmas when I was four and he was fourteen. Our parents had just married—he's my half-brother from my mother's side. I had crawled beneath the Christmas tree to look at the name on the biggest present. Leroy had tried to get as far back as me, on his belly like a salamander, and he said, "It spells Bibichka," which means grandma in Czech, but he bumped the tree on his way out and it would have fallen had my father not happened by and saved it.

My dad was in a bad mood, and when he saved the tree, he slapped his hand across Leroy's thigh with only the thin flannel pajamas between them and shouted, "Yeshis Madia! Get out of there!"

It was my fault. Leroy did it for me.

So, in answer to my question as we sat in the backyard of my parents' house, Leroy said, "I don't know. I have questions, and I don't see how anyone can know the answers. It bugs me when people think they do. Even Mom and Ted."

"What kind of questions?"

He crossed his arms over his chest with the joint resting between two fingers. "Well, for one thing, if I were the supreme being of the universe, I'd dole out my goodies equally. What kind of god would give more to some and less to others?"

"Sometimes less is more."

He rolled his eyes. "And I wouldn't require my creations to worship me. If they want to thank me, fine. But if they forget all about me, that would be okay, too. What kind of egomaniac creates other beings primarily so they will love and worship him?"

I knew it would do no good to argue with him.

"Why'd you come out here?"

I shrugged.

He held the joint out to me, but I said, "No thanks."

"Ever tried this stuff?"

"No."

"Why don't you? Come on. It'll make you feel better."

"Some other time."

We sat quietly for a while watching the stars come out.

"Leroy?"

"Yeah?"

I wanted to tell him I missed being close to him, I felt frightened and alone, and I needed him to be a big brother to me. I thought about the time beneath the Christmas tree. I had cried at the injustice, and he had patted my back and said it hadn't hurt and not to worry, and it hadn't been my fault. I picked at my sore and bleeding thumbs, and, instead of telling him the things I wished to say, I muttered, "I'm going in. The mosquitoes are biting."

I skipped classes Monday, Tuesday, and Wednesday of the following week to watch the war on my suitemates' television. I hadn't dressed. I wore a long t-shirt and underwear and socks. The rings of old mascara from earlier in the week added to the dark circles beneath my eyes due to lack of sleep over a new fear. Watching with the rest of the nation the triumphant toppling of an icon of one of the cruelest dictators in world history by a mass of celebrant Iraqis, I wept—not for the Americans who had risked their lives for this glorious moment, nor for the Iraqis who, for the first time, had a taste of liberty—for myself.

I rushed to the commode where I was sick for the second time that morning and for the third consecutive day.

On Holy Thursday, when I was supposed to be at my parents' house, I sat alone on the third floor of the library at my special window gazing out at the night and the lights of downtown Brownsville. I felt so far off course at the moment—and so alone—out in the middle of nowhere in a dreadful storm. Ironically, *The Complete Works of Shakespeare* lay across my legs opened to the first page of *The Tempest*; but in real life, no Prospero had used magic to rage the sea against me: it had been my own doing.

When I least expected it, Ahmed was there. He had come for me as I knew he would.

At the soft whisper of my name, I turned and recognized him in spite of the beard and mustache, in spite of the brown baseball cap pulled down deep across the brow, in spite of the baggy shirt and jeans. I stood and leaped at him and wrapped my arms around him.

I whispered at his ear. "You've come back! I'm so glad! I knew you would! I knew it! Why did you leave? Where did you go?"

"Let's go."

"Where?"

"To my place."

"But it's empty. What happened?"

"To another place. I'll explain on the way."

I left *The Tempest* on the chair as he took my hand and led me out of the building.

"You got a new car?" I asked with disappointment when he opened the passenger side and helped me into the maroon Buick Regal, which was not brand new but in nice condition. I missed his shiny red corvette.

He nodded, closed the door, and quickly made his way around the car to the driver's side. He started the engine and drove away, away from the university toward the central part of town.

Giddy with excitement and nervousness, I knew I was foolish for going with him. I knew I took a terrible chance, but I was so relieved he had come for me. "Tell me what's been going on. It smells like cigarette smoke in here."

"I had to go to Afghanistan. My grandmother died."

"Oh, no!"

"I didn't know how soon I could come back with the war going on, so I took everything with me. I'm sorry I didn't call or write to you. I've been going through a difficult time. She raised me from twelve years old, after my parents were killed. She was like a mother to me. I still can't believe it."

"I'm so sorry!" I touched his shoulder, happy now reason had apparently reentered my life. I should have been sad for him, but, instead, I smiled. My world made sense again. "You wouldn't believe how many times I drove to your house, peering in the windows, hoping I'd see some sign of you. You vanished, just like that," I snapped my fingers, "right into thin air." I glanced over at his dark face, so strange with the beard. "I broke off my engagement."

He met my eyes briefly and turned back to the road.

His silence made me angry. Maybe he didn't love me after all. Maybe he hadn't come back for me. Maybe, oh! I clenched my jaw. I couldn't stand his silence.

"Bijan and I were too different. I would have broken it off even if I had never met you. You were the catalyst. I didn't break up because I expected, I mean, I didn't think... What I mean is, I don't know how I feel, and I wouldn't be surprised if you didn't either."

I put my hand on my belly as my eyes welled with tears. I gazed at the moon. For the millionth time, I wished I hadn't left Bijan. I wished I were in his arms right then feeling safe and secure and sure about my future. I missed his smell. If only I could turn back the clock. Ahmed hadn't come back to marry me! He had only come, he had come for, why had he come back? I bit a thick piece of skin from the least sore of my thumbs.

"Why have you come for me, Ahmed? And where are you taking me?"

"I'll explain everything when we get to the motel."

"Why can't you tell me now?"

"I need to stay focused on the road. We're almost there. Be patient with me." He glanced over at me. "I'm glad to see you."

"Really?"

He nodded.

Alarm overcame me when he pulled into the parking lot of a third-rate motel and stopped at the end of a string of rooms, on the darkest corner, away from the streetlight and the traffic—the perfect place, I thought, for a secret crime. Yet, I followed him as he wrestled the key from the front pocket of his baggy jeans and then worked it into the knob of the faded, cracked door.

It was blackness inside until he found a lamp, which he dimmed to the softest level. The bed was made, but the rest of the room was in disarray. Clothes lay strewn across the two chairs by the window. Loose change, keys, gum and candy wrappers, and folded pieces of paper littered the table. White Styrofoam cups and old takeout boxes were piled on top of the dresser and the television. Cigarette smoke permeated the air, and stubs covered the nightstand, overflowing from the single aluminum ashtray. A bottle of scotch stood in the middle of the stubs beside a pair of binoculars, a cell phone, and the motel phone. Four pair of shoes crowded the doorway on the floor: sneakers, boots, sandals, and black dress shoes. In the closet hung several sets of clothes—jeans and polo shirts and button downs, but also three suits, a tux, and a winter coat. Two duffle bags, unzipped and half full, bulged from the closet floor. On the double bed lay a laptop, a digital camera, and a folded newspaper. Beneath the table between the two chairs sat a messy stash of what must have been two or three weeks' worth of newspapers.

I gave him a faint smile. "I didn't realize you smoked. Looks like you've been here a while."

"I apologize for the mess. It is difficult to go from living in a large house to a small room. I have been here a week, but it must look as though I have been here much longer."

"Why didn't you find me sooner?"

He shifted things around to make room for us, removing the clothes from the chairs and taking the things from the table and piling them onto the dresser. He put the laptop and camera on one of the duffle bags in the floor of the closet.

As he maneuvered around the room, he said, "I had some things I needed to do first. It's been a tough week." He stopped and gazed across the room at me, he by the closet where he had put the laptop, and I near the door, for I had not yet completely entered the room, though the door was closed and locked behind me. "I tried calling a few times, but I hung up when your roommate answered, and I didn't know your cell number."

I shrugged, more like a twitch. "My cell phone's always dead." I sat in the chair closest to the door. "I'm glad you found me, because I need to tell you something important."

Ahmed walked across the room before I could continue and plucked me from the chair and into his arms.

As he swept his lips across mine and I felt the sweet, warm breath that was also his, I closed my eyes. Our bodies became a feverish frenzy of hands moving over one another, of lips meeting lips, tongue, neck, ears. Then we both pulled off our clothes, quickly, feverishly. He guided me toward the bed and I fell back, pulling him to me, clinging to his neck.

When it was over, I clung to Ahmed and wished it hadn't ended. Tears gathered in my eyes. I was disappointed and far from fulfilled, and terribly, terribly frightened and lonely.

"Who are you?" I whispered, not daring to look at him. We both lay with our heads on the pillows, our eyes on the dingy ceiling above us.

"Hmm. I don't know. I have not yet completed the map of my DNA." He laughed, which made me giggle. Then he propped himself up on one elbow to gaze down at me. "But I can say this: I feel more alive in your presence than anywhere in the world."

"Really?"

He nodded and smiled.

I pulled back the bedcovers and crawled beneath them, putting my hand across his chest and nestling against him. "You confuse the hell out of me."

"I confuse the hell out of myself. Believe me, I wish I were someone else, someone who could be with you."

I lifted my head and half-sat up. "What do you mean?"

He led me back down upon the pillow and pressed his lips once more against mine. Then he said, "I wish I were marriage material. I know you want a family—you should have one. But I could never be a family man."

"Why not?" a flutter rushed across my abdomen— butterflies.

"My life is too complicated. It's not conducive to marriage and family and roots. I never thought I would find someone like you who would make me fall in love."

I smiled and then immediately frowned. "If you love me, then—"

"It's much too complicated. It won't work. Go back to your boyfriend. He'll make you happy." Bitterness crept into his voice as he lay back on the pillow and put an arm across his brow.

"But I don't love him, I love you!"

"Can't it be enough, my loving you? I didn't have to admit that, you know."

"I knew you were lying before. I knew you were. And no, it's not enough. Not to me."

"It has to be. It's all I have to offer." He resumed his position of before, propped on the one elbow. He played with my hair. "Stay here tonight. Stay the weekend. Let's have the time of our lives. But it has to end there."

"If two people love one another, they can make it work, but you have to want it."

He stood and stepped toward the bathroom. "I wish that were true."

While he was away, I decided to call Letty to let her know I wouldn't be coming back tonight. I took his cell phone from the nightstand.

"Mona, where are you?" Letty asked over the phone.

"Why?"

"Listen to me. Professor Hussain has left a message about the book."

"Oh, good."

"No, you don't understand. He says he's concerned, unless it's a novel, and it can't possibly be otherwise, because if it is, then your philosophy professor is a monster!"

"What? I don't understand."

"He said to call and he left a number. It's 458—"

Ahmed sprang across the room and grabbed the phone from me. "What have you done!" he raged at me as he

141

ended the call. "You've given away my position! No outgoing phone calls! Why didn't you use the other damn phone?"

He rushed around the room like a different person. He piled everything into the two duffle bags except for the trash. I was caught in a whirlwind of confusion. Bewildered, stunned, and afraid, I sat motionless on the bed while Ahmed flew like a madman around the room gathering things. When his personal belongings were completely packed, he spoke again, urgently, "That hard copy of my book, Mona. Where is it? It's not in your dorm."

"What? You've been to my dorm?"

"Where is it? I have no time."

"I, I gave it to a professor in the history department."

"What?" He raved about the room like a caged animal. He swept his hand across the cups and boxes on the dresser and knocked them across the room. "So distracted. It's you're fault!"

"I couldn't read it. He's Pakistani. I just wanted to find you, Ahmed, that's all. Don't you have it saved on a computer?"

"What's his name?"

"I, uh."

"His name, Mona. I have no time."

"Hussain. Professor Hussain."

"Get dressed."

142

He dashed from the room with the two duffle bags and returned as I pulled on my shorts. I barely had my feet in my sandals when he yanked me out the door and shoved me into the car. It had been five minutes past nine when I had telephoned Letty, and now it was a quarter past.

Once we were driving, I demanded to know what was going on.

He said, "I'm going to drop you off at the convenience store on the corner. You call a friend to come get you, okay?" He passed me a handful of change from his ashtray.

"Where are you going? And why? Who are you running from?"

He glanced over at me and touched my hair, and I saw tears in his eyes. He returned his hand to the wheel. "Listen to me, what I said about my grandmother? That was all bullshit! Practically everything I have told you about myself has been nothing but lies! You don't want to love me, Mona. You don't even know me."

He stopped the car next to a curbside payphone in front of a store. "Get out of my life and stay out. Believe me, the further you stay away from me, the better off you'll be. Go."

"But Ahmed!"

"That's not even my real name. Go."

He got out, ran around to my side, and pulled me out of the car and into the night. Then he avoided my eyes and ignored my shouts as he quickly got back in and sped away. I sank next to the payphone under the streetlight onto the curb.

Chapter Thirteen: More Excuses

"That must have been so scary," Yvette says when Mona stops talking.

"I was terrified."

"Did you ever find out who he really was?"

"Yes, though I wish I hadn't." Mona strokes Babs, who curls in her lap. Then she says, "I want to thank you again for listening to me like this. Do you know I haven't been outside of this house in months unless it's been absolutely necessary, to buy groceries and such? Going to your house, to the nursery, these are big changes for me, and I owe that to you."

"Why do you stay cooped up in here?"

"I'm terrified."

"Even now?"

"I have a horrible headache. Can we continue tomorrow?"

Is he living with her?

"Of course."

I don't think so.

That night lying in bed, Yvette imagines Ahmed behind her house plotting to strike. Mona could be in cahoots with her old professor, luring Yvette into their twisted lives

145

in the same way Mona was lured. Yvette can't decide whether Mona does so willingly, or if Ahmed has her under his control. Either way, Yvette feels her life is in danger but doesn't know what she'd say if she were to call anyone, including the police, for help. How could she possibly describe the meticulous net about to ensnare her?

Quit being such a drama queen, Yvette. She's just a lonely woman who needs to tell a story.

Yvette lies on her bed, thinking.

She understands loneliness. When her father died, her mother's tenderness died with him, and Yvette felt lonely even in her mother's company. She missed her father.

One summer when she was nine, her father took her to Port Aransas. They pulled the boat behind his old yellow Chevy pickup and docked it near the jetties, on the channel side. Huge barges left the harbor by way of that channel, and Yvette felt small in comparison, wondering where they were going and what it would be like to go with them. Her father said the red fish were biting in a place he knew, so he drove the boat out to the edge of the channel, and they casted out their lines using dead shrimp for bait.

She had already learned how to bait her own hook and cast her own line, but she wasn't the best at setting the hook. She'd get so excited at the slightest tug on the other end, and she'd reel like crazy, and, almost always, the fish would break loose. Over and over her dad would tell her to jerk the rod back to set the hook, but the excitement would always take over, and before she knew it, she was reeling in an empty line, but that day she jerked her rod, and it stayed arched toward the water. She had to use all her strength to reel.

"Daddy! It's a big one! Oh, my goodness! Oh my goodness!" She lodged the end of the rod against her bright orange life jacket and reeled.

For a minute they thought the hook was hung on the bottom of the ocean because the rod was so bent, but the line moved around and around, which meant a fish.

"Keep reeling, Yvette. Get him close to the boat. I've got the net."

"Daddy! He's so heavy. You should do it." She wanted to hand him the rod, but she was afraid if she stopped reeling for even a second, she'd lose him.

"You're doing good," he said. "Keep reeling. Keep your eye on the line. Don't let him go under the boat or he'll get off."

"Oh my goodness! Oh my goodness!"

"I see him," her father said. "Son of a bitch, Yvette. He's a big one. Get him over to me."

When her father got the red fish into the net and onto the boat, she was too excited and proud and happy to realize how exhausted she was. The fish had put up a fight and lay, slimy and bleeding from one eye, in the bottom of the boat gasping, like her.

"I bet he's nine or ten pounds," her father said as he worked the hook from the fish's mouth. "He's a biggun'. Good eating, too. Nice work, Yvette."

They were both so enthralled by the fish that neither of them noticed how close they had drifted toward the ship channel. A large wave crawled toward their tiny boat and lifted Yvette high into the air, directly above her father, and then she was tumbling, tumbling, floundering, shocked by the cold, blinded by the dark salt water, and struck by the hard force of the metal boat. The blow knocked her out for a few minutes, after which she found herself floating on her back being dragged through the water by her hair. In the distance their little boat was capsized and nearly sunk. The huge ships moved swiftly through the channel. A seagull flew overhead. The sun poked out from behind a cloud. Her throat and lungs were on fire.

"Daddy! Daddy?"

No answer.

Next she was slammed against something hard and lifted up out of the water. Her father was dragging her up onto the jetties and coughing and hacking up water. They were surrounded by people and assaulted with questions of concern. Yvette lay on the jetties with the stale taste of blood in her mouth. Her father panted as he leaned over her. The sun was behind his head.

Back at their motel room, she slept for a long time. When she awoke, after she remembered everything that had happened, she sat up and turned to her father.

He wept with his face in his hands as he sat on the edge of his bed. "That was too damn close," he said, with his head down. "I'm such a stupid shit. I should have known not to get us so close to those ships."

Her mouth went dry. "I'm sorry, Daddy. I didn't mean to ruin your boat." She got up from the bed and crept over to him, waiting.

Finally, he gazed up at her, his eyes red. "No, Yvette. I don't care about the boat, and I'm the one who's sorry."

She had never seen her father like this, weeping and apologetic. She licked her lips and asked, "Where's my fish?"

Now she wishes she could go back in time and throw her arms around his thick neck and tell him everything was going to be alright. She misses him so much, she misses both of her parents, but once her father died, the confident part of her died, too.

Monday morning, when Heidi and Yvette walk up to Gloria's house to meet her for their walk, Heidi is quieter than usual. The tallest and most athletic of the three, her usual prance is absent from her step.

"Everything okay?" Yvette asks her as they reach Gloria's house.

"Yeah. Fine," she says, but not convincingly.

Gloria joins them, pushing her toddler in the stroller.

Yvette asks, "Are you sure everything's okay, Heidi? You seem down."

"I just need to get the fuck out of Dodge. So did Gloria talk to you about the money ideas for the cruise?"

"I liked the nudie cookbook. We could call it, 'Afternoon Delights.'"

"Or 'Cooking in the Raw'!" Gloria says.

"'Fresh Meat and Other Dishes,'" Yvette offers.

"Let's not get carried away," says Heidi, "I was also thinking we could go to estate sales, buy things on the cheap, and sell them for profit on Ebay or Craigslist."

"Not a bad idea," Gloria says. "I read an article about people who do that for a living."

"I'll have to think about it," says Yvette. "But it does seem like a lot of work for a short cruise."

Too much work. I'm exhausted.

Heidi says, "We'll be dead soon. The cruise can't wait forever."

They walk on past Yvette's house up toward the main road. Gloria shares her frustrations with the new

150

assistant principal at the elementary school, and Heidi talks about her girls' track meet.

As they reach the corner of her block, Yvette is shocked to see Mona in her hat and sunglasses.

This is getting too strange.

"Hello, Mary," Gloria says. "Out for a walk?"

"Just a little sun," answers Mona. "I need to get outdoors more."

"Care to join us?" Yvette asks.

Please say no, please say no.

"I don't want to intrude."

"That's okay," Heidi says, patting Mona's back, and Yvette is afraid her fragile frame will fall over. "I'm Heidi. Come on. You're walking with us."

Mona has trouble keeping up with their usual pace, so Yvette and her friends slow down.

"How far do you usually go?" Mona asks, already breathing hard.

"We go all the way up to the main road, around those four blocks, and back," Gloria says. "We're nearly done. We finish at my house, down the street."

"So this is your youngest?" Mona points to the stroller.

"Jacob. He's two."

"Very cute. He takes after his mother."

"Why, thank you."

"So are you a native of San Antonio?" asks Heidi.

"I grew up in Brownsville."

"So what brought you here?" Heidi asks.

"Oh, I guess I needed a change." She stops at the end of the block.

"You okay?" Yvette searches Mona's face. It's pale in the sunlight.

She's strange, but I do feel sorry for her. Maybe she's sick.

"You ladies go on without me," she replies. "My house is around this corner."

"Are you sure? We can slow down," Yvette offers.

I can be such a bitch. She looks like she's about to pass out.

"Thanks anyway. Thanks for letting me tag along."

"Anytime."

"Absolutely."

"I'll see you later, right Yvette?" Mona says.

"You want me to help you home?"

"No thanks. I just need a moment to catch my breath."

"Then I'll see you at four o'clock."

Yvette and her friends continue toward Gloria's house, Yvette occasionally glancing back at Mona until she is no longer visible behind the line of oaks.

"She's strange," Heidi says.

"I feel sorry for her," says Gloria. "She seems so lonely."

"So why are you going to her house at four?" Heidi asks.

"Gloria's right. She's lonely."

"Don't get sucked in," Heidi says. "I mean, it's nice of you to help her, but don't let her get too dependent on you."

"Exactly how do you do that?"

"Space out your time with her."

Yvette is late to Mona's house, and she can tell Mona was worried she might not show. Yvette hadn't decided herself whether she would show until the last second, so sure had she become that Ahmed was there, a spider on the edge of its web. She considered making an excuse to cancel, but the last time she tried, Mona threatened to come to her house instead.

And that would be all I need. Her popping up at my place all the time.

"Oh, good," says Mona, opening the door. "I almost called. By the way, I haven't heard your dog in a while."

Yvette keeps one hand on her cell deep in her pocket, ready to call 9-1-1.

"He's at the lake with the rest of my family." Yvette crosses the room and sits in the wooden chair.

"So you're alone? For how long?"

Shit. Shut your mouth, Yvette.

"I don't know. They're not sure when they'll come home. It depends on how long the fish are biting."

"Don't you like to fish?"

"Yes. But I stayed behind to hear your story."

"That's my cue." Mona smiles. "Tea?"

Just finish the story. What happened to the baby?

"No thanks."

"Well, then. We left off with me on the curb.

"Let's see. Letty and Jan came and got me. I didn't talk much on the way home even though they expressed concern over what Professor Hussain had said about Ahmed's manuscript. I insisted it must be a misunderstanding and said nothing more. We didn't have classes on Good Friday, so I spent the day alone in my dorm room. I tried to write a paper but got nowhere. On Holy Saturday, I walked to the Chapel of the Annunciation across the street from the campus to make my confession so I could take Communion on Easter Sunday with my family. I hadn't been to Mass in weeks. Standing in line for my turn with the priest, I thought on my sins.

"As the line diminished and my turn to confess approached, I felt ill. I peered up at the life-size crucifix hanging over the high altar. 'Are you real?' I asked it, not out loud, but in my head.

"I glanced over to the back of the chapel at the Pieta—the statue of the Blessed Mother holding the body of her dead son. Without realizing it, I whispered, 'Mother Mary, are you there?' When the others in line turned and stared at me, I ran out of the chapel as though someone had shouted fire. I ran across the campus and out to the football field. I ran around the track, running the race of my life until I was too exhausted to continue.

"Easter Sunday, my parents begged me to come home, but I refused. Instead, in the dark of night, at a drugstore on the other side of town, I purchased an over-the-counter pregnancy test and took it back to my dorm. I knew I could not ask for a break from God. I had no right to ask. The lines of communication between us had been down for some time, and it would be hypocritical of me to try and mend them now when I needed help."

"But that's the best time to ask," says Yvette.

"So you're a believer?"

"Yes. You?"

"I don't always know. But then I was. I was a fervent believer. I wouldn't pray to him, though, because I felt I had gone too far to the side of evil, so, when I said, 'Please do not be a plus sign! Do not be a plus sign!' it wasn't to God, but to chance or fate or any other powers-that-be which might influence the consequences of human actions.

"But a plus sign it was."

"What happened to the baby?"

Something falls in one of the back rooms, but both cats are in the living room. Babs is in Mona's lap being stroked by her dry, bony hand. Boots lies curled on top of one of the boxes recently added to the stacks in front of the fireplace.

"What was that?" asks Yvette, standing.

"I don't know." Mona rises, too. "Wait here."

Mona leaves, and Babs turns to Yvette, staring at her, in cahoots with her mistress. Babs dares her to go and follow Mona, but Yvette misses her chance. The crazy woman appears in the room, laughing, as though someone has told a good joke.

"You won't believe what happened."

No. I won't.

Mona takes her seat, and the one-eyed cat hops into her lap. "It was a book. I was reading a novel before you came. I put it back on its shelf, but it fell over. Not enough books to fill the shelf, I guess. Sorry. Please, sit down."

Liar.

Chapter Fourteen: Abduction

On Easter Monday, I skipped my classes, but in the afternoon, hunger and a lack of food in both rooms of the suite forced me to walk down to the dining hall to get a bite to eat. After I had gotten my sandwich to go, I caught a glance through the window of Bijan sitting at a table inside.

He sat with three other guys and a girl, and they were eating and laughing together. I didn't recognize his friends. I hid behind the shrubs by the window and stared. He looked stunning and surprisingly happy. He had gotten on without me, as I knew he would, but it hurt to be confronted with this truth. Gazing at Bijan for a moment longer, streaming tears, a new thought came to me, and I turned and walked briskly away.

I would erase my mistakes and start over. I headed to my dorm room and, quickly, without thinking, looked up the number to the nearest abortion clinic, dialed, and made an appointment for the following week.

Around four o'clock, as Professor Hussain had not returned any of the messages Jan and I had left on his answering machine on Saturday, I tried phoning his office again.

"Who is this?" asked the nasally voice of an older woman.

"I'm a student."

"Haven't you been watching the news, Hon'? Professor Hussain and his family were killed this weekend in a car accident."

"Excuse me, *what* did you say?"

"I'm so sorry to be the one to break it to you, Hon'. I know he was loved by all of his students."

"What happened? I don't understand."

"He and his family were on their way out of town on Saturday when they collided in a freak accident with two other vehicles," explained the woman. "There were no survivors."

"None? How many were killed?"

"It's all over this morning's paper. Perhaps it would help you if you read about it. I'm sorry, but I have to get this other line. Professor Hussain's classes are cancelled today, but we will have subs tomorrow, and counseling for his students is the top priority in our Careers and Counseling Office. Good bye."

Had it not been for my full bladder, I might well have fallen asleep in the pleasant waiting room of the abortion clinic. I tapped on the window over the counter.

A lady slid the window open. "Yes?"

"Um, I need to use the restroom, so, I was wondering, if you want me to go in a cup, can I do it now?"

"Sure." She handed me a sterile collection cup. "Go through this door on your right and take your first left. I've put your name on the label already, so simply leave the sample on the vanity for us. We'll take care of it from there."

I returned for my purse, when another woman entered the waiting room. The woman, like me, had come alone. I turned and went through the door.

I took a right but saw no door on my left. I wandered down a corridor, confused. Finding the first door on the left, I tried the knob. It was not locked.

A nurse pulled me away as I heard a woman scream. "Stop! I don't want to go through with it!"

"You aren't allowed in there," the nurse said. "Are you lost?"

"Yes. I'm looking for the restroom."

"Follow me."

The nurse walked quickly while I tried to keep up, and she opened the restroom door. I thanked her and stepped inside.

Later, in the examining room, I asked the same nurse, "Do you think I'm doing the right thing?"

"I'm so sorry you heard that. Do *you* think you're doing the right thing?"

I couldn't breathe. "I don't know, but I'm not ready to be a mother."

"You'll feel better when it's over."

"I will?"

"Everyone does. Society makes you feel guilty, but this is your right, your body, okay?"

"Okay."

"Everything from the waist down comes off. Cover with this and wait for the doctor. Okay?"

"Okay."

"You okay?"

"Yes."

When the doctor entered, he introduced himself as he foraged around the room, opening and closing cabinets. He asked, in a cavalier tone without looking at me, if I was sure I wanted an abortion. He mumbled as though he were unaccustomed to talking.

"I don't know."

He stopped. He reached up into the top cabinet, stretching his arm and nearly missing, for he was short, and then, having successfully snatched the plastic wrapped hose or nozzle, he muttered, "Aha. Got it." Then he walked out of the room briefly, and then re-entered, again without looking at me. He took a clipboard from the vanity, snatched a pen from the pocket of his white coat, and then asked, "Where were we?"

I pulled the paper cover more closely around me and mumbled, "You asked if I was sure, and I said I didn't know."

"Well, most girls have second thoughts. It's natural. But overall, do you think this is what you want?" His small mouth and large, spectacled eyes resembled an insect. His hands worked busily at the clipboard, like a fly cleaning itself.

I shrugged, but he, not having seen, continued to fill out the form on his clipboard.

He asked, as though he had forgotten his original question, if someone were going to drive me home after the procedure.

I said no, no way. "No one knows I'm here. This is confidential, right?"

This so startled the doctor that he stopped writing and stared at me. "No? Well, you won't be able to drive yourself, and we don't have a recovery room available. Can you call someone to pick you up? That's what most of the girls do. No? No one? Then we better reschedule when you can have someone drive you. When you've finished dressing, go see the front desk, and Molly, err, uh, Matilda, uh, Monica will help you reschedule your appointment."

Without giving me an opportunity to reply, the doctor fled the office and left me alone.

I dressed and ran the hell out of there. The doctor had seemed like a character from a futuristic dystopian novel. I had come to the wrong place. I wanted badly to see my own doctor, but was too embarrassed.

When I got to my car, I found a note stuffed beneath one of the windshield wipers. It said: *I know what you have done.*

Glancing around the parking lot, I saw no sign of someone driving off or running away. Probably anti-abortionists trying to scare me. Or could it have been he?

That evening, Letty and Jan returned to the dorm to find me in bed with swollen eyes. I was past tears and said I wasn't feeling well. Letty sat at the chair by her computer and Jan plopped on Letty's bed across from me.

Jan said, "Something's not right about Professor Hussain's death. It can't be a coincidence he and his family are dead after reading Profeesor Jaffar's book, especially after the strange phone call. He called Professor Jaffar a monster."

"You should call the police, Mona," insisted Letty.

"No way. I'm too scared to get involved. And don't you guys dare! We have no proof there's a connection."

"I'm with Letty. I think you should call the police. If you don't. I will." Jan hugged her knees to her chest. "Poor

Professor Hussain and his family. If I hadn't recommended him to translate that stupid book, they might still be alive."

"Please, guys, I'm begging you. Don't do anything yet. Let's think more about this, okay?"

I had to cry and go down on my knees and make myself sick to get them to agree not to call the police. I promised I would go when I was ready, and so the two at last agreed.

My professors were surprised to see me in class, and two of them told me I wouldn't pass if I didn't get my papers turned in. They asked if anything was wrong. What could I say? My philosophy professor got me pregnant and then killed a history professor and his family? It sounded preposterous. And I had no proof.

In the evening I walked to the library, determined to start on the first of two British literature papers. I dared not go to my usual spot on the third floor. Instead, I found the books I needed and carried them downstairs to the main study area of the library.

I sat alone at a long table, facing the main entrance, like one condemned and awaiting her sentence, half expecting Ahmed to come up from behind me and convince me to go away with him again.

Two other students sat with their backs to me at the next long table, and an older woman sat at the corner of a third; yet, I felt alone. I tried to focus on my research but found myself continually checking behind me and screening those entering the building.

I thought I saw Ahmed, so I hid my face and pretended to read while keeping an eye on the figure approaching the stacks. It weaved through the aisles to my right. I gathered my things, about to leave, when I realized it wasn't Ahmed after all.

After two hours, I gave up, not having written a word. My thumbs and one middle finger bled again. I left the library books on the table, grabbed my legal pad, dorm key, and pen, and headed toward the main entrance.

As I passed the circulation desk, Bijan entered the library with a girl. I turned and hid behind the reference section where I waited until they passed.

I watched them through the books as they sat together at the very table I had just left, the girl in my very seat! They opened their books, leaning toward one another, and exchanged a laugh. She punched his shoulder in a teasing way, and he shook his head, smiling. I watched them for several minutes, hoping to discover whether they were more than study partners, when I became aware of a piece of paper taped to my jeans on the side of my thigh.

I pulled it off and read: *I'm watching you.* It was written in the same hand as the note left on my car in front of the abortion clinic! I dropped my notepad and pen, gasped for air, and then darted around the stacks in the reference section, trying to catch sight of the culprit.

He turned the corner on the aisle over. He was wearing the same baggy jeans, but a different shirt and cap. I ran to catch up as he moved toward the periodicals. I caught up to him and grabbed his arm, only to find a face I didn't recognize.

I apologized and said, "I thought you were someone else."

I walked, red-faced and jittery, back to where I had dropped my notepad. The pen had rolled out of sight, so I took up the pad, and headed out of the library.

I reached the main entrance and gave a quick glance back at Bijan. He stood up, mouth agape, watching me leave. I wanted to go to him, to see if he could possibly forgive— but I didn't. What I had done was unforgivable. I walked away, and when I was out of the building, I let the floodgates down, and ran, at my top speed, back toward my dorm.

As I ran across my dorm parking lot, a car whizzed in front of me and nearly ran me over, causing me to fall back on the grass at the edge of the lot, stunned. I got up and stared as it stopped, perhaps to see if its unintended victim were okay. Waving at it, about to move on, I noticed by the light of the streetlamp it was a maroon Buick Regal!

I dropped my notepad and took off running toward my dorm. The Buick Regal turned around and drove to the front of the lot, its headlights shining on me as I scrambled to unlock my dorm room.

The suite was empty. On Wednesday nights, my suitemates went out together, and, as of late, Letty rarely came home before midnight, spending all her time at Jan's apartment.

I turned on all the lights and brought the television from next door into my room where I sat on my bed beneath the covers with the remote, needing to divert my attention. As I searched for a show like *Friends* or *Seinfeld*—to make me laugh and forget the dread—a figure at the glass sliding door leading to the patio made me shriek. I jumped from the bed toward the bathroom and peeked through the window. I couldn't see anything because all the lights were on, so I rushed around, turning all but the bathroom lights off, including the television.

I stood in the middle of the room, trembling and waiting. I didn't see anything. I wondered if it had been my imagination. I checked the lock on the sliding glass door. It had been unlocked! I immediately, desperately, as quickly as I could, locked the door and closed the blinds.

I froze, unable to breathe, at the thought of an intruder in the suite. Then, regaining my senses, I grabbed the heavy iron from my walk-in closet and carried it around the rooms with me. I searched underneath the two twin beds in my room, moved the clothes around in the closet, and checked the shower and the toilet stall. Then I crept into my suitemate's room, carrying the iron as I searched underneath each of the twin beds. Trying the knob to the front door, I found it, to my great relief, locked. Then, taking a deep breath, I checked the closet.

As I reentered my suitemates' room from the closet, I heard footsteps on *their* patio. The thought that their sliding glass door might still be unlocked made me freeze with fear.

In the next instant, I saw movement out by the shrubs. I couldn't decide whether to go for the lock, the phone, or the front door. If I ran out the front, he might catch me in the parking lot. If I ran to the phone, he might enter through the patio doors.

I ran for the lock. My fingers shook so badly I couldn't even move the lever on the lock on the first try.

I heard a sound and screamed.

Once I got the lock secured, I shut the blinds and ran back into my own room. Afraid to call the police, because it might have been nothing, I called my mom.

I said, in the most natural voice I could, "Hi, Mom. It's me."

"Hello, Mona. How are you?"

"Oh, stressed with school and stuff, but hanging in there. I was wondering if I could come home this weekend."

"You don't need to ask permission to come home, silly." Then she asked, "Are you sure you're okay? You sound funny."

"I'm okay."

"Listen, is there something you want to tell me?"

"Everything's fine. I'll see you Friday night."

As I hung up the phone, I heard a rattle on the patio. Afraid to open the blinds, I took my pillow and bedcovers and slipped into the bathroom, where I locked the doors leading to both rooms of the suite. I left the lights on, lay in the middle of the floor, curled beneath the covers, and tried to go to sleep, thankful there were no windows. I continued to hear noises, so I lay still until I fell asleep.

Around midnight, I was awakened by loud pounding on the bathroom door leading to my room. *Bam, bam, bam!*

I clutched my pillow and said, "Who is it?"

Bam, bam, bam!

"Who is it?" I cried again.

"It's Letty, who do you think it is? Let me in! I'm about to pee in my pants, for Heaven's sake!"

I let her in. She hurried into the stall and closed the door. "What in the world are you doing? *Sleeping* in here?"

"I heard noises on the patio. I was scared. I'm so glad you're home."

"Why didn't you call the police? Why don't we call them now?"

"What good would that do? I'll be even more frightened. He might find out, retaliate. No. I'm not ready to go to the police, okay? Not yet."

I climbed into my bed, and, as I arranged the covers over me, I noticed something that made my jaw drop. *The sliding glass door to the patio stood ajar.*

I jumped up, quickly pulled it closed, and locked it. "Letty?"

My roommate was at the sink, brushing her teeth. "Hmm?"

"Did you open the patio door?" I said this as I entered the bathroom.

"Nuh-uh." She spit and rinsed. "Why?"

I shut and locked the bathroom door.

"What are you doing?" Letty asked.

"The patio door was open."

"Maybe you forgot to close it earlier."

"No. I am absolutely positive I closed and locked it. He could be in there right now."

"Come on, Mona. You're scaring me. I was just in there. There was no one." Letty unlocked the door and returned to our room. "See? No one here."

I told her to check everywhere as I ran frantically through the room. I checked my suitemates' room again as well since they were still out. Only after I had seen firsthand there was no one else in the suite did I return to my bed, and only after another hour of lying still listening for noises and staring at the patio door did I fall asleep again.

I barely made my classes Thursday, and that evening I tried to work on my British literature paper in the library, but the same eerie feeling I experienced the night before kept me from focusing on my work.

Friday evening at home, after dinner, as my parents and I sat watching television while Leroy smoked his pot out back, my mother turned to me where she sat beside me on the couch and asked, "Mona? Is there something you want to tell me?

Could she tell already? I asked, "What do you mean?"

"Come on, sweetie. You know you can talk to me, don't you?"

I jumped up from the couch, near hysteria, and ran to the bathroom where I was sick.

My mother followed and knelt on the floor beside me. Putting a hand on my shoulder, she leaned over and said, "I know, Mona. I already know."

"How?" Before my mother could reply, I was sick again.

"It wasn't hard to figure out."

"How could you possibly know? Do you sense things?"

"Leroy told me. I already suspected as much. Your poor thumbs say it all. You should know you can't tell Leroy your secrets."

"Leroy?" I quickly ran through my last conversation with him in my head. Had I told him? Had I even known then?

My mother said, "Well, we haven't seen him for over a month."

"Who, Leroy?"

My mother chuckled. "No, silly. Bijan."

It dawned on me my break up with Bijan, and not my pregnancy, was the subject of our conversation. I relaxed my shoulders, took a nice big breath, and said, "I've been meaning to tell you. I just didn't know how. I knew it would break your heart. And Dad's, too."

"It's your heart I'm worried about, little girl."

I shuddered and hugged my mother as we sat on the floor of the bathroom.

Alone in my room, I continued to fear Ahmed might be lurking outside the house, ready to strike. When Leroy came inside and shuffled off to his room, I followed and stood outside his door for a few minutes before I worked up the nerve to knock.

"Yeah?"

"Can I come in?"

"It's open."

He wore plaid boxers and a white cotton t-shirt and stood pulling the covers back on his bed.

"I can't sleep."

"I can roll you a joint in a jiffy. You'll be lights out before you know it."

"No thanks. I'm scared."

"Of what?"

"I hear noises outside my window."

"Why do I feel like I'm having a flashback? I'm suddenly fifteen years younger and my little sis is asking to sleep on my floor."

"Can I?"

"Are you serious?"

"Yes."

He shrugged. "I don't care. Just leave me a path to the bathroom."

"I know. You don't want to step on me. I remember."

We both smiled.

"Thanks, Leroy."

"No problem."

I returned to my room for my pillow and blanket. He left to use the restroom, and when he came back, I was nearly asleep on the floor.

He whispered, "Ready for lights out?"

"Ready."

He flipped the switch, leapt to his bed, and then said softly, "Good night, Mona. It's nice to have you home."

"Good night." I closed my eyes and said, without thinking on it too long, "I love you."

He was silent. Then, when I was about to give up, a surprise. "Love you, too, sis."

I spent Saturday and Sunday in the library writing the first of two British literature papers, and, for once, I was able to focus on my work and finish the job. Saturday night I slept on Leroy's bedroom floor again, where I had the best sleep in weeks. My parents begged me to attend Mass with them Sunday morning, but I lied and told them I was going to church in the evening after I finished my paper. Sunday night, after a quick taco from the student center, I returned to the library to finalize my paper before typing it on Letty's computer.

I spent the next several evenings catching up on class work, regaining my focus and excited to be productive again. My professors were pleased to see me in class with the late work in hand.

A week before final exams, as I gathered my things and prepared to leave the library, I saw Bijan with the same girl as before, walking down the stairs and exiting the building. An impulse came over me, and I decided to follow. I kept my distance as they strolled across the parking lot and climbed into Bijan's car. Because I had come straight to the library from the drug store, I happened to have my car parked in the same lot, so I followed them.

They drove to an off-campus apartment complex not too far from where Bijan lived. I watched them get out of the car and enter a downstairs apartment, unable to believe he would go inside with her at this late hour. Curious to see how late he would stay, I parked a few doors down. I could see the girl go to the kitchen window, but, beyond this, nothing.

She had to be a study partner. Surely he wasn't dating anyone so soon after our breakup. Yet, I had slept with a man—twice—and was carrying his child. I was such a hypocrite, such a self-centered jerk. Growing more and more anxious as time passed, I wondered how I could have messed things up so terribly.

It was May and hot and muggy, so I rolled down my window to let in the breeze. It wasn't one of those electronic ones. I had to crank it down by hand. Before I knew what was happening, a medicinal cloth covered my mouth as I was pulled out of my car. I kicked and hit and tried to bite the hand holding the cloth, tried to scream my muffled cry, but I gradually lost consciousness and fell limp in the arms of my captor.

When I awoke, I was sitting in a maroon Buick Regal driving down a highway in the early dawn next to the man I knew as Ahmed Jaffar.

Chapter Fifteen: Roommates

"**O**h my God," says Yvette. "How did you get away?"

"It was horrible."

"Tell me."

"It's so late. Can we continue tomorrow? I feel too weak to go on."

Are you serious? "Of course." *No backbone.*

As Yvette reaches her van, she gazes back at Mona's house wondering again why the strange woman has decided to share her story with her. She's lonely, no doubt, and likely half-mad, but Yvette senses another purpose drives Mona each day.

Why is she telling me?

She heats a chicken pot pie from the freezer and turns on the television to the Home and Garden network hoping to distract herself with shows about backyard makeovers and kitchen remodels. But as each episode ends, she realizes she's missed the entire transformation. Her mind is possessed by Mona's peculiar tale.

Is the story true? Why would she make it up? And if it is true, why must she tell it to me?

Yvette lies in bed wishing for sleep, still possessed by Mona's narrative. She may not understand why Mona is telling it to her, but she knows why she is listening. She's possessed and has no choice.

After her morning walk with Heidi and Gloria, Yvette calls Devin.

"Hey, Yvette. Are you on your way?"

"No, Honey. I'm not."

"I knew it. I knew you weren't coming."

How could he know? "I told you I wasn't feeling well." *Liar.*

"You had already decided you weren't coming. The kids are going to be disappointed."

"Devin, listen. I'm coming. I don't know when. There's a lot going on."

"Yeah? Well, good. There's a lot going on here, too, and you're missing it. Did you know Casey can cast her rod all by herself? She baited her hook, but you didn't see it."

"Hell, Devin, you've missed tons of firsts. Quit making me feel bad. If you'll recall, you couldn't make it the day we got Casey."

I had to get her all by myself.

"You won't let me forget."

"Because you force my hand. You have no clue how much I do for our kids." *How dare you insinuate otherwise.*

"You're the one who's clueless. About our marriage, about this trip, about everything. I'm sick of being your

177

damn roommate. You've pulled yourself away from me, and now the kids, too. I knew you weren't coming. I fucking knew it."

"Devin, I—" Yvette can think of nothing to say.

"I gotta go. Make sure you water the tree."

Yvette gets up from the chair, tears raining down her cheeks like the falls at Big Bend, and runs to the front yard, where the gaping grave waits for sod. Roommates? Is that what he thinks they have become? She waters the tree with the hose and looks warily at its drooping branches, more willow than oak. She and Devin hoped in spite of its weepy appearance the tree would live, Devin pissed at the city workers, even though the tree had been planted on the easement. Now they must give it extra care. Devin had been watering it, but Yvette had been too busy. If it dies, it will be her fault.

All my fault. How can it be so easy to screw up?

She turns off the water and returns inside, her face dripping.

She lingers in each of her children's bedrooms, missing her family. She makes Matt's bed and picks up a few dirty clothes from his floor, noticing they are stretched and worn and in need of replacement. He is as tall as she and still growing. She steps on a Lego part and picks it up. It's Darth Maul's light saber. She puts it up on his dresser next to the Lego Star Wars characters and the Lego Death Star.

General Grevious glares at her as though he knows she has let her family down.

We were gonna watch the entire saga together before spring break's over.

On her way to Tommy's room, the baby pictures hanging on the wall in the hall give her pause. More tears build up in her eyes. What a sweet family she has, and she isn't with them. As Devin said, she's missing important moments having stayed behind. She enters Tommy's room and smiles at his collection of rubber ducks—a werewolf duck, a Frankenstein duck, a mummy duck, and a regular duck. He's her collector. A jar of bottle caps, a mug of different shaped erasers, a bowl of tiny plastic ninjas, and a few soda cans turned into funny characters crowd his desk. She bought the desk so he would have a place to draw, but it is always piled with his collections.

My little hoarder.

Further down in Casey's room, she is pleased her daughter straightened up before leaving. Her desk is organized, and except for the pile of stuffed animals left on the bed, everything is in its place. As she's about to leave, her eyes rest on a family photo on the dresser.

Her skin's not much darker than mine, though Tommy has the really fair skin from the Palmer side. Matt's got my olive complexion.

She slumps onto the bed and the pile of stuffed animals.

She pulls up her legs and lies on Casey's bed, smelling her. She hugs the bunny and the bear and the, what in the hell is this, a platypus? Yvette has taken her family for granted lately; yet, she almost died delivering Tommy. He was in intensive care for several days because he was taken prematurely. If things hadn't worked out just right, they wouldn't have their sweet Casey.

I had to pick her up all by myself. But I'm so grateful to have her.

She thought it would be months, even years, so when she got the call from the adoption agency, she was unprepared. Devin was out of town on a business trip. The case worker, who had inspected their home and had interviewed them a week earlier, said they could wait a few days, that a foster family could likely keep the baby, but Yvette couldn't wait to see her, couldn't wait to hold her in her arms, so she said no, she'd meet them.

Unlike her boys, who were born bald, Casey had a head of thick black hair. Her brown eyes were more attentive, too, being a few weeks old. The biological parents had already signed the papers relinquishing their rights and had left before Yvette's arrival. She thought then she would have done the same, unable to bear the sight of her daughter leaving with a stranger. Yvette never learned their reason for giving up Casey. She did find out Casey had been hospitalized with pneumonia for three weeks. Perhaps the young couple discovered they were not yet ready to be parents. Perhaps they weren't financially able to give her proper care. Maybe their marriage was in jeopardy, and rather than put the baby through a divorce, they decided to place her with a couple in a stable marriage.

Whatever their reason, Yvette was grateful to hold her precious baby girl. She loved her boys, was devoted to them, but didn't want to go through life never knowing the love of a daughter. She cried the day her case worker handed the baby over. She cried tears of sorrow for the parents, who would never know her, and tears of joy for herself and the unbound happiness flooding her life.

She must remember to be grateful and to treasure her family every day. She should be with them now. She would go to Mona's one more time, and then she would join her family.

When Mona opens the door, she has a slice of cake on a plate in her hand. "Come in. I made this for you."

Liar.

"Thanks." Yvette takes the plate and follows Mona inside.

"And here's some tea." Mona lifts the glass from her chair and hands it to Yvette.

"If we don't finish today, I'll have to come next week," Yvette says, taking the tea.

"Oh, I'm so close to finishing!" Mona sounds panicky. "Can't you change your plans?" She wrings her hands, her ratty pink robe flying about her as she paces the living room. Neither of them has sat down.

"I'm sorry, I can't."

Mona paces and mutters and wrings the bony fingers so hard they might crack. "Oh, this won't do. This won't do at all. What's so important you can't come at our regular time tomorrow?"

Spooky and strange.

Yvette bites her bottom lip. "I'm supposed to meet the rest of my family at the lake."

"The lake? Yvette, believe me when I tell you it's imperative you hear the rest of my story. It's a matter of life and death."

Is Mona threatening her? Her fingers tremble as she sets the plate down on the floor beside her empty chair. "I'm sorry. I can't. Now, please, calm down. Perhaps I should go."

"No! Please! Fine. Have a seat."

No backbone.

Chapter Sixteen: The Reveal

Once I could speak, I asked, "What are you doing? Where are you taking me?"

He fixed his eyes on the road ahead. "I'm saving my child from a murderess."

My jaw dropped open. "You bastard."

"Yes, Mona. I am wretched and forever doomed, like ninety percent of the world's population."

"How are you so sure it's yours?"

"Don't play games with me. You may have deceived your young boyfriend, but it won't fly with me. I was going to spare you, you know—even when I learned you carried my child. But once I saw you set out to destroy my seed, I had no choice." His voice softened. "I never meant to bring a child into this world. I dreamed of it when I was a boy, but since becoming a man, I haven't wanted to force another life into the horrors of existence. Life is too painful and too cruel and better left unlived. People who intentionally propagate are themselves cruel.

"But now I've become selfish. I want to live on through this unforeseen progeny of mine, to pass on my studies, which are to be my legacy, and so, I will show you everything, because everything he or she learns must come from you."

"I wasn't going to go through with the abortion."

"I can't take the chance. I'll keep you with me until I see the child safely born."

"And then you'll let us go?"

"Yes. After I have shown you my work."

I thought of opening the door and jumping out, but we were going too fast, and I was afraid another car would hit me. I had learned never to get into the car with an abductor, because, once you did, you were dead. I had always planned to scream if someone ever tried to take me—to scream and kick and fight like mad—but I hadn't had the chance. The scenarios in my mind had never included chloroform. "You're going to kill me, aren't you? You're going to kill me!"

With agitation, as a parent might speak to a bothersome child, he said, "I might kill you if you don't stop screaming."

I could not steady my breaths—I was hyperventilating. Then I had this calming realization: He will not kill me as long as I am carrying his child.

I closed my eyes, and even though the lines of communication had been down for some time, I prayed silently: *Please get me out of this God, and I will try harder to be good. Please get me out of this and I will be your servant, your instrument, your whatever you want. I will be open to your will and I will obey your rules. Just please, please, please get me out of this! And, in case I wasn't clear, I mean get me out of this* alive.

Ahmed glanced over at me and said, "It's not logical I should love you. I don't know why I do. But I swear, Mona, it's true. And I will not harm you. But, please, don't look at me like that. I am not the monster you think I am. Once I tell you the true story of my life, you will see, and perhaps you will no longer abhor me."

I wanted to ask if he had killed Professor Hussain and his family but was afraid of the answer. "I don't abhor you," I said.

He glanced at me with a smile. He relaxed his shoulders and sat back in the seat. "I lied when I told you my name was not Ahmed. At the time, I didn't know you were pregnant, and I wanted you to hate me because I loved you. My life would be pure drudgery for you because I'm committed to a higher purpose. But I like to hear you say my name. Will you say it?"

I wanted to refuse. "Ahmed."

I immediately regretted not having said it more lovingly, more enthusiastically. I had angered him. He kept his eyes on the road and spoke no further.

After several minutes passed, I broke the silence. "Will you tell me where we're going?"

"To Mexico City, to my lab."

"You have a lab in Mexico City?"

"Yes, a little garden home, where I do most of my research. It's where I took Fatima, the Afghani girl. In fact, she is there still."

"What? Still there? Then she wasn't a spy for the Taliban?"

"No, no, no, no, no," he shook his head as he chuckled. "That was my invention when I considered you a subject. I created a story about myself to attract you to me. Don't worry. Now you will learn the truth."

"Are you two still lovers?"

"No."

I found myself in the bewildering position of both wanting and not wanting to know the truth, and of both believing and not believing its deliverer.

Ahmed said we had several hours of driving time, so he would first get us a bite to eat, and then he'd tell me his story.

He pulled into a drive-thru at a Taco Cabana and ordered breakfast tacos for us. He had warned me not to say anything; he had a gun beneath his seat and was an expert at using it. He told me he would never use it on me, but at the person in the window. When he asked what I wanted to drink, I laughed. It was my nerves that made me laugh.

186

My mouth was dry from the chloroform, and I had a horrible headache. "Diet Coke."

At the window, I wavered as he spoke to a Hispanic girl wearing a nose ring and a tattoo of a butterfly on her arm. She was chubby and cute, and certainly not deserving of death, but I still wavered. As I was about to get my courage up and take a chance, the girl handed over the food and drinks and closed the sliding window. My chance was gone.

Ahmed handed me the drink and a taco, took one out of the bag for himself, opened it, and took several bites as he merged onto the highway.

"I was born in a small village outside of Swabi. Although my parents were poor wheat farmers, my mother was educated, and I suppose she wished the same for me. Her sister married a doctor and had a son my age—an only child, like me—and they invited me to come live with them in the big city, Peshawar, when I was seven." He sucked at the straw in his drink, and then continued. "I visited my parents on the weekends, which I was glad to do, but during the week, I attended school. I loved school, and I excelled in every subject, especially science. Once I learned to read, I read everything, including the scientific books in my uncle's collection. After two years, he allowed me to help him in his lab, and I became his assistant.

"My cousin Syed was glad because he hated science. We were opposites—he preferred the liberal arts—but we had a lot in common and became excellent friends. Before I became the doctor's apprentice, we were inseparable, and, even after, we played and fished and swam together. He knew how to make me laugh and have fun. He was crazy. Still is. Such a vivid imagination."

Ahmed changed lanes to pass the car in front of us, and then moved back over to the right lane.

"When I was twelve, my parents left me with my aunt and uncle to join relatives in Afghanistan in their war with the Soviets, and my cousin and I begged to go, but we were denied this opportunity to fight. We stayed in Peshawar with his parents while my parents were dying for their cause. I came to hate Islam. My aunt and uncle did not seem to mind."

"I thought your grandmother raised you after your parents died."

"No. My grandmother died shortly after my parents. Hand me another taco."

I took one from the bag between us and gave it to him. "Why did you have to lie to me? Why couldn't you tell me the truth?"

"I must maintain distance between myself and my subjects, so I lie to them. Otherwise I could not continue with my research." He drank more from the straw.

I couldn't finish my taco. Instead, I chewed on my middle finger as Ahmed continued.

"When I was eighteen, my uncle registered me with a university in Peshawar to study medicine, but I continued to live with him and serve as his apprentice until my second year, when I secured an internship with one of my professors and could no longer work with my uncle. The professor paid me to live on campus so I could be more available to assist him. He introduced me to my real love: genetics.

"We performed many beautiful experiments on rats and guinea pigs and other small creatures. We published three articles together. My aunt and uncle were proud. Meanwhile, Syed continued to live with them while also studying at the university. He pursued his degree in political science.

"As I became more and more successful in the lab, I became less and less attached to people. Syed and I rarely had time for one another, and, since I lived on campus, I hardly ever saw my aunt and uncle. I liked it this way, though, because it allowed me to dedicate my entire being to my studies, for I had become fixed on this notion that I would one day obliterate disease from humanity through my studies of genetics."

"Wait a minute. So you didn't fight against the Soviets when you were a young teen?"

"I told you before. All I said to you then were lies. They were part of the seduction."

"I believed you."

"You lie often enough, you get good at it."

"Did you go to college in Canada and do graduate studies at Berkeley?"

"I started at the university in Peshawar, and then, when things went sour there, I transferred to Mexico City. I fell in love with philosophy. I found other scholars who believed as I believe. Most of my recent publications have been in the field of philosophy. But my book will be my great contribution to science, to humanity."

"What do you mean went sour?"

"Let's just say my research ethics and those of my teachers were different." He changed lanes again to pass another car.

"What kind of research did you do?"

He ate the last of the taco. "Genetics. Like I said, I started with the goal of ridding humanity of diseases passed through DNA. We studied inherited traits in mice and monkeys, which, after a while, seemed a waste of time. Human DNA was and is my concern. I became interested in whether one could inherit a predisposition toward suicide—this interested me because my parents were suicide bombers during the Soviet-Afghani conflict. I studied genetic samples of suicide victims. The university didn't like it."

"How is what you were doing any different from forensic medicine?"

Ahmed gave me a sideways glance. "The only way I could gather data was to steal it."

"How did you do that?"

"I had to watch the papers and other media for stories of people who had taken their lives. I had to search in the obituaries to find the funeral times and locations. Then I had to wait and dig them up in the night when no one was around."

"You dug up dead bodies?" My mouth gaped.

"It wasn't easy. It took a great deal of my time. But I knew it was for a good cause, so I continued. I gathered valuable information I am using in my current studies.

"I always put the bodies back immediately, without leaving the cemetery; but one time I didn't, and I got caught. I was expelled. I couldn't get accepted anywhere else after that, but my cousin had connections at the National Autonomous University of Mexico. I dared not make the same mistake twice, so I borrowed money from my cousin to rent a garden home of my own not too far away from the campus. This way, I can do what I want without others looking over my shoulder. In exchange for the money my cousin gives me, I do favors for him now and then."

"What kind of favors? Drug-related?"

He laughed. "I wish. No, Taliban. He's the fourth in command. He never finished his degree in political science. He got too caught up in Islamic fundamentalism. My obligation to Syed is the reason I had to leave so quickly after that first night we spent together. It's why I can't make outgoing calls on the cell you used at the motel. I have another cell for outgoing calls."

I stared at him with astonishment. "You work for the Taliban?"

"Not on a regular basis. I don't believe in their cause or share their ideology. I do it for the money and out of loyalty to my cousin, who has been my one friend. I feel it is my duty to repay him for what he and his family have done for me."

I stared at him for several minutes, studying his face, his profile, as though I were seeing him for the first time. It took me a few long moments to draw this conclusion: He wasn't the Taliban spy's lover; it was I. *I was the Taliban Spy's Lover.* I whispered, "Oh my God. Oh my God."

"We're near the border. Once we cross I won't have to deal with these stupid drivers. Mexicans are much better."

"Don't I need an ID and passport to get across? Did you bring my purse?"

"That would have been stupid. Of course I didn't bring your purse. Once you are reported missing, your true identity is a liability. Remember, I have connections—more benefits from helping my cousin every now and then. I am a professional at deception, and I'll take care of everything. You will be asleep when we drive through the border patrol. You will be my ill and pregnant wife on medication. I, your husband and doctor, have what I need to prove it."

"No, I'm too nervous to sleep. Are you kidding?"

He gave me another sideways glance. "I cannot take the chance, Mona. I have to do it."

"Do what?"

He didn't answer right away. Then he said, "Use the chloroform."

"No way. Please, it's disgusting! I promise not to say a word! I'll pretend to be asleep. I'm a good actress."

He didn't reply.

"Ahmed, come on! We love each other, don't we?"

He didn't look at me.

"Don't we?"

He didn't answer.

A thought occurred to me. "Isn't chloroform dangerous for the baby?"

He shook his head.

I hyperventilated again. I tried to slow down my breathing and convince myself I was going to survive. After several minutes, he pulled over at a roadside rest area.

"Stay here. I'm going to use the restroom."

"I have to go, too."

He acted as though he was getting out of the vehicle, and I was already creating a plan of escape. But he didn't leave. He pressed the automatic locks. Then he took a wet cloth from a Ziplock bag in his blue jean pocket and, before I realized what he was doing, he had it over my mouth and nose, his other arm wrenched around my neck holding me still and preventing me from hitting him.

I stomped the floorboard with my feet and fought to free my arms. It took less than a minute for me to go limp in his arms. The last thing I remember is my own piss wetting my shorts.

I awoke in the middle of night in the cab of the truck nauseous. He handed me a paper bag and said, "Do it in here."

I grabbed the bag.

When I had finished, he pushed the button on his door to put down my window. "Toss it."

I had been so conditioned not to litter, that I hesitated.

"Toss it. It reeks."

I threw it out the window, wishing I had had a chance to attach a note, wishing someone would find my message in a bag and know it had belonged to me.

"Please don't do that to me again. It tastes so terrible and it scared the crap out of me and it's made me sick."

"You didn't vomit because of the chloroform. I had to give you a more powerful, longer-lasting drug. I have more if you don't cooperate."

I was wearing different clothes and smelled clean.

"You bathed me?"

He smirked but didn't reply.

I shivered as I wondered what else he had done to me. I had a purple mark on my arm where he had injected the needle, but nothing else looked suspicious. I asked where we were.

"Approaching Mexico City."

"I've got to use the restroom."

"Twenty minutes."

"I don't think I can make it. Please, Ahmed."

He didn't look at me, and I could see I would have to wait.

I lay my face against the cool window pane and sought the moon. The night was foggy. I couldn't see the moon. Other cars passed us on the road. We were surrounded by hundreds of city lights. But I felt so alone. I touched my stomach, so sorry for the innocent child inside me.

A while later he asked, "Hungry?"

I shook my head.

"I've got hamburgers and cokes here if you want them. You haven't eaten in two days. You must be hungry."

I almost laughed. I turned the back of my head to him and stared blankly into the fog and searched for the moon.

"I want you to understand the importance of my work, and so I need to give you some background before you see my lab. My studies of the dead while I attended the university in Peshawar provided me with persuasive evidence that a gene exists in humans which causes them to eventually commit suicide."

I fixed my eyes on the dark of night, pretending not to listen.

"In the majority of the suicide victims, I discovered the 5-HT2A receptors had the same genotype—the 102 C allele possessed a C/C structure, and this was not true of those dead bodies which had been murdered or had died of natural causes, such as a heart attack. The 5-HT2A receptor—I'm talking about trystophan hydroxylase—regulates serotonin, which is a neurotransmitter. Over the years I have obtained subjects, determined their 5-HT2A genotypes, and then conducted experiments using drugs which both increase and decrease levels of serotonin."

"You find people willing to let you use drugs on them?"

"No. Of course not."

I gave him a sharp glance. He was serious.

"I was fortunate to obtain a set of female twins early on in my research. They weren't my first subjects. I made several mistakes when I was getting started. By the time the twins and their friend came along, I knew better what to do. All three were sixteen years old. I had discretely taken a blood sample from one of the twins at a park they frequented. It was fairly easy to do, as with you and your broken wine glass."

My brows shot up, and he grinned.

"And since they were identical, I knew if the one had the gene, the other would have it, too.

"I had been going about for two years searching for a subject with the right gene and here was not one, but two! I was thrilled, as you might imagine. And so, because I needed a control, I took all three from a party one night. This was in Mexico City, before I started branching out.

"I tried to increase the levels of serotonin in my three subjects using fenfluramine. This worked in my control, but not in the twins. A PET scan of their brains showed the fenfluramine had no effect on the serotonin levels in the twins.

"My control lost her appetite and lost weight, but my twins craved carbohydrates and, when I offered food, ate voraciously. Then I had this revelation: when I increased the fenfluramine in the twins to dangerously high dosages, their serotonin levels decreased. The drug had the opposite effect on them than it did on the control.

"I observed the twins become more and more crazed as their serotonin levels dropped. They became more violent—not just with me, but with each other. Additionally, the degree of their self-mutilation increased to near fatal. Within two months of this higher dosage, both twins committed suicide, within two days of one another."

"What? You allowed this? You didn't put a stop to your experiments to save them?"

"No. You see, I already knew it was a matter of time before they would do it anyway. Why not with me, where they could help the rest of humanity?"

I shuddered, tasted blood in my mouth, and yet I chewed on my cracked lips.

"I decided to reduce the levels of serotonin in my control, but I could not get her levels to drop as low as that of the twins. I exposed her to greater stress through threats, violence, rape, sleep deprivation, starvation—but nothing I did provoked her to commit suicide despite the severe melancholy she had sunk into after the death of her friends. She later died of starvation."

I felt a flutter in my abdomen. I rolled down the window and vomited.

"Shit! It's all over the damned car." He hit the steering wheel with his hand.

I told him I couldn't help it.

He grabbed several lunch sacks from the glove compartment and put them on the seat beside me and said, "Use these next time."

I took one, but it was too late. I didn't need it anymore.

"Jesus Christ, Mona. It's all over the fucking car." He sighed, and then, after a moment, he continued. "Anyway, this is important, so try to listen."

He had said those very words in class a couple of months ago. It felt strange comparing then and now.

"I spent several more years trying to reduce the levels of serotonin in my subjects by various means, but none of the experiments successfully ended in suicide until I fell upon a group of drugs which together will block the reuptake of the neurotransmitter. All this time I thought low levels of serotonin had caused the suicidal acts, but I had been wrong. I soon discovered it wasn't serotonin levels which caused suicide, but its faulty reuptake.

"The 5-HT2A receptor with the 102 C/C allele failed to effectively utilize the serotonin. It worked, instead, like a hole in the bottom of a boat. So, when I used this new drug combination to block the reuptake of serotonin in the control subjects, they began to display suicidal tendencies. Two out of five completed the suicide, and I felt I had made an important breakthrough."

"What happened to the other three?"

"They each died of natural causes. One of them died from heart attack, and the other two from starvation."

I bit such a large piece of skin from my middle finger that it smarted and brought more tears to my eyes.

"Your habits of self-mutilation are what initially attracted me to you—after your beauty."

"What?"

"You bite your lips and phalanges. Have you ever bitten a toe?"

My mouth fell open.

"While searching for subjects with the suicide gene to see if a group of drugs regulating the reuptake of serotonin might prevent a person already suicidal from following through, I found Fatima. I was hoping to make you a subject as well. Your moderate forms of self-mutilation were a clue you might possess the gene."

"Oh my God! Oh my God!"

"Relax, Mona. I fell in love with you. You carry my child. I wouldn't use you now. You have to teach our child about my important work. Perhaps he or she will continue it. Maybe by then, the horrors of my project will be less important than the results. The ends will have justified the means."

"I can't believe this!" I wanted to scream he was crazy, mad, insane. But I was afraid of the consequences.

"I have made wonderful progress with Fatima. She has minimal food and water, little human interaction, no hope to speak of. I administer pain treatments regularly. Yet, I continue to inject her with the drug combination, and, so far, she has not committed suicide."

"Oh, God!"

"But be forewarned, you do carry the suicide gene. I tested your blood from the broken wine glass. You, like I—in the absence of a cure—are irrevocably doomed."

I wanted my mother and father and brother. I longed to be safe at my parents' house eating a Sunday noon meal after Mass, watching the television, and making wedding plans. I doubted I would ever see Bijan or my family again. If Ahmed did not kill me once his child was born, he would certainly keep me his prisoner, for he had divulged too much information to ever set me free.

At last he pulled into the cracked driveway of a dilapidated two-story garden home in front of the biggest pothole on the street of potholes. The small, leaning houses crammed together on the south side of downtown, north of the university. The tiny yard was covered with rocks and cactus and two overgrown weeds. By remote, he opened the garage door, which served as the great mouth that would gobble us up. It creaked and groaned and seemed to suck us in, its paint peeled, cracked, and less white than dingy gray. The white stucco exterior appeared in slightly better

201

condition, but the red Spanish-style roof tiles appeared worn. I doubted they offered much protection from the rain.

When we entered the house from the garage, my stomach lurched. The front door had been nailed shut with sheets of plywood, as had the one window beside it.

The living room was being used as a storage room. There were bookcases filled with books, vases, platters, pots, figurines, and folk art. On top of the bookcases and end tables and coffee table stood cardboard boxes, an empty birdcage, a chandelier, a television, the white elephants and lamps I had seen at his house in Brownsville, two stuffed animals—taxidermy style: a wild hog and a giant snake—mounds of newspapers, videos, CDs, and heaps of handwritten papers. As we worked our way through the maze of stacked possessions toward the kitchen, past the sofas from his old place crammed in front of the stone fireplace on the farthest wall, past oil paintings above the mantle, stacked in front of each other without design, I met the surreal eyes of the Muslim woman veiled in the geometric design—the eyes that had watched me without warning fall in love with their monstrous owner.

I trembled as Ahmed took my hand and led me to the back rooms. First came a kitchen and eating area. The blue and yellow tiles must have been beautiful at one time, but now were chipped and cracked and crumbling along one spot behind the stove where sheetrock and stud were

202

exposed. A spider crawled out of the gaping hole and made its way to the corner of the stove.

At the back of the eating area, on the same side as the boarded up entrance, a side door led to the backyard, but it, too, was covered with boards and nailed shut, and the windows over the kitchen sink were barred with iron rods on the inside. Through the heavily barred kitchen window, the only window with a view to the outside, I saw an overgrown backyard with a six-foot falling wooden fence around it. The one tree was dead.

Across from the eating area and behind the fireplace were the stairs leading to the upper floor. To the right of this staircase were a closet and two rooms—a bathroom and a back bedroom, which extended out past the kitchen. In addition to a double bed and large armoire, there were a sofa and television and several works of art on the walls. It was the only orderly room I had seen so far.

"This is where I live," he said, waving his hand at the back room. "My lab is upstairs."

I shuddered at the prospect of a tour.

"It's awfully quiet up there." He lifted his face toward the ceiling. "Last time I came home she was calling for me. I don't hear her now."

I peered up at the ceiling, too, as though it might offer insight into the state of his other prisoner, my fellow victim.

"Shall we go up?" he asked.

I backed away from him. "I'm scared."

"Then wait here."

When he reached the top of the stairs, I ran through the narrow path in the living room to the garage to make my escape, but I could not open the door leading to the outside. I searched frantically for a button, tried pulling it up with all my strength, but the door wouldn't budge. I thought of driving the car through the door. I climbed in the driver's side, but the keys were gone, and the garage door remote control was nowhere to be found.

Finding a syringe filled with liquid lying in a leather bag on the floorboard, I snatched it up and put it in the pocket of Ahmed's shorts, which I had been wearing since I had awakened from my drug-induced sleep. Then, full of desperation, I bore all my weight on the horn of the car. It bleated like a lamb before the slaughter.

He was there before I saw him, pulling me from the car and back into the house.

When we were in the back bedroom, panting, he said, "I thought you said you loved me."

"Yes. But I'm also frightened of you."

He gave me a hurt look. "Come on, I told you I would not harm you. I brought you here to show you my important discoveries. The people in this neighborhood know little of me, but one day they will be surprised to learn a great man lived among them—for while the nature of my work forces me to live in the shadows, one day when I'm long gone, and maybe when our child is full grown, the world will be bustling with the knowledge on their tongues and lips that I, Ahmed Jaffar, provided—knowledge which will dramatically change the future of the human species. I might even find the cure in time to save your life, or the life of our child."

He took my hand, "Come upstairs and let me introduce you to Fatima."

"She's alive?"

"Yes, though very weak. My experiment so far has been a success." Unbelievably, he chuckled. "She is always so glad to see me, just like a dog. She used to leap up from the bed and run to the bars of her chamber and thrust her arms toward me, begging for me. She likes it when I bring gifts. Sometimes I bring her crayons and paper, books, and cheap toys. She begs me for these things and expresses the greatest gratitude when I bring them. Just like a dog. She likes it when I go into her chamber with her. She can't keep her hands off of me. But today she is weak. She stays on the bed, but I can see her eyes following me with their brightness. She is still glad to see me. She whimpered when I sat beside her on the bed. She touched my hand, smiled with her eyes at me, whimpering."

I fought the impulse to cringe. "I don't want to meet her today, Ahmed. Please let me sleep awhile. I'm so tired. I'm afraid once I go up I will never be able to sleep again. And right now I need to use the bathroom."

He opened the door for me, and I entered the room. I found the light and then slammed the door shut, locking both doors. I knew it would do me no good to lock myself away in the room, though there were locks on both doors—the one leading to the bedroom and the other leading to the hallway. I would surly starve as others of his victims had in the lab above. The bathroom had no windows leading to the outside. No escape at all.

I found a roll of toilet paper in the cabinet beneath the sink, and I hid the syringe inside it and placed it in the back of the other rolls. I hoped to find another hiding place for it later.

When I came out, he had pulled back the covers on the double bed. He had a look on his face that said he wanted me—a look that, weeks ago, had sent ripples of pleasure through my body. I could not imagine going on like this, indefinitely. The tears of utter exhaustion flowed from my eyes. He came to me and wiped the tears away with his thumbs as he held my head with the rest of his fingers. He did this gently, lovingly, and I could see he did love me, if such a monster could. He caressed my cheeks, moved his fingers through my hair, and all the while I stood, trembling and sobbing, and unable to believe this is how it was going to be.

Chapter Seventeen: The Ghost in the Window

The vibration of Yvette's cell phone in her pocket pulls her from Mona's story. "It's Devin, my husband," she says. "Excuse me a moment."

"Hey," Yvette says softly into the phone. "I'm at Mona's. Can I call you back?"

"Who's Mona?"

Yvette meets her neighbor's glare.

"You told him my name?"

In the phone, Yvette says, "A friend. She's a friend."

Geez. Don't everybody freak out at once.

"Call me tonight. We're heading out on the boat, and we don't get reception out there."

"Everything okay?" Yvette asks.

"Nothing different. The kids wanted to chat. Call us tonight." He hangs up.

When Yvette looks up, Mona is leaning over one of the stacks of boxes, glaring at her.

Spooky. Spooky and strange.

"He doesn't know who you are. I call you the neighbor lady."

"I know what you call me."

The blood rushes to her face. "So, how did you escape? How did you get away from Ahmed?"

Mona walks across the room, with her back to Yvette. "I'll tell you what happened, but I have to tell you in the order the events occurred so you will understand why I did what I did. That's the whole reason I brought you here, Yvette. I needed to explain myself so you would understand in the end."

"What do you mean you brought me here? I delivered a package, remember?"

Mona faces her. "Oh, yes. You'll have to excuse my nerves. I never can relax."

Too strange. Did she set me up? "But you're safe now, right?"

"No. I've been running all my life. I'm so tired of running." She steps back to her chair and sits down. The one-eyed cat hops in her lap.

Taking her seat, Yvette asks, "You mean he's still after you? All these years you've been running from him?" She initially suspected Mona was in a witness-protection program, but not for the first time she fears the strange scientist might still be looking for her. What if the person she saw through the slats in her backyard fence was Ahmed Jaffar, stalking her? Another chill worked itself down her back all the way to her toes like the cold breath of someone standing behind her.

Is he here? Living with her?

"He's a ghost, and so am I, but after I tell you my story, I can finally rest in peace."

"I'm listening," Yvette says, on the edge of her seat, ready to run.

"I'm too worn out to go on today. Come back tomorrow."

Yvette bites her lip. "I'll come tomorrow, but then I really must join my family."

In the evening, Yvette calls Devin, and after hearing from each of the kids their stories of fish that got away, of alligator and bobcat sightings, of Frodo Baggins jumping from the boat to fetch a Frisbee, and other tales that make her wish she went with them, Devin comes back on the phone.

"Hold on, I want to get out of this tent. I need to ask you a question, and I want the truth."

"Devin, what's wrong?"

"Tell me the truth, Yvette. Are you having an affair? Tell me straight out. I can't stand it anymore."

If it weren't for Devin's shaky voice, Yvette would laugh. "How in the world could I possibly have time for an affair?" She wishes she could show Devin her calendar and how just about every day of every month was loaded up with kid activities, doctor and dentist appointments, Cub Scouts and Girl Scouts and robotics, and the list went on. "Sweetheart, I can't believe you are asking me this. Oh, Honey, no. I love you. How can you even think such a thing?"

If I were going to muster up the energy to have sex, it would certainly be with my own husband.

He doesn't answer.

"Devin? Are you there?"

"I'm here."

"I had no idea you've been thinking this way. Roommates? How long have you been upset?"

"You don't know what it's like Yvette, wanting you and not being wanted back."

"Oh my God! Oh, Devin! Listen to me, Honey. I'm coming up. I'll get in the van right now."

"No, that's okay. Don't come tonight. I don't want you on the road this late. Maybe tomorrow?"

"Yes. But I have a commitment in the afternoon. I'll come after." She waits, unsure if he is still on the line. "Devin?"

"Yeah?" he asks in a broken voice.

"I love you, and I'm so sorry."

"Talk to you tomorrow."

Hell.

Nausea sweeps through her. How have things gotten this bad? At what point did her marriage fall apart?

Between thoughts of her husband's pain and Mona's story, Yvette can't relax. She peers through her windows a dozen times searching for signs of Ahmed Jaffar, and as much as she wants to water her vines, she's too frightened to go out into the backyard with Mr. Baggins gone. She heats up a chicken pot pie from the freezer and watches an old episode of *NCIS*, which is about a stalker. Restless and afraid, she invites Heidi to come over and watch programs recorded on her DVR, *Oprah* and *Modern Family*, to help keep her mind off things.

As they drink a bottle of wine and munch on microwave popcorn, Yvette tells Heidi a little about Mona.

"Don't you wonder why she's telling you this?"

"Absolutely. I've been asking myself that this whole time. Any ideas?"

"I have no explanation. And that's what scares me. What's her motive?"

"Maybe she's lonely and bored. Maybe she's making it up."

"Maybe she's nuts. You should be careful."

"She knows where I live. I can't not show up. If she's crazy, she might do something."

"She could be telling the truth. It could be a cry for help."

Heidi tells Yvette she's thinking about leaving her husband, Bill. She says she loves him and has forgiven him

212

for his affair. She has hurt him back with her affairs and is no longer interested in sleeping with other men. But she feels like he doesn't love her anymore, and it hurts her to be around a man who doesn't want her.

"Have you talked to him about these feelings?" asks Yvette.

"No. I'm too scared."

"He might be hurting, too. Don't leave expecting him to beg you to stay. Talk to him and find out what he really wants."

"Easy to say."

"I know." Then Yvette tells Heidi a little of what Devin said.

"Make love to him the first chance you get," says Heidi. "It sounds like he feels the same way I do. Let him know you still want him."

Tears rush to Yvette's eyes. "You're right. That's what I'll do."

Lying in her bed late at night, Yvette realizes she has taken for granted how much Devin has fulfilled her and helped her to feel secure and complete. He came along at the end of a bad relationship with a guy who cheated on her and within months of her mother's death. At that time, she had erected walls around herself, afraid of loss, distant to the rest of the universe, a dust mote blowing haphazardly in the wind with no course, no purpose, no reason for being. Anyone else might have given up on her, but Devin persisted, for who knows why, and after four years, convinced her to marry him.

I love you Devin. I'm so sorry.

When Yvette pulls up to Mona's house and climbs out of the van, she sees, without a doubt, a face staring at her through one of the bedroom windows.

And the face is not Mona's.

He's a ghost, and so am I.

If she has suspected Ahmed Jaffar is living with Mona, she hasn't really believed it, or she never would have returned to the house. Now, with indisputable evidence that someone besides Mona is inside the house—not in the yard, which might be explained by a yard boy—Yvette must act.

What to do? Yvette stands frozen on the sidewalk in the warm afternoon staring at the ghostly figure in the window, and the figure stares back. A baseball cap pulled low over the eyes makes it difficult to tell the gender of the figure. Then it does something shocking: it waves.

Is it taunting her?

Yvette takes her cell phone from her pocket, ready to call 9-1-1. But what would she say? She has no idea who this is waving at her. She gets back in her van and drives away.

At home she wishes she can call Mona, but Mona refused to give Yvette her phone number—saying it was a matter of life and death. Then, Yvette thought she was a lonely drama queen who made mountains out of molehills.

She has read stories of people who fall in love with their abductors. There is even a syndrome. She Googles it: The Stockholm syndrome. This is what she reads from the *Mental Health Matters* website:

After their rescue from two bank robbers in Stockholm, Sweden in 1973, the four hostages surprisingly supported their captors even though their captors abused them. One victim even became engaged to one of the robbers and helped with his legal fees.

Psychologists were familiar with the phenomenon long before 1973, particularly in cases such as
•Abused Children
•Battered/Abused Women
•Prisoners of War
•Cult Members
•Incest Victims
•Criminal Hostage Situations
•Concentration Camp Prisoners
•Controlling/Intimidating Relationships

Some psychologists explain this phenomenon as a survival mechanism

related   to   adaptation   and   natural
selection.

The mention of prisoners of war reminds Yvette of the night she met her grandfather, who was a prisoner in a concentration camp during the Second World War, and this sheds some light on Mona's moody behavior. She also recalls how then, like now, she was drawn into a story and possessed by it.

Her mother flew her to Maine to see him ten years after Yvette's father died because he was at death's door, though with him, at least they had some warning. This was two years before her mother's heart attack, when Yvette was twenty-two.

The old man's room was dark, except for a bedside lamp. Thick curtains covered the tall, narrow windows from floor to ceiling. Yvette's grandfather sat up in bed leaning against a pile of pillows. He had a few gray hairs on his head, thin, like fishing string, and a pair of reading glasses on his crooked nose. From pajama sleeves, his bony, wrinkled wrists rested on a pillow across his lap with a half-finished crossword puzzle.

His voice was raspy but clear when he said to her mother, "Well, who's this looker?"

"This is my daughter, Yvette."

"Yvette is a French name referring to a yew tree," he said. "The yew is one of the few true evergreens in Western

Europe and is a symbol of death and rebirth. Do you want to know why?"

Yvette nodded.

"Papi is a walking dictionary," said her mother.

"Its branches grow down into the ground to form new stems, which then rise up out of the ground to form trunks. So you see? Death and rebirth."

"How interesting. I never knew."

"Papi, Yvette is going to sit with you for a while so I can help in the kitchen."

"Good, good."

Her mother left to help her sister-in-law cook their meal without so much as kissing her father. She hadn't seen him in twenty years.

"In France, Yvette also means beautiful, which seems fitting here, my dear."

"Thank you." She sat on a chair beside him. "Are you working on a crossword puzzle?"

"You're a bright one. You deduced that by the one lying half-finished across my lap."

"We can't all be as bright as you."

"Okay, I like you, too, Yvette. You'll do."

"How is it you've come to be known around here as the walking dictionary?"

"Quite a misnomer since I can no longer walk and haven't in three or more years."

"The name must be an old one, then," Yvette teased.

"Even the word dictionary in regard to me is a misnomer because my knowledge base is not of all words in one language but of many words in many languages, though I happen to be familiar with a series of French names, mostly female, because of my former, more prurient, interests."

"Knowledge is knowledge, right? But you must have another motive in learning many words in many languages other than prurient interests."

"Yes, clever of you to deduce that. My native language is German, and after escaping a Jewish ghetto in a small German town, I eventually found myself in the U.S. army training at Camp Ritchie for counter-intelligence. In addition to English and German, I picked up French because of a brief stay I had in Paris. I also knew a bit of Russian because of a grandmother who spoke nothing else. And so, the army sharpened my language skills by depositing me behind enemy lines where I had to converse with native-speaking peoples in a way that appeared natural or die."

"So your knowledge of words saved your life."

"And it continues to, even today, in the admittedly less stressful form of crossword puzzles."

He doesn't know he's dying. "So now we've come full circle."

"Unless you wish to hear more about my life in between, then yes."

218

With little encouragement from Yvette, Ludwig Weishaupt began his tale of his experiences as a German Jew turned American soldier during World War II.

"I was born near Bremen. In 1937, a German soldier for the Third Reich announced on his loudspeaker all Jewish men age eighteen and older must come out onto the square. I had just turned eighteen and was frightened to go, so I hid in the attic, thinking it would be better to die in my home than out on the street, but my father and two brothers went. The Jewish men were made to lie face down on the cobblestone to hear the news from Hitler. Each household must send one Jewish man to work in labor camps for the German army. To frighten us, the soldiers shot every tenth man lying on the cobblestone. One of my brothers died that day. We weren't allowed to bury his body. My other brother was taken to a labor camp and we never heard from him again.

"My parents had relatives in California, and they had been writing back and forth to these relatives to get them to sponsor me to the United States. In 1938, after much paper work, disappointments, and near-death experiences, my visa was finally received from our relatives in the mail.

"My aunt and uncle treated me like a slave. I felt grateful and resentful at the same time, so, when an army recruiter came to our area in 1941, I enlisted, mostly to flee.

"I didn't know I was leaving one kind of prison for another. I'm sure you've seen enough movies about basic training to get a sense of how an enlisted man is treated. First your superiors break you down and humiliate you. Then, like a dog, they train you to be loyal to your pack. You grow to love your alpha leader and to feel you would do anything for him. It is not for your country you put your life on the line, but for the love and gratitude you feel toward your commanding officer, who has become your god.

"My knowledge of various languages was quickly noticed, and after my basic training, I was sent to Camp Ritchie to be broken in and trained all over again under new leadership. My first assignment was to drive a loudspeaker car along the front lines in Germany to convince the German soldiers to surrender. I barely escaped with my life and after had to spend a few weeks in a psychiatric ward in Paris. That is where I learned the origin of nearly every female French name, a skill which helped me into more than one nurse's bed.

"I returned to Antwerp a month later but then was captured during the Battle of the Bulge. I was taken to a prisoner-of-war camp not far from my hometown near Bremen, but, fortunately, my Jewish ancestry was never discovered or I would have been killed. I used my training to gather information and to keep up the morale of the other prisoners, but at one point it was discovered I was an intelligence officer, and then I entered the lowest point of my life."

Ludwig stopped speaking. Yvette was imaging the war-torn world of human suffering he had sketched for her, and so this sudden silence drew her back to the surface.

"You don't have to go on, if it's too difficult."

"Cathartic, dear."

"Then, by all means, continue."

"As an intelligence officer who spoke many languages, I was too valuable to the Germans to kill, so, instead, they tortured me. First, they broke me down by forcing me to carry the bodies of dead prisoners—both Jews and Ally soldiers—to a heap on the outskirts of the camp. Then they made me the bread deliverer to the other prisoners. I was told I must give one loaf to be shared by eight men, and if I didn't throw the bread into the mud for the prisoners to dig out to eat, I would lose my genitals.

"This second job was far worse than the first. The corpses were already at peace. I didn't have to watch their suffering. But this second job was pure hell. What made it hard for me was the gratitude the prisoners felt toward me: Even though the bread was too little and was covered in the dirty slush of mud and human excrement, they thanked me with tears in their eyes as they gobbled up their crumbs. If I had had the means, I would have killed myself, but the German soldiers were too clever for that.

"Before we were liberated in the Spring of 1945, a new German commanding officer took over the camp, and perhaps because he saw a fellow lover of languages and books and all arts, he took a liking to me. He moved me out of the stables and into a barrack with my own cot. He invited me to his quarters to play chess and listen to German opera, of which we both knew all the words. He fed me expensive wine and cheese and, occasionally, a full meal. I grew to love the man, even though he was my enemy and I could hear from my barrack the oppressive and brutal tactics he carried out on my fellow prisoners. I was the chosen one, and though I sympathized for the other prisoners, I was glad I had been so blessed to have found favor with this man whom I loved like the religious do their gods.

"I soon came to understand his attentions did not come without a price. He expected certain favors in return. At first, the favors were simple enough: playing chess, working jigsaw puzzles, reciting his favorite poems in multiple languages. But he wanted more from me, and I, not wanting to lose my special privileges, gave him what he wanted until he grew tired of me and put me back in the stables with everyone else.

"One day before he put me back with the others, he gave me a pistol. He told me we needed to cut our overhead. We didn't have enough bread for the prisoners and he wanted me to shoot one of them. He brought out two of the weakest prisoners. They were barely able to walk and were nothing but bags of bones by then. Herr Schneider told me to choose who should live another day and to put a bullet through the head of the one who should die."

"Oh my God," Yvette murmurs. "What did you do?"

"I was so confused and frightened. I knew both men. One of them, Howie, said, 'Shoot me. I want to die. Leave my nephew to live.' And Jerome, the nephew said, 'Please don't shoot us. Please let us both live.'

"Herr Schneider stood a distance from me holding a bigger weapon than mine, and he shouted, 'Choose one or I'll shoot you!'

"Warm piss flowed down my leg. My hands shook so badly, I could barely hold the gun straight. First, I pointed the gun at Howie's head. I glanced back at the German commander to see him smiling with pleasure. It was beyond my comprehension he could find pleasure in this. I no longer wanted to live in a world where people like he existed. I put the gun to my own head and pulled the trigger. Nothing happened. The gun wasn't loaded. Before I could ask why he had done this, the commander shot the two prisoners. Howie and his nephew, Jerome, fell to the ground. I looked up at Schneider. He was angry and smug. He told me it was my fault he had to kill both of them because I disobeyed his direct order and he needed to teach me a lesson. Herr Schneider ordered me to stand there and watch the two prisoners die. They pulled themselves across the dirt and held one another while death slowly took them. All three of us wept, and long after the men were dead, I continued to weep. The commander returned me to the stables with the other prisoners who hated me by that time as much as they hated Schneider.

"The other prisoners abused me, for I was a traitor to them, and I would have died from their abuse had we not been liberated within three weeks.

"Eventually, I was sent by the army to train recruits near Galveston. That's where I met your mother's mother. We married and had three children and had a beautiful life together until she died twelve years ago. I have one daughter who never visits and a son who is dead, but I feel fortunate Bobby and his wife take care of me. He is a good son."

When Yvette later asked her mother why they never visited Ludwig, she said, "Because he beat the hell out of me growing up, and I've never forgiven him."

"So Bobby was his favorite?" Yvette asked.

"He was hardest on Bobby. Beat him to a pulp."

"Then why has Bobby taken him in all these years?"

"It's beyond my comprehension."

At twenty-two, Yvette hadn't drawn the conclusion she is able to draw today, that her mother had broken a cycle of abuse and escaped becoming a victim of the Stockholm syndrome. Her mother had not loved Yvette's grandfather and had not been grateful as most victims are. This would harden anyone, especially after losing a spouse. Yvette realizes her mother's rigid spine had more to do with self-control than lack of love. She wanted to spare her daughter.

Yvette's eyes well with tears. *She loved me in her own way.*

And now Mona may or may not be a victim of the Stockholm syndrome. Yvette rereads the screen several times, wondering what course of action she should take. If Mona were still Ahmed's prisoner, and if she were suffering from the Stockholm syndrome, she wouldn't tell Yvette her story and risk exposing her abductor. Maybe she has come to her senses and is in need of help. Maybe she's drugged Ahmed, or killed him. Yvette nearly calls the police, but she has so little to go on. Yvette is about to call Heidi to ask for an opinion, when her home phone rings.

"Why didn't you come up to the door?" Mona asks. "I saw you come and leave."

"You saw me?"

"Yes. I waved to you, but you didn't wave back."

"That was you in the window?"

"Who else would it be?"

Liar!

Yvette knows it was not Mona but doesn't want to challenge her, fearing she will no longer reach out to Yvette—if that's what she's doing. She suspects Mona is crying out for help, but has to be subtle, and she must be keeping Ahmed at bay, by drugging him. Or he's sick, dying, making it possible for Mona to tell her story.

You poor thing. No wonder you're so strange.

Yvette considers again that Mona might be working with her abductor, luring Yvette into a trap, but since she can't be sure of Mona's innocence or guilt, she doesn't want to cut herself off from her. One thing is for certain: Yvette will never go to Mona's house again.

Never.

"I came back because I was weak and dizzy. I needed to come home and rest."

Liar.

"Do you still plan to come over?"

"I don't think so. Not today." She needs time to figure out what to do.

"What? This can't be! Yvette, I'm so close to finishing. What will I do? I guess I could come to your house again. Should I come right now?"

"No. I might be contagious."

"If you are, then I've already been exposed. What would it matter?"

"My house is a wreck."

"Do you think I care?"

If Mona is still a victim, the distance will help her toward recovery. On the other hand, if Ahmed is living with her, and if he isn't drugged or sick or dying, he might follow her here. "Could you tell me your story over the phone?"

She is quiet on the other end.

"Mona?"

"I'm here. I don't know, Yvette. What if we're overheard?"

"How? How do you mean?"

"The phone lines could be tapped."

Poor, paranoid woman.

"By whom?"

"I don't know."

"I don't think so, Mona. Besides, if someone tapped your lines, they would also have your house bugged. I don't think so, though."

"I don't know."

"It's the only way I can hear the end. I don't know how long it will be before I'm well."

With the doors and windows locked, cell phone close by in case she needs to call 9-1-1, and Devin's pistol in a drawer beside her chair, Yvette listens to Mona's voice drone over the phone like a dying bird.

Chapter Eighteen: The Lab

Ahmed kept me locked inside the bedroom with access to the adjoining bath, but the doors leading to the hallway from both the bath and the bedroom were bolted shut. The one window over the sofa on the back wall was boarded on the outside, and six iron bars were screwed in across the front on the inside. He brought me three meals a day, which he left me to eat alone, but most nights he came and slept with me.

The first time he brought me food—the morning after our arrival at his secret lab—I refused to eat.

"Do it for the baby," he said.

"I can't. I'm too upset. I feel nauseous. I want my mom and dad!"

"You'll see them soon enough. After the pregnancy, you and the baby will return." He left and bolted shut the door.

The next time he entered the room, I said, "Ahmed, don't you realize what you're doing is wrong? Don't you understand you can't just kidnap people and do what you want with them, no matter how good your intentions may be? I know you have grand ideas about solving genetic problems and stuff, but you can't do it this way. Don't you see? You can't destroy life in your hopes of saving it down the road."

"Isn't that what you were planning to do? Abort our child to save your own future dream? Besides, the people I choose to use in my research are the vilest, most worthless of the species. Fatima was a slut and a cheat. The twins were sluts and were stupid. I've known dogs smarter than those silly girls."

"What about me?"

"I misread you. That's why you're no longer a subject."

"But, initially, you thought I," my voice fell off. "Human beings are human beings!"

"See how nicely she contradicts herself?" He let the plate of food drop heavily upon the coffee table. It nearly broke. Then he stormed out, slammed the door, and bolted it behind him.

I had not left the bed except to use the bathroom and to drink a few sips of water when, two days later, Ahmed came into the room, picked up the plate of food—still full and sitting on the coffee table where he had left it—and threw it across the room. The plate shattered into fragments, and food dripped down the walls.

"I told you to eat. Don't you care about your own baby growing inside of you? Selfish bitch! Eat, I tell you, or I will force it down your throat!"

"Let me go and I'll eat," I said weakly.

"I told you, I will let you go after the baby is born, when I'm sure you won't terminate the pregnancy."

"Both me and the baby?"

"Yes."

I knew he was lying, but I was desperate to believe. "Promise me!"

"I promise."

"Really and truly?" I sat up in the bed, dizzy. "Because, Ahmed, you know I wouldn't do anything like tell the police, don't you? You're the father of my baby. I want you in our lives. Blood is thicker than anything. You are as much my family now as my mother and father and brother. We should get married, as soon as possible, before the baby comes." I loved him once, so it was possible he might believe I could love him again. To make my speech sound more convincing, I added, "I'm so impressed with your work, even though it was hard for me to understand and appreciate it before. I was shocked—you must understand. But now I realize the good it will do in the end."

"You're just saying that, Mona. I'm not stupid."

"Ahmed, I'm serious. You must understand I'm not scientific minded. When I look at people, I think of their souls, and I think of them as creatures of God, each one special and loved by God. But I am beginning to understand a more scientific viewpoint, to see how silly this whole God

230

thing is. I'm beginning to see the value in sacrificing a few members of our species for the good of the whole. We are just animals, after all, right? What could be the difference between sacrificing a rat and sacrificing a human being, especially when we're talking about a major improvement to the entire species?"

"You're a good actress."

"It's just taken me a while to understand and appreciate your way of thinking. You're so much smarter than I am. And how can you blame me for being frightened? If the tables were turned and I was the scientist, well, don't you see you'd be frightened, too? Without any power over your own life?"

"Don't be frightened. I've told you I love you and I won't harm you or the baby. Don't you believe me?"

"I'm trying to. It's hard when you tricked me before, about fighting in Afghanistan against the Soviets."

"I told you things were different then. I didn't love you then." He moved closer to me.

"You still love me now?"

He sat down on the bed. "Yes." He kissed me tenderly and then looked at me, as though he were waiting for my reaction.

"Please, Ahmed. Kiss me again. I'm so frightened. I need reassurance." I pretended to enjoy it, and I half-believed in my own lies. "Say you love me," I pleaded.

"I love you. And our baby."

After he had finished with me, he asked, "Will you eat?"

I nodded, burying my face in the pillow.

"What's the matter now? I thought we understood one another."

"We do. Really, Ahmed. I'm just so relieved. I was so frightened before. I'm crying tears of relief."

A few weeks later, I asked Ahmed if he could get me something to do. I had watched every English movie in his collection. "What about an art set? I need something to do with my time."

He fell for it, and so after he brought me the set and while he was away from the room, I created a distress note, but as soon as I dropped it into the commode, the paper, unprotected, disintegrated. So, a few days later, I asked him for a box of Ziplock bags.

"You always give me so much food, but then I get hungry later, before you've come back, and the food tastes stale. If I could have a few plastic baggies, the food would stay fresh longer." The next day he left and returned with the Ziplock bags.

"Thank you," I said nonchalantly. "Put them on the coffee table. I'm almost done with this masterpiece."

"What is it?"

"A picture of my family—my mother and father and brother and me. See the bump? I'm pregnant with our baby."

"I'm not in it."

"That's because I'm not finished with it, yet."

When he left, I took the note I had been drying beneath the bed with my name, the date, and "Mexico City garden home north of the university," folded it carefully with the word "Help" visible on the outside of the fold, tucked it into one of the plastic bags, and hurried to the commode where I flushed it down. This brought me hope and made me extremely happy for several days.

I asked him for other things, like books. "I need to distract myself. I need to do something to pass the time until you set me free."

"I have a bunch of philosophy books—interesting works which I taught in my classes. You're interested in existentialism, but have you read Nietzsche? Or Schopenhauer?"

I shook my head. "That's fine, I guess, but what I'd really love is a novel. I want to read literary classics, so I won't get too far behind in my studies. Pick me up a few at a bookstore, will you? Some Dickens. Or, perhaps Dostoevsky."

"I'll see what I can do."

"One other thing. It's stuffy and hot in here. Aren't you going to let me out for fresh air and sunshine? For a few minutes? You can put tape over my mouth or whatever—I promise I won't scream—but I need to see and smell the outdoors."

"I'll think about it."

Not a week later, he returned with Dostoevsky's *Crime and Punishment*. He had a smile on his face. He knew it would please me.

"Oh, Ahmed!" I got up from the sofa. "Thank you! Have you read it?"

"No."

"Well, I'll tell you all about it when I'm finished." I was delighted by the thickness of the book.

A few days later, I screamed at Ahmed as soon as he walked in the door. "Did you ever think it was their religion that made them do it?"

"What?" he asked.

"Your suicide-bombing parents!" I shouted. "It wasn't their DNA! It was their ideology!"

He slapped my face. "Never speak to me like that."

The next morning, I found spots of blood on my underwear. I cried out to Ahmed from the bathroom with such a wail, he rushed downstairs directly to me.

"What is it?" He stood in the bathroom doorway, panting.

I stepped from the panties, his long shirt hanging down to my knees, and showed him the blood.

The look of anguish on his face equaled mine, but he whispered, "It's okay. You need to stay off of your feet for a while." He whisked me up into his arms and then gently laid me on the bed. He put *Sleepless in Seattle* into the VCR and brought me iced tea and cookies on a tray and set it on the bed. Then he leaned close to me and said, "Don't get up for anything, okay? You call me when you need something. You and the baby will be fine." He had tears in his eyes.

That night, as I neared the end of Dostoevsky's novel, Ahmed came in from the shower, wearing his white briefs as usual, and readied the bedcovers for sleeping.

"You're going to bed already?" I asked.

"Yeah, I'm sleepy."

"Do you mind if I keep reading?"

"Go ahead."

It felt weird. We were like an old married couple.

"Ahmed, can I ask you something?"

"What is it?"

"Have you ever thought about giving up your research, leaving the Taliban, and living a normal, everyday life without fear of getting caught?"

"Of course I have."

"You still can, you know. You still have the choice to leave it behind."

"My research gives me a sense of purpose. Without it, life would have no meaning for me."

I felt sorry for him then.

One day as Ahmed used the bathroom, the toilet overflowed, and when he used the plunger to fix it, one of my distress notes floated to the top of the commode. I was watching a movie and didn't know.

He stood in the doorway between the bath and bedroom. "What's this?" He had the note out of the bag. It was damp, but the words were legible.

"I don't know," I cried. "You should ask your other prisoner."

"She doesn't have little plastic bags, Mona. You do. What are you trying to pull?"

"Well, it didn't work, so no use getting mad about it. I thought it would go down, but I guess you can't flush plastic." I was trying to hide the fact that I had already successfully flushed a half a dozen notes.

"No use getting mad? No use getting mad?" He raised his fist.

I knew I had to be brave, to not give in to the trembling. "Listen to me, Ahmed. You have got to understand. No matter how much I love you, as long as you keep me prisoner, I am going to try to escape. It has nothing to do with my feelings for you. It has everything to do with my desire for freedom. I wouldn't expect any less of you."

My direct method worked. He didn't strike me. He crumbled the note in his fist, took up the box of baggies from the coffee table, collected the art set, and stormed out. He returned and took up the painted pictures scattered around the room.

"Not my family one, please! Ahmed, please don't take the family painting! I promise you I won't eat a bite if you do."

But he wanted to punish me, so he took it, ripped it to shreds, and left the room, bolting the door behind him. "You can forget all about your fresh air and sunshine!" he called through the door.

That evening, he didn't return, and, in a moment of despair, I took up the twenty-one inch television, ripped it from the VCR, though it was as heavy as three bowling balls and nearly put me in labor, and hurled it with all my strength against the barred window. The glass in the window cracked, as did the glass screen of the television, and fell across the sofa and tile. But the boards and the bars didn't budge. I cried out, in case I might be heard. I cried out frantically. Then I heard the woman upstairs crying out, too, repeating my words in the same tone. She was my echo, as I yelled,

237

"Help me! Is anyone there? Help me! Help us!" It was like yelling into a canyon.

Then the automatic garage door opened. I panicked and ran into the bathroom and locked myself inside. I could still hear Fatima's shrill cries, my echo.

"He won't kill me," I reminded myself, trying to keep from shaking. "He won't kill me until after the baby comes." I thought of the syringe, which I had moved weeks before beneath the mattress on my side of the bed and which I had come close to using many nights while he slept beside me. But I was always too afraid. I wasn't sure what the syringe contained, though I hoped it was the same drug he had used on me during the awful drive down. I believed it was the same drug, because when he had found it missing the day he brought me to his Mexican lab, he had questioned me about it.

"Please, God," I whispered in the bathroom. "Don't let him kill me!"

When he entered the bedroom, he called out to me in a voice enraged. He beat on the bathroom door, cursing me, demanding I come out, but I crept into the tub, curled into a ball, and waited, fighting hard not to hyperventilate.

"Fine, have it your way," he said after several minutes, and then things were quiet.

When I awoke a few hours later, I could hear Ahmed cleaning the mess.

The next morning, he said, more gently, through the door, "Come out and eat. I promise I won't hurt you. You should know I wouldn't do anything that might harm the baby."

My legs were cramping, and I was hungry. I knew I had to come out, and the longer I waited, the weaker I would be. I had to come out.

Appealing to him through the closed door, I said, "Ahmed, I'm sorry. I'm sorry about the mess. I'm sorry about the television. I just want to be free. Do you understand? If you'll let me go, I promise I won't abort the baby. I wish you would trust me."

"Trust you, after what you pulled last night?"

"Take me away from here and marry me. Please! Let's live a normal, happy life. Don't you want that? Don't you want to be happy?"

"I am happy here with you. I thought you were, too."

"I am. Sometimes. When I forget I'm your prisoner. I am happy. But then I remember, and I yearn to be free."

"A few more months. A few more months and you will have your freedom."

I opened the door. "Promise?"

"Of course." He took me in his arms. Both of us were partly aware we were playing a game—a fantasy game—but neither of us wanted to face the truth. We clung to one another. Ahmed kissed my cheek, then my lips. I clung to him and pushed reality out.

Ahmed had shaved his beard and had cut his hair, so he resembled the man I once loved. Oddly, over the next few months, there were moments when I would forget the terrible things he had done—continued to do—and I would convince myself he was good. He believed he was helping humanity. He believed he was noble and full of purpose. I thought I might believe these things of him, too.

There were times, when he made love to me, I pretended everything was okay, and I felt something like happiness. Sometimes he brought me gifts, like another television—it was a nineteen-inch and didn't give as clear a picture as the previous, but still, it was better than nothing. He bought a few more videos in English—*Back to the Future*, *The Breakfast Club*, and *Caddy Shack*. I finished *Crime and Punishment* and started Nietzsche's *The Birth of Tragedy*. Sometimes we shared a laugh, which felt creepy later when I reflected: here we were laughing together, making love, eating, and doing normal couple things, all the while she was up there, the woman whose desperate cries had joined mine that terrible night I threw the TV into the window.

At other times, I was aware I'd transferred my disgust for Ahmed onto his other victim. I wavered between these moments of delusion and reality. Sometimes I sighed

240

and rolled my eyes when I heard the woman crying for him. Once I muttered, "Damn bitch!" I came to hate her, for the Afghani spoiled the romantic dream; but then I would have a moment of recognition and feel ashamed of myself and sorry for Fatima. What if I had been the one up there and Fatima down here in the comfortable room? I wondered if I weren't losing my mind.

Most of the time, I felt hopeless, thinking I must soon die, but often I believed I would one day see Bijan again. Perhaps no one would ever find those notes I had flushed down the commode; but believing someone would find them and I would be saved was necessary to my sanity.

One afternoon, he came in the room where I sat on the sofa with my feet on the coffee table and a book in my hand.

I said, "I think I understand what Nietzsche is saying."

"Oh yeah? You think so, huh?"

"I do. Test me. Ask me questions, Professor."

He laughed. "Questions, eh? Hmm. Okay, here's one. What does Nietzsche say about science and art?"

"He says science folds in the face of logic, and art is a beautiful alternative, a happy drug, the elixir of life."

"Very good. I'm impressed."

Oddly, I blushed. "But there is something you might explain to me. I don't understand how he can go on and on praising art, and yet he bashes Christianity as anti-life. If he believes God is imaginary, why does he make a distinction between art and religion? Wouldn't he see them as one and the same?"

"He says the creation of another world—an afterlife—makes real life meaningless. Christianity condemns the passions and requires suffering and self-sacrifice. That's what Nietzsche objected to. Art doesn't require the same kind of contempt for the here and now. It revels in it."

"But that's not true!" I took my feet from the coffee table and sat upright. "Art doesn't celebrate the here and now. Are you kidding? Do you think I read Dostoyevsky's big fat novel so I could revel in the here and now?

"If there is no God, art and religion are exactly alike. The difference is once you finish a novel, it's over. Once the curtains close on stage, the drama ends. But God you have with you always. And I *do* feel him, even now, while I'm acknowledging he might not be real, I still feel him. He's my imaginary friend."

I looked at Ahmed, my other imaginary friend, and burst into tears.

Ahmed sat down on the bed and said, "I take it you're not impressed with this fellow, Nietzsche."

242

After keeping me captive for six months, Ahmed did something surprising. He let me roam the house freely. At first, he did this when he was home; but after a week or more, he stopped locking me in the bedroom before he left.

Once, when he was gone, I completed an assessment of the downstairs. The door to the garage remained locked. I could not get through.

I pulled at the boards on the front and side door and window, but they wouldn't budge. I needed a hammer to remove the nails.

I studied the bars on the other windows. No escape through them.

I searched the entire downstairs for keys, money, a phone, anything.

Ahmed had no land phone line, no computer, nothing which I could use to call for help. I kept an eye out for his cell phones.

I explored the closet by the second day to see, since it backed up to an exterior wall, if I could gradually break and dig my way through. Back in the furthest corner beneath the bottom steps of the stairwell was a hole in the foundation about two feet long and ten inches wide and four feet deep. Inside this hole, which had been covered with a piece of plywood, were human bones.

It was time to go upstairs.

I crept up the stairs, filled with terror, and hoping to God Fatima was still alive.

A sink and toilet stood in the middle of a large steel cage precisely above the facilities downstairs. There were no walls except for the one exterior wall the cage backed up against. Six of the studs from where the interior walls once stood remained. The entire floor was one open space except for the bars in the middle. On the outside of the cage was a writing desk beneath a window, which to my astonishment, was not barred. When I inspected it more closely, though, I found it locked down by a deadbolt which required a key. To the side of the desk was a long table to the right with a microscope, test tubes, knives, and other lab equipment.

Inside the cage, the woman was drawing on the wall above her bed. She was sallow, her face a skeleton, her arms mere bones. She wore a full brown skirt to her ankles and a brown scarf over her head, her long, scraggily hair falling down her back to her hips. Her blouse might have once been white, but was now dingy and nearly as brown as the skirt. A girl in her twenties appeared an old woman. Squatting on the bed facing the wall up near the wooden headboard, she held a crayon in her hand, which brought my attention to the wall.

Fatima had created a mosaic on the wall of her cell as high as she could reach. She had used crayon and lead and ink. Faces peered out from everywhere, all different—some big, others as small as the palm of her hand. There must have

244

been hundreds of these faces. I wondered who these people were. Then the woman, who seemed more an old, decrepit monkey the way she crouched on the bed facing the wall, spoke.

"What took you so long?" she said in a raspy voice.

"What?"

The woman scratched at the wall with her red crayon and then turned to face me. She crawled like a monkey to the edge of her bed.

"I said, what took you so long?"

"I don't understand."

The monkey-like Fatima climbed from the bed and walked—which was obviously very difficult for her weak frame—over to the bars of her cell. "Come closer."

I took a step toward the bars, but kept my distance.

"I have something to tell you," she said. "Something important."

I moved closer to the bars. The woman reeked of urine and sweat and bad breath. "I'm glad you're okay. I'm so glad you're alive. I want to help you." I grabbed the door of the bars and tried to pull it open. I turned around, scanning the upstairs for a key to the padlock.

Fatima sighed. "He keeps the key in his pocket at all times. Come closer. It's a secret."

I stepped closer. The crouching woman reached her thin hands through the bars and grasped me by the throat.

"Ahhh!" I grabbed the bony fingers of the prisoner and pried them from my neck, choking and coughing as I took several steps back. "What are you doing? Are you crazy? What did you do that for?"

The woman spit at me. "Come in here with me. You'll see."

I used my shirt to clean the spit from my arm. "You don't understand. I want to help you. He's had me locked downstairs."

"I know what you've been up to. I hear you down there." The Afghani grabbed the bars in her hands, leaned her body and head back, and laughed a rueful cry. "Hahahahaha! Hehehe! Hahahaha!" Then her laugh turned into screams. "Heeee! Ahhh! Ahh! Get out! Get out!"

I ran down the stairs and stood in the back room—my room—dumbfounded. The woman stopped screaming. I searched for something to throw through the upstairs window to bust it open, thinking I could use the bed sheets to lower myself down. The nineteen-inch television in the bedroom would be light enough to haul up the stairs and heavy enough to bust the window. Before I could enact this plan, however, the garage door rattled its warning. So I hurried to the sofa in the back room, flipped on the television, put in a movie, and waited for him.

Exuberant now I had a firm plan of escape, I smiled sweetly at Ahmed from the sofa as he came through the living room and entered the back room. Rubbing my belly, I said, "Want to feel the baby? He's kicking up a storm."

Ahmed sat on the sofa beside me and put his hand to the round, hard hump. "I don't feel it."

"Wait a minute. Shh. Wait."

Then there was a jolt from inside me. "Wow," said Ahmed, smiling. "He's got strength in those little legs."

"Now you understand why I can't sleep well. Imagine being kicked in the sides all night long."

"The little devil."

I didn't shudder, as I did when my efforts at self-delusion failed, because my plan so elated me. I wrapped my arms around his neck and returned his kisses.

He said, "I've brought you presents."

"What? What did you bring? Tell me you brought chocolate. Please let it be chocolate!"

He left the room and reentered with two big bags, which he sat on the floor. He bent over and pulled out a box of chocolates.

"Oh, Ahmed! I absolutely love you!" I jumped from the couch and embraced him. Taking the box, I returned to the sofa and gleefully tore open the chocolates. "Yum, yum, yum! I can't wait to try these. Thank you so much, darling!" I was ecstatic. Not only did I have a solid plan of escape, I had chocolate.

"There's more." He lifted two cotton maternity dresses from one of the bags.

"Yay! Clothes that fit! Now I can stop wearing your raggedy shorts." I immediately tore off his old clothes and slipped one of dresses over my head. It was white and soft and comfortable enough to sleep in. I turned around and modeled for him. "What do you think?"

"Very nice."

"Why, thank you."

"I only bought two, but you could wear each one a few days before washing. I also bought more underwear, since you complained about the others."

"Thanks!" I had hoped I could send out clues to the world by getting him to buy things for me, like I read once in a novel.

I sat on the sofa in front of the movie and ate the chocolate while I thought about my new plan. I thought I might wait another day or two, I didn't know. I might not be free, but as long as I forgot about the woman upstairs, I was comfortable. I spent my time watching movies, reading novels, flipping through fashion magazines. I rarely cooked, and Ahmed never asked me to clean. I made our bed and occasionally cleaned the bathroom, and that was it.

More importantly, I was frightened of what might happen to me if I did not succeed. What terrible punishment would I be made to endure? Perhaps I would wait a few more days, or weeks, before making my escape.

But then Ahmed told me he was planning to take Fatima off her meds to see if she would commit suicide. He said he had found another subject with the suicide gene, and he wanted to try his experiment on her.

"When, Ahmed? When will you bring the new subject?"

"Perhaps as early as tomorrow."

This meant Ahmed would no longer try to keep Fatima alive. I couldn't let that happen.

"I better go up and check on her. I've brought her a few things, too."

"What did you bring for her?" I couldn't believe I was jealous of her still.

He said, "More crayons and pencils and a couple of bananas. She loves bananas because her teeth and gums are in such poor condition."

He left the room.

I put my hands to my cheeks. It had to be tonight. Fatima would die otherwise.

I went to the bathroom and then climbed in bed.

He had returned to the bedroom. "What are you doing?"

"I'm tired. Growing your child is difficult work." I turned to face the wall, my back to him. The television continued to play a movie.

He turned off the television and the light and left the room, and I tried to go to sleep, wanting to get my rest before the big moment—what would be my last attempt to escape, whatever the result.

My thoughts returned to the woman above me. Could I live with myself if I didn't intervene?

As I lay in the silence, I recalled the many evenings Ahmed had made me listen to his perverted scientific studies. He spoke passionately, gesticulating, and frequently pacing the floor, as he described in great detail the chemistry he believed took place inside the brains of his subjects.

Three or more hours passed before he came downstairs and climbed in bed beside me. He didn't make the demands of me he made most nights. I lay there, relieved, my hand on the syringe beneath the mattress, waiting.

Chapter Nineteen: Escape

When Ahmed's breathing became regular, I took a deep breath, reminding myself I could do this, and turned in the bed to face him. He lay on his stomach, his face sweetly nestled against the pillow. If he had made demands, he had also brought me pleasure and had often made me feel loved. It was strange, I knew, even as I thought it. But we had managed to develop a sick kind of love for one another, and leaving him was not easy. A sob formed in my throat as I found his arm, counted to three, and then jabbed the needle and thrust down the syringe. He bolted up onto all fours, like a bobcat.

"What the hell!" he reached across the bed and tried to grab me.

I dashed to the bathroom and shut and locked both doors before he could disentangle himself from the bedcovers. I turned on the light and waited. I could only hope the drug would knock him out.

"What are you up to? What have you done! You little bitch! You little bitch! What a liar! What a good actress you've been, telling me you love me! And all the while you've been plotting against me."

He jiggled the doorknob and poked inside the hole to press open the lock. I grabbed the lock with my fingers and fought to hold it in place. My hands were shaking so terribly, I could barely grasp it.

Then he gave up on the knob and returned with a hammer, which he must have stored in the locked garage. He beat at the door slow, hard, terrible blows. He would knock a hole in the door in no time, and there was nothing I could do to prevent it. He struck the door to the hallway, so I stood near the other door, the one to the bedroom, and waited. Five, six, seven blows, and the door was cracking open. He put his eyes up to the crack he had made and stared at me.

I screamed.

Then he stumbled back. The drug began to take effect. I waited to be sure. I crept up to the door to listen, trying to peer at him through the crack.

There he was—his face inches from mine. Before I could respond, he hit his fist through the crack and grabbed my shoulder. "You bitch!" he cried again, but he slurred his speech, and his grasp on my shoulder weakened.

Sucking in too much air too quickly, I broke free from his hand, and my abdomen felt like one huge contraction. I clutched it and then bowed over and fell down into the tub.

I lay there, regaining control over my breathing. I could not have this baby now. It was much too soon. I still had a month to go. I had to escape with Fatima tonight. It was our only hope for survival. I pulled myself up and walked to the door and listened. I heard nothing but his heavy breathing. Through the crack, I saw him sprawled on the floor.

I hoped he wasn't faking it.

I decided it was now or never.

I considered searching for the car keys and the remote to the garage door, but as I had never succeeded in finding them before tonight, I did not think it wise to waste valuable time. I found the key to Fatima's cell in his coat pocket—I'd seen him put it there before. Then I pulled the sheets from the bed and tied the flat and fitted ones together, over and over, so the knots were secure.

Ahmed's body lay slumped in the hallway by the entrance of the bedroom and bath. I bent over, grabbed him beneath the armpits, and dragged him near the bed. He was heavy, and I could only move him an inch at a time. Once I had his hands near the foot of the bed, I took the lamp from the nightstand and used the cord to tie his hands to the bedpost on the bottom near the floor. I tied four loops tightly around the wrists and then made several knots to the post. I ran to the kitchen, deciding to use the cord to the toaster to make another binding to buy myself more time; I knew once he awakened he would hunt me down.

The binding didn't look like much. I was wasting my time.

It dawned on me I should kill him, so I ran to the kitchen for a knife. I stood over him for several minutes, trying to pick a place to stab him. I decided on the chest. Raising the knife, I took in air and held my breath, but I could not bring down the knife. It was too much, taking a human life. Instead, I kissed his cheek.

I twisted the cord around the frame of the bed so Ahmed couldn't simply lift the bedpost to become free. I pulled them to make certain they were secure, and then I gazed at him one more time. How handsome and sweet he seemed lying there, and how strange it felt to be leaving him! Doubts plagued me—perhaps I wasn't doing the right thing. No! I wanted my parents! My brother! Bijan! Full of determination, I took the sheets and the nineteen-inch television up the stairs.

Fatima peered at me through the bars of her gate with hope in her eyes, as though aware of what I was doing.

"I'm getting us out of here." I used the key to open her cell.

Fatima burst into tears. Time was of the essence, and I needed her to compose herself, but she stood, slumped in her cage, bawling.

Quickly, I hurled the television through the window. I had half-expected an alarm to go off, but there was nothing

254

but the crash of the glass and the thud of the television hitting the ground below.

I fastened the sheet to the leg of the desk near the window.

"Come on, Fatima. It's now or never."

Still sobbing uncontrollably, the monkey-like woman climbed out, holding the rope of sheets. When she landed safely on the ground amid the broken bits of television, I followed. Halfway down, my abdomen contracted again, and I nearly lost my strength, but I held on, clutching the sheets with both hands, leaning against the exterior stucco wall. Quickly, I slid down the sheets to the ground below, where the glass from the window lay scattered across the yard of weeds and tall grass in the dark of night beneath the one dead tree.

I cradled my belly with both hands as the contraction grew intense. For a few minutes, the pain wrapped itself around me, then relaxed, let me go, and I could once again stand upright. I ran to the side of the house looking for a gate. To my dismay, the gate was locked. Fatima and I pulled at it. When it didn't budge, we ran to the other side of the house. No gate. We were trapped in the backyard.

One side of the fence warped and hung, and as I wrestled with the pickets, the weathered wood scratched my hands, arms, and legs. My back and abdomen ached. I cried from frustration and pain, but also with determination. I would not let this stupid fence defeat me. I had come so far. I gripped the wood, briefly startled by an insect wrapped in white spider silk, another fellow victim. I grunted and pulled at the wood.

Fatima understood what I was doing, and together we pulled a picket free, but, as I lifted it in the air, I lost my balance and fell back in the grass. Fatima helped me climb back to my feet and we pulled at the next picket. Our hands and arms bled where the boards and rusty old nails scraped. We had to pull four of the boards down in order to fit through, and then we ran, so happy and anxious and excited, like dogs, to the back door of the neighbor's house and pounded on the door.

"Help us!" I cried when the sleepy, shocked faces at the window peered out at me. "Ayudame!" I knew few Spanish words and wasn't sure if I pronounced them correctly. "Por favor! Ayudame!"

Fatima, my little echo, cried out, too.

A woman's voice came through a crack in the door. The door remained chained. "No tengo teléfono, señora." Then the door slammed closed and the other faces at the window disappeared.

Luckily, the gate to their fence was not locked, so we entered the street and hurried to the next house. Guessing it was approaching midnight, I agreed if strange foreigners were to knock at my door, bleeding and in a state of panic, I, too, would think twice about inviting trouble into my home. But I had to try again. I had a vague idea where I was and in what direction I needed to go to find the police. We would get only so far on foot.

We stole to the front door of the next house. This particular house appeared more neglected than the others, so I hesitated. I could see by the light of the moon and a dim lamp several yards away on the corner the house across the street had a few potted plants in front and the driveway was swept clean, unlike this other house, which did not have grass growing in the yard. Struck with indecision, I bit at the inside of my mouth, and at last walked up to the door of the more neglected house.

An old man, perhaps seventy years old, opened the door and bared his toothless grin. He had short white hair growing in a semicircle around the bald spot on the top of his head and dark brown skin and even darker eyes, which were bloodshot, and he stood slightly bowed, small and thin. He said something I couldn't understand. I smelled the alcohol and mistrusted the gummy grin.

"Teléfono, por favor?"

"No teléfono. Pero, mira." He pointed to the corner, about six houses away, where the dim lamp illuminated the pocked street.

"No comprendo."

"What do you say?" Fatima squeaked.

The man crept out from the door and onto the porch beside us. He shuffled his feet and put a grubby hand on my shoulder. "El teléfono." He pointed with the other hand to the street corner. I understood now. He was telling me there was a payphone on the corner.

I said, "I don't have any money, señor. No pesos. I need help. Ayudame. We need the police. Do you have a car? Can you take us to the police?"

"No tengo el carro." He shuffled back into the house behind the door.

"Please, wait!" I cried. "Por favor, señor!"

Fatima joined me. "Please help!"

He said something back to us and then reappeared behind the door. He held coins out for me to take. "Por el teléfono."

"Oh, thank you! Gracias! But señor, where are we? What do I tell the police?"

"No comprendo." Then he shuffled out of the door, closed it, put one grubby hand on my shoulder and another on Fatima's, and together we hobbled down the driveway and into the street. "Vamanos," he said gently.

The old man limped, took small steps, leaning his weight on us and grunting. This was clearly difficult for the old man. I helped him along as best as I could. When we came to the phone, I put the coins into the slot. Then he took up the phone and spoke into it.

I glanced back at Ahmed's house. Mortal fear pulsed through me at the thought of his finding me again. The old man hung up the phone.

"Are the police coming?" I asked.

"Sí."

"Gracias, señor. Gracias."

I then took the phone and pressed zero, hoping to call my parents collect, but the operator spoke no English. I recited the number of my parents in Spanish over and over, but she kept saying words I couldn't understand. I handed the phone to the old man, saying "Ayudame."

He took the phone, listened, and the hung up.

"No! I need to call my parents."

He shrugged and said, "No comprendo." Then he put his hands on our shoulders and we lumbered back toward his house, back in the direction of my captor.

He opened the door to his home and beckoned us inside. I was scared to go into the home of a stranger, but in I went and Fatima followed.

The brown tiles on the floor were cracked and chipped and had tattered rugs scattered over them. The furniture in the living room appeared equally worn. A sofa and chair with holes in the upholstery faced a small television perched on a table in front of the stairwell beside the fireplace. On the mantle stood several religious statues, and above them, hung a crucifix. The old man led us to the table in the nook in front of the kitchen. The resemblance to my prison made me shudder, for the floor plan was identical to Ahmed's. We sat at the wooden table. There were four chairs. I wondered if he lived alone.

He pointed to the bowl of fruit between us and offered us some. The apples and bananas and oranges looked ripe and good, but I was too afraid, too nervous, to eat, but Fatima took a banana and ate it quickly, like a starving dog. She ate a second, leaving the peelings on the table. My abdomen tightened again, and I bent over and gripped it with my hands. The man's eyes widened. I held on to my belly with my jaw clenched. Then, when the pain released me, I sighed.

"I'm okay."

He stood, dragged his feet to the kitchen, and returned with mugs of hot coffee.

"Gracias." Against my better judgment, I drank a few sips.

He sat again across from me and gave me his gummy grin. Smiling back, I wished I could communicate, for my mind had wandered off in all kinds of terrible directions. I wished I had been able to talk with the telephone operator. I now feared the police might think I was responsible for Fatima's abduction. What if they thought I was her captor? How could I defend myself in a language I did not know? And Ahmed had connections. What if he were able to convince the police I was the villain? I had heard horror stories about Americans who were held in Mexican prisons despite their innocence. Panic overwhelmed me as I broke into a nervous sweat.

I decided we should leave before the police arrived, so I stood up, saying, "Gracias, señor, and adios. Fatima, we have to go." I took her hand and pulled her through the front door.

The old man called out to me in Spanish, but I took Fatima's hand and ran down the street and around the corner. Hearing his shouts, I followed the next block of houses, running in a state of frenzy. Then another contraction gripped my abdomen, and I had to stop, bowed over, clenching my jaw.

Fatima glared at me. "It's coming?"

"I hope not."

A car turned toward us, so we ducked behind scraggy shrubs. A police car passed, the contraction ceased, and then we continued blindly down the dark street.

We ran up another block and came upon a plaza full of activity. A well-lit bodega poured music onto the plaza, and people dressed in Halloween costumes were going in and out. A group of young people, about my age, sat together smoking on benches in front of the bodega. The men, covered in white powder and wearing skeleton costumes, and the women, dressed as witches, laughed and spoke loudly among themselves, apparently drunk. I was afraid to go to them—I thought they were laughing at us—so I led Fatima past, further down the crowded plaza. At last I saw a church, and I hurried to it.

We found the old wooden cathedral doors locked. I pulled at them in frustration. We crept around to the side of the church, looking for a rectory. We faced a narrow passageway between the church and courthouse. No light illuminated the path so even as we took a few steps into it, we walked in perfect darkness. Clutching my belly, I blindly moved forward with Fatima's hand in mine, staying close to the stone wall.

Another contraction forced me against the stone wall, and a low moan fled from my throat. Fatima echoed me and squeezed my hand. I clenched my jaw and bore the pain as tears streamed down my cheeks. Eventually the pain left me, so I pushed myself back onto my feet. Then I saw a door. I squeezed the handle, pressed my weight against it, and, to my surprise, it gave, and we stumbled inside the church and fell in a heap on the floor.

The church was dark and cool. I climbed back onto my feet, closed the door, and felt my way into the sanctuary, pulling Fatima behind me. My hip hit up against what I soon realized was a pew.

"Come sit down," I said.

The fear had not left me, but I felt safe for the moment.

After another hour of weeping and praying in the dark church, I stretched out, exhausted, on the hard, narrow, wooden pew. Fatima copied me, keeping her face near mine. I wouldn't let go of her hand, afraid she would run away. I knew she knew we had escaped. I wasn't sure if she was glad to be free, but I did know she was incapable of taking care of herself, so our lives were in my hands alone.

Chapter Twenty: Fatima

"What happened to Fatima?" Yvette asks Mona.

"She lives here with me. I'm sorry I lied, but I was afraid you wouldn't stay to hear my story if you saw her. Most people are frightened by her appearance and her strange behavior. She never recovered."

"What? She lives with you? Can I meet her?" So that explained the sounds Yvette has heard in Mona's house, the face behind the fence and in the window. They belonged to Fatima. Yvette is awash with relief.

"Of course. You can come over now, if you'd like."

"I'm leaving for the lake, remember?"

"I thought you weren't feeling well. You're still going?"

"I don't want to disappoint my family." Yvette winds a strand of hair around her finger, thinking.

"Come by on your way. Fatima would love to meet you after all these days of hiding."

Yvette considers Mona's invitation. On the one hand, she's something like a reader with the rare opportunity to meet a character in a fantastic story. Fatima in her house? Fatima the monkey-like woman who was held in a cage for so many months? Yvette's curiosity overwhelms her. She wants to meet Fatima.

On the other hand, Mona could be lying and luring her into a trap. Yvette has this fleeting thought, which resists becoming a revelation: Mona's not a victim of the Stockholm syndrome; it is she, Yvette. And here she goes, possessed, walking into Mona's trap.

"Does anyone else live there?" Yvette asks.

"No. The cats, of course."

"What happened to Ahmed?"

There is silence on the other end of the phone.

"Mona? Are you still there?"

"Yes. Listen to me Yvette. Ahmed is still looking for me and for my baby."

"Where's your baby?"

More silence.

"Mona, is your baby still alive?"

"Yes, she is. I want to tell you what happened to her. I need to tell you what happened to her. Oh, Yvette, I can't possibly tell you over the phone. Come over and meet Fatima, and I'll tell you the rest of my story."

Yvette glances at the clock. It's after five. It will take her two hours to get to Choke Canyon. "My family's expecting me."

"I'll be quick. I promise. Please. This is so very important. Soon you will understand why. I know it's hard to trust someone you've just met, but you have to believe me. Come now, or as soon as you can."

Mona's desperation alarms her. "What about the men's deodorant in your medicine cabinet?" Yvette's face flushes red. She hadn't meant to say that question aloud.

"It was left here by the last renter. He left lots of his things. I was in a hurry to get the place. I told the owner I would rent it as is. I was desperate."

Yvette is torn. She doesn't want to let down her family, especially Devin, but they've made many trips to the lake together, and it's good for the kids to have time alone with their father. Yvette has gone without Devin on numerous Cub Scout and Girl Scout trips. Missing out on this one spring break vacation isn't such a big deal. She's dying to know the end of the story. But Devin thinks she doesn't care about their marriage. If she doesn't go to the lake, it could break his heart. Yet Mona sounds so desperate.

But what if it's a trap?

She has 9-1-1 on speed dial. She'll take Devin's gun. She can do this.

"Okay, Mona. Let me call my husband. I'll be over in a minute." She has no choice.

Devin isn't happy to hear Yvette isn't coming, but he also doesn't seem surprised. She promises she'll make it up to him, to all of them, and says she isn't feeling up to it.

Full of self-loathing and armed with the gun and the cell phone, she climbs in her van and drives to Mona's.

You're a liar and you have no backbone.

Yvette is surprised to see suitcases leaning against the stack of boxes in Mona's living room.

"All packed, then?" She takes her seat.

"Nearly. Tea?"

"No thanks. I just had coffee."

Mona is dressed today in her cream blouse and tan pants, and her hair is in a clip: the top pulled taut and the back long and aimless.

"Where are you moving to?"

"I'm still working out the details," Mona says enigmatically. Then, "Are you ready to meet her?"

Yvette nods, her hands in her pockets, her heart fluttering out of control. She feels something like an aneurism on her left temple.

Mona floats down the hall like a white ghost and returns as airily holding the arm of the person in the green track suit she calls Fatima. The person is nearly bald, with a clump of dark hair hanging from the back of her head like a samurai wrestler. She also has no eyelashes and peculiarly splotched eyebrows. Her dark skin hangs on her thin frame and is red and shiny with oil, even on her scalp, as though she rarely bathes, but she doesn't smell. Fatima carries Boots in her arms, her head down. When she gets closer, Yvette realizes the shimmering on her skin is baby oil. Maybe she has a skin condition, and the oil is to help with it.

Yvette stands up, unsure of what to do. All she can think is, poor woman. Oh, you poor thing.

Mona helps Fatima sit down in the chair Mona usually sits on. "It's okay, dear." Mona puts a hand on Fatima's shoulder. "Yvette is our friend. Please sit down, Yvette. This is Fatima. Fatima, as you already know, this is Yvette."

"Casey's mother," Fatima mutters.

Mona's brows lift. "She rarely speaks to anyone but me. She must like you."

"She knows Casey?"

"They've spoken through the fence."

Fatima strokes the cat in her lap.

"Do you want to show Yvette your art?"

Fatima shrugs. "She can go. I don't mind."

"Yvette can go? Do you mean to your room?"

Fatima shrugs.

Mona turns to Yvette. "Would you like to see her room?"

Yvette nods and follows Mona down the hall, still wary of a trap. Fatima doesn't follow, but slouches in the chair stroking the cat with her head down. Yvette has been dying to see the rest of the house.

Oh shit oh shit oh shit.

First and foremost, she is relieved no crazy man awaits her with an ax or a gun or a syringe, as she has imagined.

Second, she is struck by the art covering the wall—not on paper tacked to the wall, but on the wall itself. It is everywhere and consists of different mediums: crayon, chalk, water colors, pencil, and marker—all in unbelievable detail. So many faces. So many people Fatima must have known or seen in her life.

Mixed in with the faces are other images, mostly of gravesites. Tombstones and flowers and people bent over the graves. Crosses, skeletons. A repeated image throughout the room is of a tiny baby. Mona's baby.

Creepy. Why is she in a graveyard? Is she a ghost?

Now Yvette notices the bed. On the pillow is a life-size baby doll wearing the clothes from the UPS box delivered to Yvette. She had forgotten about them.

The doll is creepy, and Yvette expects its eyes to open and words to come from its mouth.

Spooky and strange.

"Fatima loves that doll," Mona says when she sees where Yvette's eyes have lingered. "I'm no psychologist, but it seems she has reverted to a childlike stage in her life, before all the trauma with Ahmed."

"Who sent you the baby things? And why?"

"I sent them to you. I wanted you to bring them to me so I could tell you my story. I didn't recognize you when you came to the door that day, and I'd been having the strangest nightmare."

"Really? You set me up? Why me?"

Mona averts her eyes. "I'll explain. I promise. But let me finish first."

What is going on here?

Yvette shakes off the uneasiness. More alarms sound in her head than ever as she tries to guess why Mona has chosen her. "What happened to Fatima's hair?"

"She pulls it out."

"Oh my God."

Poor thing. Oh, poor thing.

"I know. I've had to be careful not to leave scissors and knives lying around, or she'd cut it off. But I can't stop her from plucking it. She plucks her eyelashes and her eyebrows, too. I don't know why. I suppose it could be due to nerves, like how people bite their fingernails. I bite my cuticles, as you know from my story."

"But her hair. She pulls her own hair. That's awful. Poor thing. Oh." Yvette's tears brim over. "Have you taken her to a doctor?"

"No. I'm afraid they will deport her. She's not a citizen, you see. Her student visa expired over ten years ago. But we have seen a trusted counselor. Fatima is stable."

You call that stable? "What about her family?"

"She says she has none. They're all dead. Killed by the Taliban. She screams in her sleep, and I don't know if her nightmares are of Ahmed or war-torn Afghanistan or both."

"You aren't frightened having her around? Couldn't she hurt you?"

Mona smiles. "No. She's harmless. And we love each other like sisters. But I was frightened of her at first. Before I knew her, I didn't know what to expect."

"I can imagine."

Spooky and strange.

"Let's go back and sit down, and I'll finish my story."

Yvette follows Mona's airy figure down the hall and back to where Fatima slouches in the chair.

"Come, dear," Mona says. "Back to your room. I don't want you to hear all these bad memories."

Fatima gets up and without looking at Yvette carries Boots to her room, then, stopping in her doorway, she turns. "I draw dead people. I don't want them to be forgotten. Some are Ahmed's other victims. I saw many he hurt and killed. Before Mona came.

"Some are people in Afghanistan killed in war. Some are girls murdered by the Taliban for wanting an

271

education. Or their families murdered for wanting their daughters to have an education.

"And some of the faces are of me, of all the different women I had hoped to be. One day, one day, but not to be. This is me. Fatima."

She plucks a strand of hair from her head and stuffs it into her mouth. Then she walks into her room and closes the door behind her.

She eats her hair? Yvette's eyes brim over once again. *Poor, poor thing.*

"That was different," Mona says. "The longest speech I've ever heard her make to anyone besides me. She must think highly of you, Yvette."

"I can't see why."

I'm a liar and I have no backbone and I'm not there for my family. My husband thinks I'm having an affair. I thought I was in a cage. My mind was in a cage. I was free and didn't know it.

Mona shrugs and returns to her chair. "Where was I?"

Yvette sits down. "You had escaped, and you had gone to the church and fallen asleep on the pew."

Chapter Twenty-One: The Day of the Dead

A few hours after dawn, an abrupt contraction woke me, and I clenched my jaw and balled my fists till, at last, it subsided. I slowly sat up on the pew and looked around. The morning light streamed in through stained glass windows. A boy in a white robe with his back to us on the altar lit the candelabras. Such a sight after our terrible captivity! The thin frame raised the flame with subdued reverence. I wanted to embrace the boy and his sweet innocence. People entered the church. A mass would be starting soon. I woke up Fatima, took her hand, and led her quietly across the church to the back. There, I asked the people coming in if they knew English. At last a young man, a teenager, said yes.

"Do you have a phone I can borrow? We're in trouble and I need to reach my parents."

"Okay. Sure." He took a cell phone from his pocket and handed it to me.

"Thank you so much!" We stood in the back of the church while I made the call home. I could barely press the numbers because I trembled so.

As soon as a voice answered on the other end, I cried, "Mom?"

"Who is this?"

"It's Mona!"

"Mona? Oh my God!" This was not my mother's voice.

"Aunt Rachel?"

"Mona, where are you?"

"I was kidnapped by a maniac and taken to Mexico City. Please let me talk to my mom or dad. I need help. I have no money and no way to get home."

"Can't you go to the police? Where are you?"

I glanced at the teenager, who was listening. Others also were beginning to notice us. I walked to a quiet corner and whispered, "I'm at a church. I'll wait here for my parents. I don't want to go to the police. I'm afraid. I have another one of his victims with me and she's an Afghan. I don't know what the police will do with her. Please put my mom or dad on."

"Oh, honey, I wish I could."

"Why can't you? Aren't they home?"

"Oh, Mona. Something's happened."

My heart lurched. "What?"

"Last night, oh Mona. I can't tell you over the phone. Tell me where you are and I'll come get you."

"Tell me."

"Last night someone broke into your house and killed your parents. Leroy, too."

I fell to my knees and dropped the phone. The boy who loaned it to me rushed over and picked it up.

"Hey, did you break it?" Then he noticed me. "Hey, are you okay?"

I came to my senses and grabbed the phone. "I need to use it once more. Aunt Rachel?" The call had ended. I quickly redialed and said, "Aunt Rachel, get away from that house. I was taken by Ahmed Jaffar. He has Taliban connections. You aren't safe as long as you are in that house. He will kill you next."

"Tell me where you are."

It dawned on me we might not be able to get Fatima with us across the border. Even I had no identification. Plus, by bringing my aunt here, I might be placing her in greater danger. If the Taliban had killed my family, they may also have bugged the phones. If I told my aunt where to find me, would Ahmed find me first and kill my Aunt Rachel in the process?

"Hide, Aunt Rachel. My parents' phone is probably bugged. Please take care." I hung up and returned the phone to the boy. "Thank you."

"Do you need help?"

"I need to get to Texas. Do you know anyone who can take me without papers?"

The boy shook his head.

The priest emerged in the foyer. He was tall, thin, and very old.

"Do you speak English?" I asked.

"Some," he said.

"Oh, thank God. I need help."

"What is wrong?"

"I was kidnapped and brought here from Brownsville. I just escaped and need to get home but have no money."

A group of people gathered around us, listening.

"We must call the police."

"No."

"Why?"

"I'm afraid. My friend, who was also abducted, is from Afghanistan. She's been abused and traumatized and can barely speak. I'm afraid they will deport her to Afghanistan or worse, detain her for questioning and consider her a threat. What will happen to her then?" I lowered my voice to a whisper. "I don't even think I can get her across the U.S. border legally. Can you help us?"

"I think you should speak with the police, but now I must say the mass. Stay and we'll talk more after." He fell into line behind the usher boys carrying the crucified Jesus.

I thanked him, but decided to wait outside and come back in an hour. I was angry with God over the murder of my family and wanted to have nothing to do with him.

Outside in the bright day, people wearing costumes gathered in the plaza for the festival of the Day of the Dead. Some of the costumes were colorful and beautiful, in every shade from turquoise to bright pink, with elaborate ribbons and feathers and shiny sequins. Two little girls wore white angel wings made of real feathers. A grown man wore a flamingo neck and head as a hat. Others were of the horror variety—store-bought masks of werewolves and skeletons and zombies. One person looked as though he had a hatchet stuck in his head. Fatima in her dirty tattered skirt and I in my blood-stained maternity dress fit in well with this group. Other costumes were simple—Batman, Spiderman, and witches.

As we crossed the plaza, I stepped on a Mardi Gras mask with gold feathers. I picked it up. It was beautiful. I put it on Fatima to hide her gaunt face, fearing an Afghan would attract the attention of the authorities.

She pulled it off to study it.

"Keep it on. It's safer that way." I took it from her hands and put it back on.

"Can't see," she said.

"I'll lead you."

I took Fatima's hand and led her through the crowd of the plaza. Fatima was used to going whole days without food, but I was famished, since Ahmed had made sure I never missed a meal for the sake of the baby. I watched the festival around us and salivated at the sight of the roasted corn and turkey legs the costumed wearers carried from the marketplace. I saw a garbage can and inside found a half-eaten cob. I ate some of it and offered the rest to Fatima. She ate, too.

Up ahead near the tables, barrels, and wagons of the market, I saw the back of a man who resembled Ahmed. I stopped, frozen. I didn't wait for him to turn around. I took Fatima's hand and dragged her to the other side of the plaza, behind the church, and into the cemetery.

People in costume gathered among the graves. We walked past them to a place lined with a copse of trees to hide until the mass was over.

I sat with my back against the thick trunk of a tree and broke into sobs. Fatima lay beside me on the ground, her face, free of the mask, in the soft dirt. I cried for my parents and brother, whom I missed so much, and for Fatima, whom I should have helped sooner, and Fatima surprised me by stroking my hair. When at last I saw people leaving the church, we returned to the priest.

The priest told me he knew a man who might be able to get us across, but he warned us it would be very dangerous. I smiled. Coyotes and the border patrol were a welcome danger compared to Ahmed and the Taliban. He said to come to the confessional on Tuesday and he would tell us what to do.

"What's today?"

"Sunday."

"Where will I go until then? I have no money."

"We are a poor parish. I have nothing to give you. I'm sorry. There is a shelter for women and children a few blocks east toward the university. Come back Tuesday, at four thirty, when my friend returns, and I will introduce you."

I took Fatima back to the copse of trees in the cemetery to wait. I was too scared to go to the shelter, thinking Ahmed would expect it. I thought about my parents and brother until I ran out of tears. We eventually fell asleep on the ground.

Sometime in the night, a sharp pain in my back woke me. It came again every few minutes, and I realized I was going into labor. Although I tried to be quiet, my uncontrollable moaning woke Fatima. Her eyes told me she understood what was about to happen. I wished then we would have gone to the shelter. There was no time to go for help now.

I took off the underwear I wore beneath my dress and sat on the ground with my knees bent, legs open. The baby was coming whether I was ready or not. In between contractions, I ripped the bottom of my dress into strips of cloth. Fatima did the same to her long skirt. The pain became so great, I cried and screamed.

"Push," Fatima said. "You will be okay. I will help you."

I met her confident eyes and was thankful she was with me. She took my knees in each of her hands and said again to push. I was afraid something would go wrong, and I felt weak, like I would faint. Within an hour, my little girl was born. The placenta came next. Fatima gnawed the umbilical cord with her few remaining teeth and then buried the placenta in the loose dirt. I wiped the precious baby with a strip of cloth and put her to my breast.

Fatima smiled with tears running down her face. "She's beautiful."

"She is beautiful," I whispered, weeping tears of happiness and gloom, for my parents and brother would never gaze on the sweet bundle in my arms.

Fatima embraced me and the baby and then wiped my forehead with one of the strips of cloth. After a while, Fatima fell back to sleep, but I did not. I stared at my daughter's sweet face wishing I could protect her.

Daylight shone brightly in the early morning as we left the shady copse of trees in the cemetery and followed the sidewalk toward the shelter. We could not last in the cemetery beneath the trees. We needed food, and my back was sore from sitting on the ground. I walked briskly through the plaza with my sweet bundle wrapped in the strips of cloth in my arms and Fatima beside me, wearing the mask. I worried Ahmed was lurking and waiting at the marketplace where I thought I had seen him. Fortunately the crowd of the festival was as thick as it had been the day before and there were others along the streets walking with us, so I soon felt a blanket of anonymity enveloped us. I had once read Mexico City was the largest in the world, and as we hastened along the busy sidewalk and congested streets, I couldn't be more grateful.

I could see signs pointing to the universidad, which I knew meant university, and soon I could see the campus. I wasn't sure which building was the women's shelter, so I asked the others on the sidewalk. A woman pointed across the street.

Before we stepped off the curb, I saw Ahmed walking in front of the shelter. His cap was pulled low over his eyes, but I knew it was he. If so many others hadn't been standing with us, Fatima and the baby and I would have been easily spotted. He was no more than twenty yards away! I pulled Fatima in the other direction, hiding in a clothing shop. After an hour, the owner kicked us out, and so we scuttled along the sidewalk toward the university.

A few more blocks to go, and we could lose ourselves among the buildings. If Anna—that's the name I gave my baby—kept quiet, we could hide between the stacks inside the library. There would be a theatre, a chemistry lab, empty classrooms, dormitory study halls, and a host of nooks and crannies for us to hide until Tuesday.

When we neared it, music emanated across the campus. I followed the sound and discovered a festival taking place in an open field. Large cardboard dolls resembling skeletons, colorful paper flowers, and booths with folk art, food, and drinks lined the perimeter of the field. Clowns and dancers and jugglers amused people walking by the booths. Musicians, dressed like the dead, played on stage for a giant crowd of picnickers seated on blankets in the grass. One blanket lay abandoned with half-turned cups of beer and a big mustard stain in the middle. Someone might have been coming back for it, but I snatched it up and wrapped it around my baby.

I found a heavily populated area and sat on the grass with Fatima beside me. She was curious about the baby, so I let her hold her. Fatima's tears ran down her chin, visible past the edge of the mask. I wondered what she was thinking and feeling.

"Are you okay?" I asked her.

"Stupid question," she replied. She seemed to have moments of such clarity at times and at others such absolute confusion, like a toddler or an elderly person suffering from senility.

While listening to the music and keeping a watchful eye on the crowd around me, I nursed my baby, covering my breast with my hand. When she pulled from the breast, I burped her and changed her makeshift diaper. Then I stretched my legs out in front of me and lay Anna across my lap. I felt less frightened sitting there with the music, the dancers, the artwork, and the laughter of so many others. Fatima lay down beside me and fell asleep.

By dusk, the crowd had moved around and shifted, but the numbers had remained fairly consistent, and the music had played continually. Many of the students danced in a space in front of the stage, but most of them ate and drank on their blankets in the grass, or walked around the booths on the sidewalks buying, eating, drinking, dancing, and talking with one another. When a group beside us got up and left, I quickly collected their trash and picked through it for food, hoping the others around us wouldn't take notice. I didn't want to be asked to leave.

After a while, we got up to use one of the portable restrooms set up behind the food booths. I made Fatima go inside with me. I was afraid she'd leave or think I'd left her. She held the baby while I went, and then, squeezing in the corner, I held the baby while she went.

The portable bathroom was foul and disgusting, so I quickly opened the door for fresh air. I was startled by a man waiting outside. At first I mistook him for Ahmed, and I let out a shriek. Fatima shrieked, too, my little echo, in her bird-like cry. He apologized, and I smiled, embarrassed.

Luckily, the sidewalks continued to be heavily populated, though markedly less than they had been during the early evening. I continued to feel safe in the crowd but glanced behind me every so often for that image I most dreaded, half-expecting to find it slouching behind me in the shadows.

I found a new spot for us in the grass and listened to the music and the festival with the crowd. After midnight, the crowd dispersed, the musicians having already packed up and left. I changed the makeshift diaper on Anna, and then Fatima and I followed a group of girls walking across campus. They led us to their dormitory. I prayed Anna would keep quiet so no one would notice the little bundle in my folded arms. Unlike my dorm back in Brownsville, the building had a main entrance and hallways leading to each room. We roamed the hallways for a safe place to sleep.

Riding the elevator to each of the eight floors, I finally found the commons on the first floor—I had missed it the first time around. It was dark and vacant, so I crept over to one of the sofas and slept on one end with Anna in my arms and Fatima slept on the other. Fortunately the sofa faced the television on the back wall, away from the entrance, so anyone who happened by would not see us unless they took the time to check over the back cushions.

My baby awakened, hungry, before dawn, so I nursed her, dressed her in a fresh diaper, and found a restroom for Fatima and me. There, I rinsed the soiled makeshift diapers so I could reuse them later when they had dried, then quickly we left the dorm before we were discovered. We walked aimlessly around the campus till dawn, and then we sat on a bench in front of La Biblioteca, the library.

By dusk, we walked from the campus toward La Catedral Catolica de la Santa Maria, to return to the priest for help. I could not keep going on like this, lurking in between buildings and sleeping in nooks and crannies, nursing and changing diapers on public benches, and eating from garbage cans. We were so hungry. But most importantly, I was worried because I could no longer get my baby to latch on and nurse. Her wails frightened me and drew attention to us. We had to ask the priest for help even though it was not yet Tuesday.

We fell into a line of people parading down the street toward the plaza by the church. Apparently, the Day of the Dead festivities would continue.

After several blocks, we walked with a singing and dancing group behind the church to the cemetery, where people dispersed to different gravesides with their flowers, sugar skulls, and other gifts for the departed. We returned to the line of trees and rested awhile, but Anna wouldn't nurse, and her skin felt hot. Frightened for her then, wishing desperately I could get her to a doctor, I stood up and paced around the trees with my little sleeping ragdoll in my arms wondering what I should do. How would I find a doctor and how would I pay and how would I keep us hidden from Ahmed?

A few yards away, I saw a young couple approach a site which was still fresh, the mound the size of a baby. Even from where I stood behind them, I could read the tombstone: "Mariana Elena Cardenas; 10-2-2003 to 10-25-2003."

The couple, their faces tear-stained, stooped over the mound and crossed themselves before adorning the grave with fresh-cut flowers tied with a pink bow, a rattle affixed to the ribbon. The man kissed the woman's forehead, whispered in her ear, and she nodded. The woman took two fistfuls of dirt from the little mound and moaned through her tears. The man's tears fell more heavily as he tried to comfort her. I clutched my baby in my arms.

Then something happened to me. I realized I had nothing to give to my daughter. I was penniless, without parents, trapped in a foreign country with a disturbed Afghan I wished to protect and a madman hunting us down. As much as I loved my sweet precious girl, I knew this couple could give her a better life, since she was sick and needed medical attention. It would have been easy for me to keep her at the risk of her own well-being, but I knew in my heart doing so would be selfish. If Ahmed found us, she'd never have a chance at happiness. My love was so great for this tiny life, that I found the strength to let her go.

While the couple knelt at the grave trying to get a grip on their pain by saying their sweet nothings to their lost child, I placed my sleeping, listless baby into the woman's purse, which lay near her in the grass. Then without hesitation, I ran away pulling Fatima with me as fast as I could, before the couple could stop me and before I changed my mind. Their voices called to me over the graveyard, but the crowd of dancers and singers absorbed us, and we could not be found.

Chapter Twenty-Two: Choke Canyon

"So you never saw her again?" Yvette asks Mona.

Mona turns her face away as the sobs wash over her.

"I'm so sorry. I don't know what to say," says Yvette.

"Do you think I made the right decision?"

Yvette wants to reach out and touch Mona, to pat her shoulder or squeeze her hand, but she feels awkward, and so instead crosses her arms. "Of course. You did what was best for your baby. That couple in the cemetery probably gave her a good life."

"Do you think people who adopt are capable of loving their children as much as those who have their own?"

"Absolutely."

"How can you be so sure?"

"Because I'm living proof. My sons are my biological children, but I almost died giving birth to Tommy and was told I would bleed to death if I ever became pregnant again. My uterus had thinned. But Devin and I had always hoped for a big family, so we adopted Casey."

"And you love her as much as you do your sons?"

"Absolutely." *She's my sweet, precious girl. My only girl. I love her so much.* "And I bet the couple at the gravesite couldn't be more grateful for your baby. I bet they loved her with all their hearts."

"But they didn't." Mona crosses the room to the window behind the stacked boxes and luggage.

"How can you know that?"

"You can't imagine how hard it is to give up a child."

Yvette can no longer see Mona's face, which is turned to the window. There couldn't be much to see in the backyard other than dead shrubs and dirt. "I think I can imagine. I don't know if I could have been as selfless as you were."

"Fatima and I went into hiding once we got back to Texas. My aunt helped us. About five years ago, my aunt offered to help me search for Anna by hiring a private detective."

The hair on Yvette's neck stands on end. Slowly, she climbs to her feet, then goes stiff, like a statue. "And what did you learn?"

"It took the detective a couple of years to track her down."

"What happened to her?"

"The man and woman in the graveyard that day ten years ago were American, even though both were originally from Mexico. I can only guess they were too emotionally distraught over their recent loss to keep Anna."

Yvette's heart thumps loudly in her ears. She's dizzy, about to faint. She takes a wobbly step toward Mona, the stacked boxes between them. "So what did they do?"

"They took her first to a doctor and then to an adoption agency. In San Antonio."

Yvette's mouth drops open. She rushes a hand to cover it. "Do you mean St. Jude's? It's the only one here."

"Yes."

Yvette can't speak, and both are silent for a long moment. Finally, Yvette asks, "Why did you choose to tell all of this to me, Mona?"

Don't say it. Please don't say it. Lie to me.

Mona turns from the window and meets Yvette's eyes with her own. "I think you know why."

Yvette stumbles from the house to the van. Her hands tremble as she fights to unlock it and climb inside. She hits her head on the top of the van but can barely feel it as she struggles to fit the key into the ignition.

Mona leaps across her front yard waving her arms like a mad woman. "Wait! Yvette, wait! Stop!"

Yvette speeds away, away from the house, away from the street, away from the neighborhood, away from the city. She drives directly toward Choke Canyon. She needs to warn her family. Casey.

For two hours she drives like a moth to light, half-blind, scared, trembling like no other time in her life. She hadn't seen this coming, the emergence of Casey's biological mother, if that's who Mona is, into her life. It could all be lies.

Please be lies.

But what would Mona have to gain by lying? Maybe she's crazy. Maybe she wants attention. Maybe she needs drama in her life to make her feel alive.

Yvette does not want to accept the possibility that Mona is telling the truth and a madman is hunting Casey.

It's dark when Yvette pulls into the state park, her head and throat aching from the constant flow of tears, her shoulders and neck sore from tightly gripping the wheel. She wipes her face with a tissue and stares at herself in the rearview mirror. She looks ill, with dark circles beneath her eyes and pale skin. Her mouth drops open as she realizes she has the mad look of Mona.

Spooky and strange.

She pulls herself together and checks in at the main office, gets the number of Devin's campsite, and then drives through the dark winding roads, illuminated by street lamps and the bright lanterns of other campers. When she reaches the right spot, she sees Matt standing on a pile of rocks with a bandana around his head and a stick jutted toward the sky like the statue of liberty. Yvette bursts into tears.

Casey lifts her head from a collection of shells, squinting against the bright light of the lantern hanging on a post near the picnic table, and hollers, "Mom!" Her skin is dark from the sun, darker than usual, and her hair is a matted mess.

Tommy beats her to the van. "Whydja come! Why are you here? Are you staying with us tonight? Dad said you weren't coming! Are you okay? Why are you crying?"

"I'm so glad to see you guys. I missed you!"

Mr. Frodo Baggins wiggles his little tubular body in excitement and tries to pull away from the spot where he is staked and leashed beside the tent. A garland of brightly lit Teddy Bears along the top of the tent further illuminates the campsite.

Yvette climbs from the van, hugging each of her kids. She kisses the tops of their heads.

"Matt, let me see where you got hooked."

He rolls up a dirty leg of his jeans and points to a scab on his shin.

"Does it still hurt?"

"Nah. It's fine."

More tears fall from her eyes as she kisses each of them again, giving Casey an extra firm hug. "Where's Dad?"

"On the pontoon getting it ready," Matt says. "We're about to go night fishing. Are you coming?"

With his flashlight pointed on the ground in front of him, Tommy runs to the shore where the pontoon boat is docked, shouting, "Dad! Mom's here! Mom's here!"

The breeze from the lake is cold as all of them, including Mr. Baggins, head out from the shore on the boat. Devin looks good in his jeans and camo vest with his face unshaved and the gleam of the lights in his blue eyes.

I love you, Devin. I'm so sorry.

"Fifteen minutes later, and we would've missed you 'til late tonight."

She wants to tell him what she knows and to share some of the terror clutching her heart, but she doesn't want to frighten the children. He must think she's crying because of what he's said to her over the phone about their marriage, so he doesn't ask why she looks ill. He seems happy she's upset, and smug. "I wanted to surprise you."

Liar.

But I can't explain in front of the kids.

"We're leaving in the morning," he says. "First thing. You came for nothing."

"Hey, Dad!" Tommy shouts with the face of a conspirator. "Let's show mom the you-know-what!"

"Can I drive, Daddy?" asks Casey. "Tommy got to last time."

"For a bit. Come on, Captain Casey." He stands and helps Casey behind the wheel, quickly whispering in her ear.

293

Then he says, "We're going to show Mama the baby ducklings."

"Yeah!" Matt says, smiling. "They're *adorable*."

"Ducklings? I can't wait."

Yvette stands behind Devin, behind Casey in the captain's chair, holding on to the side of the boat. She wraps one arm around Devin's waist. Two other boats with bass anglers troll along the shoreline with their lanterns held high; otherwise, the lake is quiet.

She whispers to Devin, "I need to talk to you. I'm frightened."

"I'm sorry I said those things. Don't be frightened."

"It's something else."

"What?"

"Wait until we're alone."

"You're scaring me," he whispers at her ear.

I'm scaring myself. Scared shitless.

She squeezes him from behind. "I love you."

Devin slows down the boat. "Okay, guys, the baby ducklings should be right through here, at the back of this cove. Mama, you better go up to the front of the boat where you can get a better look. Matt, use the spotlight."

The boat slows to a crawl as they leave the open water of the lake and skirt through willow tops toward the lonely cove of a tiny, grassy, tree-covered island.

"It's getting a little rough out here," says Devin.

"Stump!" Matt calls from upfront, the ever-vigilant one; the most cautious, anxious, worry-wart Yvette knows besides herself. He points to the left, so Devin helps Casey move the boat to the right.

Devin says to Casey, "Why don't you and Mama go up front by Matt and Tommy so you can show her the ducklings?"

"Okay!"

More conspiratorial tones ring from their voices. Standing in their fluffy, cumbersome life jackets, her three children joyfully point their fingers in the direction of a log.

"See them?" asks Tommy.

"Where?" Yvette scours the log and shoreline illuminated by the spotlight.

"Oh my God!" Matt exclaims. "Right there, in front of your eyes!"

Yvette moves closer to the front of the boat, holding on to a bolted chair to keep her balance against the waves. "I don't see anything."

A loud splash and the flash of an alligator make her scream and jump back.

Shit! I can't take this right now!

Laughter all around.

Be strong for the kids, Yvette.

"Ducklings, huh?" says Yvette in a voice of mock-reproach. "Well, I heard you guys, too. I wasn't the only one who screamed."

"That was Casey!"

"Nuh-uh, Tommy! I was trying to scare Mom!"

Yvette skips around and tickles each one. "Just you wait, when you least expect it, I'm going to get you good!" She thinks what a good actress she is. She embraces Casey and kisses her sweet little cheek.

Act.

"That's what you always say, Mom," Matt complains.

"Okay, everyone," Devin says. "Back to your seats." Then he adds, "I know you kids wanted to fish tonight, but now that Mom's here, what do you say we go make a fire and roast s'mores."

"Yeah!"

"Awesome!"

"Let's go!"

Back at the camp, while the kids roast marshmallows at their campfire, Yvette and Devin sit close together in lawn chairs, a sleeping bag draped over them, facing the lake with the kids and dog in view and the sparkling stars and crescent moon above. Flakes of brightly lit ash jump from the fire like fireflies, and a swirl of smoke lifts up toward the sky. Yvette wishes they could stay at the lake forever.

In a hushed voice, Yvette tells Devin about Mona's story. She can't tell it with Mona's details; that would take days. Also, she's interrupted several times by the kids wanting to give her more marshmallows and s'mores than she can eat, but she knows they've missed her, so, in spite of the terror in her heart, she keeps her patience and gives them the attention they need. For once, she's glad when the kids get caught up in their own arguments—whose marshmallow is most burnt, who caught the biggest fish, what names they'd assigned to the fish, and so forth. And in between their burnt offerings, she whispers a short, choppy version of Mona's story to Devin.

At last, she draws this conclusion: "I think Mona is Casey's biological mother—at least she seems to think it, and that's what matters."

"What does she want?" Devin whispers, the lines in his face deepening. He looks like an old man. "Do you think she wants Casey?"

"I don't know. Oh, Devin. What are we going to do?"

"Call the police. As soon as we get back tomorrow. We're going to call the police and tell them everything."

At one point, Casey asks, "Are y'all talking about Cruella?"

Yvette makes light of it. "Just about our neighbors in general, sweetie."

Liar.

"That's called gossip," Matt chimes in, holding up another burnt marshmallow proudly.

"That lady's weird," Tommy says.

"No she's not!" Casey says. "She's nice, Tommy. You even said so. Not to Frodo Baggins, but to us."

Devin leans forward. "Why do you say she's weird, Tommy?"

"Every time Casey and I are trying to play in the backyard, she wants to talk to us."

"What?" Yvette's back stiffens. "You've never told me that. What does she say?"

"She calls us darlings." Casey giggles, imitating Mona's voice. "Listen, my darlings."

Oh God. Please say it's not so. She talks to them?

"Casey, come and sit on Mama's lap and tell me what she says." Yvette pats her thighs and then helps Casey up onto her lap.

"She says, 'Listen, my darlings, I'm here if you ever need anything.'"

"She says to never get in a car with a stranger, even if they got a gun," says Tommy.

"Sounds like good advice," Devin says.

"But it's constant," Tommy says. "I don't even like to play back there anymore."

"I like her friend," Casey says. "She looks funny but she's nice. She lets me pet the cats. Cruella says she has special needs, like Santiago. You know him."

"Pet the cats?" Devin raises his voice. "You've been in their yard?"

"When the ball or Frisbee goes over," Tommy says.

Oh God have mercy.

"Don't ever do that again," Devin says.

"You're the one who told us we should always get our toys," Matt says. "Remember that time the football landed in Mrs. Turner's yard? You were mad we didn't go get it."

"I was wrong. From now on, tell Mama or me, and we'll go do it."

In the tent, Yvette can't sleep. She worries if getting the police involved will end in Fatima's deportation. Even though she doesn't trust Mona, she feels sorry for her and for Fatima and doesn't want to make their lives more miserable.

What does Mona want?

Was it to warn her Ahmed was searching for her? Was it to take Casey? Was it all a strange, sick game? But mostly, as she lies on the hard sleeping bag with Casey's warm body snuggled against her, her head resting on

Devin's solid arm, she worries if Mona may have wittingly or not led Ahmed Jaffar to them and to Casey. For this last reason, she will call the police.

Yvette is awakened by a rustle outside her tent. After she gets over the surprise that she's fallen asleep, she freezes, holds her breath, and listens for the sound again. There it is: more rustling.

Did Mona follow me here?

Or worse, Ahmed Jaffar?

"Devin," she whispers, shaking him. "What's that sound?"

He sits up quickly, as though she's thrown cold water on him. "What?"

"Listen."

The sound of twigs cracking and of rocks shuffling seems to get closer.

"Probably raccoons." Devin lies back down.

But the sounds get closer to the tent, and the footfalls sound heavier than raccoons. They sound like the steps of a man.

Like Ahmed Jaffar.

Devin sits back up.

Yvette pulls out his gun and hands it to him with a shaky hand. He gives her a surprised look, but takes the gun.

Neither speaks or moves as a hand reaches for the zipper and opens the tent. Devin's finger is on the trigger.

A figure emerges.

"Matt!" Yvette cries when she recognizes her oldest. "What are you doing out there?"

"Had to take a whiz. Geez. Y'all scared me. You have a gun?"

"What's going on?" Tommy asks.

"Go back to sleep everyone." Devin puts away the gun.

Matt makes his way over the bodies of his family to the outskirts of the group to his sleeping bag. Yvette can feel Devin's heart thumping as quickly as her own as it slowly returns to a normal rhythm. Once everyone's settled again, Yvette knows she will not be able to sleep again.

"I'm scared," she whispers in Devin's ear, since she knows he too can't sleep.

Devin holds her more tightly in his big, strong arms as she melts into him, limp as a fish that has just fought the battle of its life and lost.

Chapter Twenty-Three: Vanished

As anxious as Yvette and Devin are to get back home to call the police, they are tired and the campsite is a mess. The children, who thought they were going to get to go on the boat again today, are upset it's time to pack up. It's only Thursday, they say, and spring break isn't over. Once they get loaded and put the boat on the trailer, the kids beg to ride home in the van with Yvette. With all three kids and Mr. Frodo Baggins, she waits for Devin to park the boat in the storage unit outside of the park and then follows him back to San Antonio.

The wheels turn round and round, like my mind. Jesus.

Several times, Yvette glances in her rearview mirror, worried someone could be following her. When the kids speak to her, she has to say "Huh?" every time.

"Earth to Mom," Matt teases.

Even when she goes through Dairy Queen to pick up lunch, she thinks she's being watched. The vehicle in line behind her is driven by a redhead. The girl in the drive-thru window is a redhead. Yvette has never noticed so many redheads.

The same is true of Middle Eastern men. She sees them everywhere, staring at her, and each time, she wonders, could that be Ahmed Jaffar?

When they finally arrive home, Mr. Frodo Baggins is happy to be in his own backyard, running and barking and chasing squirrels. Yvette wonders if she'll hear any complaints from Mona as she stands near her back fence, watering her vines. She waits, trembling a little. Nobody comes to the fence.

Where is she?

Several messages from Mona wait on Yvette's answering machine:

"Yvette? Please pick up the phone!"

"Yvette, it's very important I talk to you. Please answer."

"Yvette, no matter what, please do not call the you-know-who. It will make things worse, I promise. Please trust me. I'm relocating, and as soon as I can, I'll contact you."

What? Relocating?

Without telling Devin, Yvette drives over to Mona's house while Devin and the kids unload the camping gear.

This is stupid, but I don't care.

She knows she's being stupid. It could be a trap, but she picks through the front hedge and peeks into a window to the living room. The house is empty. The stacks of boxes are gone. The suitcases, gone. The two wooden chairs, gone.

Mona and Fatima have vanished.

When the police officers arrive, it's after nine o'clock at night, and, fortunately, all three kids are in their beds. One of the officers, a rugged, fit man about Devin's age, sits with them at their kitchen table taking notes. He keeps rubbing his nose and scratching the top of his head, and Yvette thinks she will wipe down the table when he leaves.

The other officer, a young Hispanic woman, walks around the house making sure the windows and doors are secure. Yvette feels embarrassed that the kids have left their bags and camping gear lying around the house, but at least the sink is clean of dishes and the bathrooms don't smell.

After telling the officers what she can recall about Mona, Yvette plays the messages on her answering machine.

"Definitely a threat," the male officer says. "Which is what we need to open an official investigation. Otherwise, sounds like no laws have been broken. You invited her into your home—no forced entry. You went of your own volition onto her premises—no abduction. But the phone message is a definite threat."

"So you'll check into this?" Devin brings the officers mugs of coffee.

"We can make inquiries. Dust the house behind you for finger prints."

Yvette notices the other officer bagging something in the living room. "Standard procedure," the woman explains. "So we can sift out your DNA from that belonging to the women in the house behind you. I'll dust for fingerprints as well. Establish a baseline."

Yvette turns to the officer at the table. "Can we have an officer watch our house, just in case?"

Please say yes. Please say yes.

"Can't justify putting an officer on watch at this time. There's no evidence this Ahmed Jaffar is even looking for you."

"Should we let the kids go to school next week?" Devin asks.

"I see no reason to keep them home," the officer says. "They're as safe at school as anywhere else. Plus, we might have this resolved by then. And then again, it could all be nothing."

Yeah right.

The next day, Yvette and Devin are both antsy around the house, glancing out windows, half the time worried they're overreacting and the other half wondering if there's something more they should do. The boys are happy to be on their X-Box live video games, and Casey sits with her Ipad researching orangutans, having decided she wants to be like Jane Goodall.

When nothing unusual happens on Friday, Yvette and Devin both feel more at ease, Yvette wondering if she has made more of this crazy woman's story than she should have. Mona never claimed to be Casey's biological mother. She was just a strange, paranoid woman who was hopefully now out of their lives.

I've made a mountain out of a molehill.

Liar.

Sshh. Stop.

So, on Saturday, Yvette decides to distract herself with a visit to the mall with the kids while Devin rests at home and waters the tree.

Everything is okay. That hamster wheel is looking better and better.

They all need new spring and summer clothes, Casey especially, since none from the year before fit. After buying a few items for the boys at JC Penney, they head to Justice, Casey's favorite store. The boys are easy to please, but Casey is developing a style based on the teens she watches on the Disney Channel and Nick Jr., and so negotiations are necessary.

Girls are so much harder than boys. But so worth it.

"I'm not going into that store," Tommy says outside of Justice. "It's for girls."

"They have clothes for boys, too," Yvette says.

"Can we go to the arcade?" Matt asks. "I have my own money."

"I don't have any money," says Tommy.

"I'll give him a few dollars if you let us go. Dad paid me for mowing the lawn last week."

Okay, I take that back. They're both hard. And both worth it.

"No way. We're staying together."

"Come on, Mom," Matt says. "It's not like you haven't let us do this before."

The arcade is two doors down, and Yvette is uneasy about letting them go, even though they have done this a million times. But the boys could be real pains while waiting for Casey to try on clothes. Plus, if anyone was in danger, it was Casey, not the boys.

We do this all the time. Quit being so melodramatic, Yvette.

"Stay together. And wait there until I come to get you."

The boys fist bump one another and head off.

Twenty minutes later in the dressing room, Casey asks, "Why didn't you say hi to Cruella?"

"What are you talking about?"

"Out in the mall. She and her friend were behind us. I waved."

307

Oh God, oh God, oh God!

Yvette can't breathe. "What? You saw them?"

Casey nods, gazing at her reflection. "Does this outfit make me look fat?"

"Take it off! Hurry, Casey." Yvette pulls and pushes and tears at the clothes against Casey's cries. Her entire body is swollen and numb with dread.

"Mom! Stop it! You're hurting me."

"Everything okay in there?" a woman asks.

"Yes, thanks!" To Casey, Yvette says, "Please, hurry, baby girl. I'm worried about the boys." She holds out Casey's pants so she can quickly climb inside.

"Just go, then. I can finish dressing."

"No way I'm leaving you alone. Come on."

"But my shoes!"

"Carry them!"

Holding Casey's hand, Yvette runs out of Justice toward the arcade, thinking what an idiot she was to let the boys talk her into this. The dark crowded room, filled with beeping and clicking and other game sounds, is like a maze as Yvette weaves through, pulling Casey behind her.

"I don't see them!" Yvette turns a corner. "Do you see them, Casey?"

Oh please God!

"No, but I dropped one of my shoes."

"Don't worry about it now."

They skirt past a group of teens when Casey asks, "Mom, why are we doing this? What's wrong?"

Yvette finds an employee, a high school boy with glasses. "My sons were here. Matt comes to here with brown curly hair. Tommy to here, blond hair, kind of long. Tommy's really skinny and wearing cut-offs. Do you remember seeing them?"

"Was the older boy wearing Aeropostle?"

"Yes. His shirt. Where did they go? Did you see them leave?"

"Their neighbor hurt herself, so they helped her down the mall to the first aid clinic."

"What? How long ago?"

"Ten minutes, I think."

"Where is it? The clinic?"

"Down past J.C. Penney on the right."

"Thanks."

I'm such an idiot! I'm a liar, I have no backbone, and I'm an idiot!

Yvette pulls Casey from the arcade.

"What about my shoe?"

"We'll come back for it."

They run past the fountain and Saks Fifth Ave., past Build-A-Bear Workshop and The Gap. As they reach J.C. Penney, a security guard stops them.

"Something wrong, m'am?"

"We're on our way to the clinic. I was told, I was told my, my neighbor was hurt. Is that the clinic?"

"Yes, m'am. Straight through the red door."

Yvette picks up Casey and runs at full speed to the red door. A hallway leads to bathrooms and a drinking fountain, and an "employee's only" room. There, the clinic! She busts through the door and looks around.

"Can I help you?"

There they are! Matt and Tommy stand next to a hospital bed, on which Mona lies with an ice pack strapped to her ankle.

"My boys!" Yvette rushes to them.

Thank you God. Thank you, thank you.

Matt turns. "Mom. Mona was hurt."

"She twisted her ankle at the arcade," says Tommy.

Fatima chuckles. "She was dancing. Dance Revolution."

"*Dance Revolution Two,*" corrects Tommy.

Yvette stares at them, taking in the scene. Fatima wears a green track suit and, over her lashless eyes, a baseball cap, reminding Yvette of why she first believed Fatima to be a man staring at her through the fence. Mona wears the floppy hat she wore to the nursery. Panting to catch her breath, Yvette can find no words, can only think what a stupid woman she is for leaving her boys alone when

310

a known threat exists, how lucky she is her children are alive at all, and she better smarten up because luck runs out.

"Why is Casey barefoot?" Matt asks.

"I dropped my shoe in the arcade. We gotta go back."

"I need to speak with you privately," Mona says to Yvette. "It's time sensitive information."

Like hell.

"I don't want to see you anymore, Mona. I'm sorry."

The kids become quiet, averting their eyes with embarrassment.

"It's a matter of life and death," she says. "Please. I just need a moment of your time."

"Put it in a letter." Yvette collects her children and leaves the clinic despite Casey's objections over leaving her lost shoe.

That night, a loud clatter sounds throughout the house. Yvette holds her breath and listens.

"What was that?" Devin turns over in the bed.

"Sshh," Yvette says. "Listen."

Devin ignores her and climbs from the covers and picks up his pistol.

Yvette follows him through the living room. They check through windows in the front and back.

The clatter comes again. Frodo Baggins runs barking from Tommy's room to the back door. Devin rushes outside, Yvette following.

Is it Ahmed Jaffar? Please protect us, oh God.

The night is cloudy, muggy, and windless, but enough of a moon makes it possible to see a figure cross the yard.

"Who's there?" Devin demands.

Yvette switches on the flood light, illuminating the yard.

"Don't shoot!" It's Mona.

"What the hell are you doing back here?" Devin shouts.

Frodo barks like mad, so Yvette picks him up. "It's okay boy."

"It's a long story. I'm sorry I woke you."

"You better start talking, or I'm calling the cops."

"Devin? We haven't met. I'm Mona."

"I know who the hell you are. Doesn't explain why you're sneaking around in my backyard."

"We had to leave the cats," Mona says. "I had no place to take them. I was just looking for them, but can't get into the house. Thought I'd climb your fence to get to the back. The side gate's locked. Never mind. I'll leave."

The kids wait near the door, huddled together. Casey is crying. "Why does Daddy have a gun?"

Mona pulls a crumpled sheet of paper from her jacket pocket and stuffs it into Yvette's hand. "I did as you asked. I put it in writing. Good night."

Chapter Twenty-Four: Warnings

Dear Yvette,

> *Burn this as soon as you're finished reading it.*

> *A few years ago, the private detective hired by my aunt to find Anna got a big break in the case. Armed with nothing more than the name Mariana Elena Cardenas from the gravesite the day I left my sick baby in the woman's purse, he at last found an adoption agency in San Antonio with records a baby Cardenas was put up for adoption the year Anna was born. Apparently, the young couple used their daughter Mariana Elena's identity to bring Anna across the border. Maybe they planned to keep her and later changed their minds. Maybe they thought she would find a better home in the U.S. than in Mexico. For whatever reason, they gave Anna Mariana's identity, got her medical care in the U.S., and then signed over their parental rights to the adoption agency.*

> *Because you opted for an open adoption, the biological parents could at any time open the records. Mr. Brody, my detective, tracked down the Cardenas couple and got them to revisit the adoption agency as the biological parents and obtain copies of Casey's file. It wasn't hard, knowing what he knew, to get their cooperation.*

For over two years, I have been keeping an eye on you and looking for a way to tell you my story. I had to explain everything so I could tell you the most important part of all, but you left before I could say it. I've been trying to get your attention, and you shun me. That's the thanks I get for trying to help you! So I've written it down here, as you asked:

Most states in the U.S. and some states in Mexico have a data base known as the Missing Children's Data Base. Mr. Brody discovered Ahmed has registered his DNA in every state with this data base. If Casey's DNA is ever run through any of them, there will be a match with Ahmed's and he will be alerted as to her whereabouts. This is why it is so important you not involve the police. They will unknowingly lead Ahmed directly to you.

As her biological father, he has rights. I have spent time researching this. Because the Cardenas's claim to Casey was fraudulent, and although neither you nor the adoption agency did anything outside of the law, Ahmed has a legal claim to Casey. He has been adept at keeping a low profile and has never been arrested or charged with a crime, so he has no criminal record and therefore the court may find no reason to keep his child from being reunited with him. You can read about cases where children raised for years in an adoptive family have been forced by the court to

315

be returned to biological fathers who never relinquished their parental rights.

I'm sorry I haven't been a nicer neighbor to you, Yvette. As grateful as I am for the good life you have given Casey, I suppose I'm jealous it couldn't be me. The jealousy and resentment are hard to contain. But believe me when I say this is my sole purpose for telling you my story: I do not want Casey in the hands of that monster.

Burn this letter as soon as possible. I will contact you when I can.

Yvette collapses on a chair. Devin gets the kids back to bed and then he and Yvette read the letter again.

"Can this really happen?" Yvette says through the thick sobs lodged in her throat. "Is this possible?" She can't stop her fingers from shaking.

This can't be happening.

Devin helps Yvette onto the sofa and sits beside her, taking her trembling hands in his. "Listen to me, baby. The police didn't take any of our DNA. It's gonna be okay."

"I saw the lady officer bagging something from our living room." The sobs break free from her throat and she can barely speak. "Casey's DNA could have been in it."

"What?"

"I asked the officer about it, and she said it was standard procedure, so they could differentiate between our DNA and that of other people. Something about a baseline."

Devin puts his face in his hands. "Oh, God."

"They won't necessarily run it through the data base, though, will they?"

"Oh, God."

"Devin, we can't let this happen. We've got to do something." Yvette crosses the room, crumpling the letter in her fist.

"Dear God."

"Let's run away," Yvette says suddenly.

"What?"

"Let's load up the kids and run away."

"Where would we go?"

"I don't know. Back to the lake?"

"Yvette, that's crazy. We can't run away. Let's go to bed and think about this tomorrow."

"I won't be able to sleep."

"Let's try. It's after midnight."

Yvette tosses and turns and stiffens at every noise the house makes as it shifts and shudders in the wind. Devin reaches across the bed and strokes her hair.

"Everything'll be okay. We have each other."

Yvette scoots across the bed closer to him, and he puts his arms around her. She hasn't been in his arms like this in a long time, and she's forgotten how good it feels, how secure she feels. Devin is her home. Wherever he is, that's where home is to her.

You are my home sweet home.

She loves him so much and doesn't want to imagine life without him, because if she ever lost him, that feeling of being all alone in the world would return.

All alone, with no backbone, a hamster in a wheel.

She needs Devin. "Oh, honey."

He reaches his lips to hers, holding her like he'll never let go. She's never been more grateful for the sweet feel of his body as she traces the line of muscles along his back.

"Oh, Devin. I'm so sorry I haven't been here for you."

"Ssh. You're here now."

"I love you so much."

"I know." He covers her mouth with his.

On Sunday Yvette and Devin take the family to a nondenominational community bible church they have attended since they moved into the neighborhood eight years ago. Heidi is there with her two daughters, and when she sees Yvette, her face falls. She approaches Yvette in the narthex outside the main room of the chapel.

"What's happened?" she asks.

"Is it that obvious?"

"You and Devin's faces say it all, girlfriend. What's wrong?"

The service is about to start and people are rushing by to their seats.

Yvette squeezes Heidi's hand. "Let's talk later."

"Lunch tomorrow after our walk? We need to celebrate the kids going back to school."

"Sounds good."

Liar. I won't be sending the kids to school.

"I'll call Gloria." Heidi and her girls leave to find their seats.

After church, Devin and Yvette take the kids to eat at their favorite restaurant, a Chinese buffet that has something for everyone. While they don't discuss Mona's letter in front of the children, they both make comments about wanting to take a family vacation soon, to get away, and so they spend the afternoon discussing what places they'd most like to see. It feels nice to Yvette, laughing and dreaming with her family, and for a little while, things seem almost normal again.

Better than normal. I appreciate this life. What an idiot I've been.

Back at home, the kids return to their electronic entertainment, and Yvette and Devin sit in the family room

319

wondering if they should call and check on the status of the investigation. Yvette does not want to send the kids to school in the morning.

I don't want them out of my sight.

"We can't put our lives on hold," Devin says. "We have to go on."

"I don't know."

"We don't even know if she really is who she says she is."

"Why would she tell me such a story if it weren't true?"

"Maybe she wants money. Maybe she's a con artist, and she got evicted before she could finish her con."

By bedtime, they still haven't agreed on what they will do, but Yvette sets her alarm and will wait and decide in the morning. Devin says he has to go into the office.

This can't be happening.

Yvette cuddles a while with each of her children, though Matt tells her he doesn't like to be mothered, and he pulls away from her hugs and kisses, saying he's too old.

"You're never too old to be my little boy," she says not for the first time as she tickles his sides.

Tommy at age eleven still likes her hugs, so she lies beside him for a while twirling his hair while listening to him tell about his video game.

When it's Casey's turn, Yvette can't hold back her tears as she lies beside her daughter beneath the covers, arms around her little body.

"What's wrong, Mom? Are you crying?"

"I'm just so happy. I'm so glad God gave you to me. Of all the people in the world he could have chosen, I'm so thankful it was me."

"Me, too."

Yvette hasn't even realized she's fallen asleep when the phone rings. The clock reads two after midnight. She picks up the phone, the caller id simply reading, "Unknown Caller."

The voice on the other end belongs to Mona. "Listen to me, Yvette. My private detective, Mr. Brody, has reason to believe the authorities plan to take Casey from her school this week. They matched her DNA to Ahmed's in the Missing Children's Data Base."

Take Casey?

"Oh my God!"

"Listen to me. We must leave tonight. Bring whatever cash you have on hand and nothing more. You are likely being watched, so do not leave by way of your front door or garage. Do not take your vehicles. As inconspicuously as possible, climb the fence to my old rent house. I should be there in ten minutes to pick you up."

This can't be happening? What is she saying?

Yvette feels numb and slow, like an idiot on morphine. She can't think.

I can't think. What is she saying? This can't be happening.

"What are we going to do? Oh my God!"

"What is it?" Devin asks.

Mona rasps into the phone, "Hide."

Chapter Twenty-Five: The Story of the Sunken Gardens

"**W**hat the hell was that?" Devin asks as Yvette drops the phone to the floor.

She tells him what Mona said, unable to believe the words as she speaks them. Her heart is racing. She can't breathe. "What do we do?"

This can't be happening.

"She said bring whatever cash we have on hand?" Devin asks. "It's a con. I'm telling you, she just wants money."

"But what if it's not? What if she's telling the truth?"

Devin storms from the bedroom to the front windows and peers out. Yvette follows. A dark sedan is parked across the street in front of their neighbor's house.

"I've never seen that car before, have you?" Yvette asks.

"No." Devin storms back to the bedroom.

"What are you doing?"

He picks up the phone off the floor. "Calling the Grays."

"But it's after midnight."

He gives her a look of exasperation.

"You're right. You're right."

Think, Yvette. Quit being an idiot.

"Sorry to call so late, Tom. The sedan parked in front of your house. It's not yours, is it? Yeah, a dark sedan. I don't know. Never seen it before? Thanks, Tom, and apologize to Tammy for me. Goodnight." Devin returns the phone to the nightstand.

"So what do we do?"

"Hell if I know. Call the police?"

"And do what? Ask if they're planning to take Casey away?"

"Ask if they have an officer on the house."

Yvette nods, waving her hands like a bird. Her body feels numb and she can't think. Time seems delayed, like slow motion on television.

I'm so numb. So confused. This can't be happening.

"What's that number?"

Yvette jogs down the hall to the kitchen and gets the officer's card from a pile of other papers and things and calls out the number. Tommy wakes up and wants to know what's going on, so Yvette walks him back to his room, tucks him in, and tells him to go back to sleep. When she returns to her bedroom, Devin seems harried and old, and she realizes he, too, has the mad look of Mona.

Spooky and strange.

"What did he say?" she asks.

"There's been a new development in the case, so they put a watch on us, but he couldn't talk about it over the phone."

"Oh, God. That tells us nothing, Devin. Maybe they've discovered Mona is the real threat."

"I don't think so." He clenches his jaw.

"Why?"

"Right before he hung up, the officer told me we needed to be sure not to leave town. He wants us to stay close by in case he has questions."

"We don't have to be in town to answer questions. We can answer questions over the phone from anywhere."

"Exactly."

"So you think Mona's telling the truth? First you say it's a con, and now you say it's not. What is it, Devin?"

Fix this, please. This can't be happening.

"Calm down." He puts his hands on her shoulders and she buries her face in his chest.

"What do we do?"

"If we go to the police, and Mona's right, we may lose Casey."

"They wouldn't take her from us after ten years, would they? That wouldn't be any good for her. They've got to know that."

Casey needs us. I need Casey.

"Do you want to risk it?"

"So we should go with Mona?"

"If she's conning us, well, it's just money. Plus, I have my gun. I think my odds of fighting Mona are better."

Fight Mona?

Yvette stifles a giggle.

I'm going mad. I'm delirious.

Yvette swallows hard. "Are we really going to do this?"

"I think we should."

Shit oh shit oh shit. This can't be happening.

"You wake the kids. I'll pack a few things." Yvette pulls on a pair of jeans in a daze, unable to believe what they're going to do.

Mr. Frodo Baggins follows Yvette as she nervously dashes around the house putting clothes, medicines, and toiletries into a duffel bag. Her mind feels blank and slow, so she has to double back to add things she's forgotten. She tosses in a few packets of Moist and Meaty, because there's no way she's leaving her dog behind. The kids walk like zombies in their PJs and sneakers to the back door, muttering their questions.

"It's an adventure," Devin says again.

"We were talking about going on a vacation, remember?" Yvette adds.

Liar.

"Now, keep your voices down. We don't wanna wake the neighbors."

The night is clear and cool, and the vines along the back of the fence have finally bloomed. Yvette can barely see them in the moonlight, but their sweet fragrance is unmistakable.

Can't we go back to me watering my vines? Can't we go back to normal? I want my hamster wheel back.

Devin pulls himself over the fence in three quick moves. The fence is old, and it moans under his weight, causing Yvette to worry they'll be heard. She stands on a chair and hands over first the duffel bag, and then Mr. Baggins, who's now on a leash and is, thankfully, not barking. Next, she helps each of the kids climb over with Devin catching them on the other side.

She's not confident she can climb the fence, but when someone walks up the driveway, she hoists her belly onto the hard pickets and flings her legs over, only to drop with a thud to the ground on the other side.

Ouch.

"Are you—"

"Shhh. Someone's out there."

The beam of a flashlight crosses the fence.

Please oh God. Please.

"Don't move or speak," Devin whispers to the kids.

Then something horrible happens. Mr. Baggins begins to bark.

Not now, Frodo!

Someone comes up behind Yvette, and she stifles a scream, but it's Mona who's come to help her up. "This way." She leads them into the vacant, dark house through the back door. They pause for only a moment as Mona collects the cats. "Casey, can you hold Boots?" Then, they exit the front door, and follow Mona to a white van, running, by the curb. "Get in."

This is exactly what Yvette has told her children not to do their whole lives: to get into a vehicle with a stranger, or with a person you don't trust. But now, she is helping them in.

"Go to the very back," she says to the boys, who find Fatima already in the third seat. Yvette and Casey take the middle seat with Mr. Baggins, whimpering in the presence of the cats.

"Pass the cats to Fatima," says Mona before climbing behind the wheel. "We don't want the dog to hurt them. Poor things. They've been traumatized, but we had no choice."

Fatima squeals with delight. She has obviously missed her cats.

Devin gets in the passenger's seat up front. "How did you get in the house?"

"Broke a window."

"Oh, God." Devin shakes his head.

"Seatbelts." Mona pulls slowly from the curb. "All the hotels in this area don't allow pets, so the landlord said he'd keep them for a week, but he refused to give us a key. I don't know if they've been fed."

"Poor kitties," Casey says.

"You kids doing alright?" Mona asks.

No one is doing alright. No one will ever be alright again.

A police car stops at the opposite corner of the intersection, and Yvette feels her teeth bite into her tongue.

"I don't think this is a vacation," Matt says. "Who are we running from?"

Sweet Matt. What do we say?

Mona turns right through the intersection. The cop follows.

Mona glances over at Devin. "I've done this before."

"What exactly *is* this?"

"Help people at risk. Let me talk to your children."

Devin hesitates, then nods.

"Listen to me, darlings," Mona says in a louder voice.

Casey turns back and exchanges a giggle with Tommy. Despite everything, Yvette cracks a smile, and she thinks to herself, we could be headed for a trap, led by a mad woman or a con artist or both, and I'm smiling.

I'm losing it. I'm mad and delirious. An idiot on morphine.

Mona winds through the neighborhood, and Yvette no longer sees the cop. "Fatima and I help people all over the city. We help women and children, and even men, who have been abused and need protection from their abusers. But your case is special. We have children at a shelter who are scared and lonely, and your parents have agreed your whole family will come and keep them company."

Liar.

"For how long?" Matt asks.

"A little while." Then she adds, "But listen to me, darlings, no one can ever know the true location of this special shelter. Otherwise, the abusers could find it and then nobody would have a place to hide anymore. So, to keep it safe, and to keep the people hiding there safe, the only way you could come to help is to sneak off in the middle of the night when no one else could see where you're going."

"Oh!" Casey says, like everything makes sense to her. "I get it."

I'm so glad she's a good liar.

"Cool," Tommy adds. "So are we almost there?"

Mona is just now turning out of their neighborhood. "Not yet, darling. We can't go there directly. We have to go to another location first. And since the drive will take a while, I want to tell you the story of the Sunken Gardens."

Yvette reaches up and squeezes Devin's shoulder, as if to ask, "Are you still sure about this?"

And, as if in answer, he squeezes her hand back, probably to say, "No, but this is the best we can do."

"Back in 1840," Mona says, "German masons quarried limestone blocks from the area by the zoo now known as The Japanese Tea Gardens."

"We've been there," Tommy says.

"Have you? Did you like it?"

"It was okay," Tommy says.

"I liked it," Casey says.

It's a beautiful place. A normal place. Take me back to normal. This can't be happening.

Matt leans over the middle seat. "They have rare specimens you can't find in many places of the world."

"Right, darling. But back then, it was just an empty hole. Then in the 1880's, the cement company used it to make their cement. At the turn of the century, this wonderful man named George Washington Brackenridge donated 200 acres of land to the city, and as you know, it, along with other land he later donated, became Brackenridge Park."

"That's where the zoo is, and the train," Casey says, petting Frodo Baggins. "The gibbons are my favorite, though

I wish we had orangutans. I want to go to Africa to study them."

"The wart hog is my favorite," Tommy says.

Matt leans over the middle seat again. "I like the anteater. Have you seen how big he is?"

Mona merges onto Highway 281 South. "Oh, darlings. I'm so glad you love the zoo. Because we're going to a place near there, but not tonight. Now, listen, darlings. In 1915, after the cement people left, another wonderful man by the name of Ray Lambert, the City Parks Commissioner, developed his concept of a sunken garden, and four years later, he invited a Japanese-American couple by the name of Jingu to come and live in the gardens to help care for them. And the gardens were then named The Japanese Tea Gardens. And, darlings, Mr. Jingu and his wife opened a little place in the gardens called The Bamboo Room where they would serve iced green tea, and they also developed a green tea ice cream, and over the years they had seven children, all living together in the gardens until 1938, when Mr. Jingu died. Well, the rest of the family continued to live in the gardens, but something horrible was brewing in the world."

"What?" Matt asks.

"World War II," Devin answers.

"Right, darlings. World War II. Now the gardener, Mr. Hugo Gerhardt, was a beloved friend to the Jingu's,

332

especially after Mr. Jingu died. The little ones would follow Hugo around as he tended to the garden, and they loved him as he did them. But in 1941, when the Japanese attacked Pearl Harbor…"

"December seventh, to be exact," Matt says.

"Yes, darling. Well, after that, the city wanted the Jingu family evicted from the gardens, and the gardens themselves were renamed The Chinese Gardens."

"How terrible," Yvette says. "I didn't know that about our history, and I've lived here my whole life."

"So what happened to the Jingu's?" Tommy asks.

"Well, there was rumor they might be put in one of those Japanese-American internment camps."

"What's that?" asks Casey.

"Like the concentration camps during the holocaust," Matt says.

"Have you learned about those yet, darling?"

"Yes," Casey says. "But I don't like to think about that."

"I know, darling, but it's important to remember bad things so people don't make the same mistakes again. So, anyway, what many people didn't know was that beneath the sunken gardens, Mr. Lambert had created a huge cellar, in which he had hidden a wine collection that had been in his family for years. Do you know why he hid it?"

"Prohibition," Matt says. "So Mr. Lambert was a bootlegger?"

My sweet Matt. Such a knower of facts.

"What are you talking about?" Tommy asks.

"Mr. Lambert was not a bootlegger, Matt, but you're right about Prohibition. Darlings, in 1919, the United States made the production and sale of alcohol, like beer and wine, illegal. Mr. Lambert had come from a family of winemakers in the Texas Hill Country, and though they never broke a law during all of Prohibition, which was finally repealed in the early thirties, he wanted to preserve his family legacy in that secret cellar. But when the Jingu's were in danger of being evicted from the gardens and taken to an internment camp, Mr. Lambert emptied the contents of the cellar, sold or gave away every bottle, now it was legal, and helped the Jingu family hide there."

"How nice of him," Casey says.

"You're so sweet, darling, and yes, Mr. Lambert was very nice. His cellar was enormous, and soon Mr. Lambert and Hugo helped other Japanese-Americans, and even German-Americans who feared the same thing could happen to them, hide in the cellar for many months. And that, my darlings, was the birth of the Sunken Shelter, the secret place you are coming to spend time."

"Cool!" Matt says.

Mona pointed to her window. "We're passing Brackenridge Park now."

Such a beautiful place. A normal place. Take me back to normal.

"And Mr. Baggins gets to go, too?" Casey asks.

Mona pauses. "If he must."

"So where are we going tonight?" Tommy asks.

"To see the clown artist."

"The what?" Devin asks.

The what?

"The clown artist, also known as the Czech Widow. Bernie Mokry. Most people call her Bernie. Bernie the Clown."

"We're going to a clown's house?" Casey asks.

"To her store, darling." Mona exits onto I35 South. "When she's not busy doing clown things, she operates a general store next to her home in a small town southeast of San Antonio called Atkins. At the back of her store is a hall she rents out for wedding receptions, dances, birthday parties, and all manner of events, and sometimes she performs at them, too. Tonight, we're going to sleep in that hall, and in the morning, she'll teach us all how to be clowns. Would you like that, darlings?"

"Sure!"

"Yeah!"

"Sounds great."

I said take me back to normal. This does not sound normal.

Yvette is bewildered, anxious to learn why they are visiting a clown, if, indeed, they are. The entire drive feels outside of time and space, like the world has frozen and Yvette is observing from outside of her own body. She can't comprehend that they are running off with Mona in the middle of the night.

This can't be happening. I feel like an idiot on morphine.

When Mona finishes her story, the van becomes quiet, and soon the children lean back in their seats and close their eyes. Even Frodo Baggins, curled in Casey's lap, begins to snore. Although Yvette feels like a physical mess, more exhausted than she has ever been, she cannot relax. She can only pray Mona is doing what she says she is doing.

Please God. Protect us.

Up front, as they drive down a long stretch of Farm Road 1346, Devin asks Mona a question in a soft voice Yvette can barely overhear. "We can't hide forever. What's the plan?"

"Ahmed has two ways to get what he wants: he can steal it or he can go through the legal system. We hide out to make it impossible for him to succeed at the first, forcing him into the courts. But we wait until Mr. Brody has enough evidence to prove Ahmed's connection with the Taliban. If we can get Ahmed indicted, we don't have to worry about him getting legal custody."

To Yvette, it sounds like everything has to work out just so, which seems impossible. They have no way of knowing what Ahmed will do, if he is, indeed, after them.

This is all so crazy. Crazy, strange, and spooky.

They pass tall silos and oil rigs and long stretches of fields and pull onto a gravelly drive. The sign reads, "Mokry's General Store and Grain." They pass the façade of the building and park around back, near the hall. A short round woman in a house coat and flip-flops steps from the back porch to meet them. As soon as they open the van door, Frodo Baggins jumps out, wagging his tail, and he runs, dragging his leash, straight up to the round woman and licks her.

"I'm Bernie," the woman says. "Please come inside out of this wind."

They follow Bernie into the hall where seven cots have been set up, each with a pillow and blanket.

Like the seven dwarves.

They are lined up in a row on the wooden floor in front of a stage. Across from the stage is a bar, and along each side of the hall are rows of tables and chairs.

"I know you're tired," Bernie says, "so why don't you go on to sleep and we'll talk in the morning. The bathrooms are over past those tables. I'll have a yummy breakfast ready for you around nine. If you need to reach me before then, there's a phone behind the bar and a note with my house telephone number on it."

Bernie leaves through the back door. Yvette and Devin take cots on either side of the three children, leaving the last two cots on the end for Mona and Fatima. As Yvette crawls beneath the blanket, she wishes she could tie her children to her so she could be awakened if anyone were to take them. She looks tenderly at Frodo Baggins curled at the foot of Casey's bed and has never counted on him more than now to protect her family.

Chapter Twenty-Six: Seven Clowns In, Seven Clowns Out

When Yvette awakes in the sunlight streaming through the quiet hall, she finds she's alone.

Where is everybody?

The six other cots are empty. Even Mr. Baggins is gone. She jumps up and looks around. The bathrooms are empty, too.

Shit. This can't be happening. Please God.

She runs out the back, across the gravelly drive, past the van, which is thankfully where they left it, and over to the house next door, twenty yards away. She is relieved as soon as she approaches the side-door window to see her family on the other side seated around a kitchen table. Mona and Fatima aren't there, but Mr. Baggins is, begging for scraps at Matt's knees. Tears brim her eyes, and she pauses a moment to catch her breath and calm her heart before entering.

Thank you thank you thank you, God.

The kids greet her, full of excitement, shouting over one another the plan for the day: they will learn how to be clowns.

"Not just any ol' clowns," explains Tommy. "We're going to learn how to juggle."

"And balance a bottle on our head," Casey says.

"And pantomime." Matt gets up and walks around the table, pretending to be trapped in a box. Mr. Baggins follows, breaking the illusion.

"A great start, Matt," Bernie says from behind the kitchen bar, fleshy arms flattening at her sides. She totters on two bird-like legs across the linoleum. "Pancakes, Yvette?"

"Sure. Thanks so much." She sits on an empty chair beside Devin and fills her plate from a stack on the table.

I have no taste buds. I am so numb. An idiot on morphine.

"Sleep okay?" he asks.

"Evidently. I didn't hear y'all get up." She puts another forkful of pancakes into her mouth.

"Good," he says. "You needed the rest."

I'm not sure I ever slept. Or maybe I'm dreaming. A nightmare. This can't be happening.

After the breakfast dishes are put away, Bernie takes the children back over to the hall to teach them clown skills while Mona returns from another room and sits at the table with Yvette and Devin to discuss an update. She has spoken with Mr. Brody. The entire San Antonio police force has

340

already been notified of their disappearance last night, and their photos are in circulation.

We're fugitives on the run. This is crazy. Strange and spooky.

Additionally, Ahmed Jaffar has booked a flight from Mexico City to San Antonio and is due to arrive today. Mona warns Devin and Yvette to turn off their cell phones and not to contact a single person. They can't risk giving away their position to the police, to Ahmed, or to the Taliban, whose help Ahmed may have solicited by now.

Good guys and bad guys are following us. Including the Taliban. Crazy.

Yvette can't help but fear Mona is the true threat, their abductor.

This could all be a trap.

"As I mentioned before, the only way in and out of the Sunken Shelter is through the theater, which is right next to the Japanese Tea Gardens. There's a concert this evening, and before the headliner performance, we will do a short show. A secret chamber off the amphitheater will lead us to the shelter. As we go in, seven other clowns will come out and leave the way we came so no one wonders where we disappeared to. It also allows families ready to be relocated an easy way out. We always time the entrance and exits this way. Eventually UPS boxes are sent to the family's loved ones, and inside is the new location."

Yvette clears her throat. "That's why you sent the box to me."

"Exactly. The stacks of boxes in the living room of my rent house were filled with contact information for families we recently moved from the shelter, as well as books I was collecting from garage sales for our library."

Please let her be telling the truth. Let her be a good guy.

Devin leans back in his chair. "What happens if Mr. Brody can't find enough evidence to indict Ahmed?"

"Fatima and I will testify against him."

Yvette's mouth drops open. "But that means…"

"Wouldn't the Taliban come after you?" Devin asks.

"That's why we hope to avoid it." Mona stares directly at Yvette. "But I will do whatever it takes to keep him away from Casey."

She loves Casey, too. She won't hurt us, will she? She doesn't want to hurt Casey.

Later in the afternoon, after a lunch of sandwiches and chips, Bernie instructs each of them to put on oversized, colorful clown clothing and wigs from a chest in the hall, and then she begins the time-consuming task of applying makeup to each of them. As she works at one of the long hall tables sitting opposite them, she explains, face close, short blond hair cropped around her face like a mushroom cap, hands working their miracle, how important the makeup has been throughout the years to protecting the identities of hundreds of people.

Bernie finishes the children first, who walk around admiring themselves in the mirrored wall behind the bar. Matt wears a jester's hat, Tommy a straw hat, and Casey a green curly wig. The makeup, along with the addition of a red clown nose, conceals their identities well. And their dramatic way of walking and swinging their arms gives them a professional appearance.

Please God. Please protect my sweet kids.

"Children are naturals," Bernie says, "which is why this makes an excellent cover for victims on the run."

At four o'clock they load into the white van completely transformed in their clown makeup and baggy, colorful clothing. The kids bubble with excitement as they wave goodbye to Bernie, and Mona pulls up the gravelly drive to Farm Road 1346.

Yvette lays a hand on Mona's sequined shoulder, leans forward, and says, "Thank you." She pulls her hand back, afraid for having crossed a line, an invisible barrier between them.

Let her be a good guy.

Mona glances back and nods in her sad clown face, the only sad one in the lot, and the adults are quiet the rest of the drive.

Brackenridge Park is packed and bustling with cars and people when they pull into a parking lot for "employees only" at the Japanese Tea Gardens. Mona gives them last minute instructions—all clowns hold hands and all animals in their crates until they reach the stage. The animal crates and Yvette's duffle bags rest on a wagon pulled by Fatima at the end of their line. They stroll between the gardens and the amphitheater to a private entrance manned by a security guard, apparently expecting clowns, and from there they are led directly to the stage.

This is so crazy. Crazy and strange. Is this really happening?

Once on stage, two men take the wagon backstage, with Frodo barking angrily, while the seven clowns perform before a huge crowd of excited people which has already begun to clap. Tommy juggles tennis balls, Casey balances a Coke bottle on her forehead, and Matt pantomimes. Fatima waves an extra-large white-gloved hand held high on a stick. Mona throws confetti into the crowd. Devin and Yvette mock fight, as Bernie has taught them. The carnival music makes their random performance look rehearsed. They are only on stage for five minutes when Mona guides them backstage.

But it felt like an eternity.

From backstage, they retrieve their wagon and enter an antechamber. Once the antechamber door is closed, Mona opens another and leads them through. They pass seven other clowns pulling an identical wagon as they take a dimly lit and wobbly wooden ramp down to yet another door. Mona pulls out a key and inserts it into the lock, opens the wooden door, and beckons them through.

The final trap?

They enter what looks like the lobby of a third-rate hotel: four sofas and two chairs in worn fabric and leather are arranged around an old wooden coffee table and console television on uneven limestone floors. Beyond the television is a common eating area consisting of six round tables with chairs, a microwave, and a refrigerator-freezer. The entire area is empty of people.

Where is everybody? This is a trap!

Mona leads them down a narrow musty hallway, also resembling a hotel with numbered doors on each side, through which Yvette can hear the sounds of television and radio and people talking.

Thank God there are others here. Our fellow prisoners?

They make a few turns down adjoining corridors until they stop at a door numbered 129. Mona takes a key and opens it.

Yvette has never seen such an efficient use of space: there's a kitchenette to the left, smaller than her walk-in closet at home, with a fridge, two-burner stovetop, sink, and open shelving holding a set of dishes. A table for four is pressed against the wall, and past it, further into the room, is a sofa, chair, trunk, and television. On the back wall past the television is a corner desk with a computer. Between the kitchen table and the sofa is a door to the left leading to two queen-sized beds and a bathroom. Mona directs everyone to wash off, change clothes, and rest and she will return in a couple of hours to pick up the clown clothes and give them further instructions. She and Fatima will be staying next door in 130.

So strange and crazy. And spooky.

Since the children are not eager to get out of costume, Yvette takes a shower while Devin washes off in the bathroom sink.

"This is really something," Devin says over the sound of the running water.

"Not what I expected."

"I think I trust Mona, but I still worry we're doing the wrong thing, running away like this." Devin wipes his face with a towel.

Please let her be a good guy.

Fearing the children may hear, Yvette pokes her head from the shower curtain with her index finger against her lips. She turns off the water and whispers, "I know what you mean. He doesn't have a criminal record and now we may." She finds a towel on a rack over the commode and dries off. "Unless we're her prisoners. It's all so strange. I feel grateful to her but suspicious at the same time. Like the Stockholm syndrome."

Spooky and strange. I feel like Mona felt in her story. It's creepy how many similarities there are.

Devin piles the costume on the floor in the corner of the bathroom. "We've gone this far. I think at this point, we have to trust her."

They change into their clothes and then force the kids, one by one, to wash off and change, too. Yvette is glad the children have no clue of the danger they're in. They hop around the room like it's the best vacation of their lives. But Yvette also knows soon she and Devin must tell them the truth, whatever that may be.

Chapter Twenty-Seven: The Shelter

Yvette and her family adjust to life in the shelter, and although it seems easy for the kids, being away from friends and family and work is weighing on the adults.

What do Devin's parents think? Have they heard about us on the news in Houston? And poor Heidi and Gloria must be beside themselves with worry.

The children make friends and spend time in the exercise room, the library, the arcade, and the commons. They sometimes have friends in their room to watch television or play board games or fold origami. One little boy named Stevie has two circular scars on his face—one on each cheek—obviously created by the end of a cigarette. He has similar scars on his arms and legs, but he has been all smiles over the week he has been around Yvette's family. His older sister, Deja, has hung around, too, and, even though she has a full figure and is pregnant, you can tell the thirteen–year-old just wants to be a little girl as she helps organize their games of hide-and-go-seek and tag with some of the others.

Poor babies.

Yvette and Devin have had a few meetings with Mona about what happens next. Each time she comes to their door, Yvette and Devin practically leap to her, dying for information. Yvette recalls the way Mona eagerly awaited Ahmed's return while living in his prison. Like little dogs, they wait and pounce.

Like Mona and Fatima did with Ahmed.

Mona brings in a lap top and opens it on the table. "I want you to meet our attorney, Edith Pearson. Come, sit."

Yvette and Devin sit and watch as Mona types on the keyboard.

"Edith?"

"I'm here. Hello, Mona."

On the screen appears the face of a middle-aged black woman with short hair and a colorful scarf.

"I have Yvette and Devin Palmer with me."

"Hello," Yvette says.

"Hi there. I managed to get a hearing scheduled in four days. According to the clerk, no claim has been filed on Ahmed Jaffar's behalf, so this may be an open and shut case, unless he appears."

"Thanks, Edith," Mona says. "Email me the specifics."

Mona types into the keyboard. "I have Mr. Brody waiting to meet you as well."

In a few moments, the white-bearded face of a man, perhaps late sixties, appears on the screen.

"Like I told Mona, I spotted Jaffar here in San Antonio at the airport a week ago and followed him to the Holiday Inn. I'll keep an eye on him."

"Edith says he's made no move in the courts."

"Naw. Ain't his style. He's looking for you. Plans to take her."

This can't be happening.

Yvette and Devin thank Mr. Brody, and Mona closes the lap top.

"How well do you know this detective? I mean do you trust him?"

"He's been a part of my life since I escaped back into Texas."

"That long?" Yvette asks. "So you must trust him."

"He and my aunt were close once. Almost married."

Yvette brought her a cup of water. "What happened?"

"His work as a police detective was too hard on her, especially after my family was killed. She changed. He retired from the force and tried to make it work with her, but he missed the action, so he volunteered for the shelter."

"He's a volunteer?" Devin asks.

"He's a good man. Helped a lot of people. Abusers have been indicted because of him. I trust him totally."

They are good guys. Thank you, God.

Yvette lounges on the sofa with a novel from the shelter library. Stevie and Deja sit at the table with Tommy and Casey folding paper into animals according to Matt's instructions. Matt stands over them, making one crease at a time, waiting for his pupils to copy him. Devin researches boat motors on the computer because, he says, the one on the pontoon is on its last leg.

"Like this," says Matt.

"What are we making again?" Stevie asks.

"A rabbit."

"Oh yeah. Deja had a pet rabbit once. Snowball."

"Don't talk about it, Stevie."

"Why not?" Casey asks.

"Our dad killed it." Stevie wads his partly-made rabbit in his fist. "I messed up. Can I start over?"

Casey gives him another slip of paper. "Why did he kill it?"

"He's mean," says Stevie. "He gave me these scars."

"He's only mean when he's drunk," Deja adds. "He can be nice, too."

"He's always mean."

"No he's not."

"Mama says he's possessed by the devil."

"So it's the devil's fault, not his. He can't help it."

Yvette looks up from her book to see Stevie crush his paper between his hands.

"I messed up again. Can I have another paper?"

"Papa loves us," Deja insists.

"That's why he made you pregnant."

Deja stands and shouts, "Shut up! Just shut up! He wouldn't be in jail if you hadn't told on him!"

Yvette and Devin cross the room to the children, Yvette putting a hand on Deja's shoulder. "It's okay, sweetie. Sit down."

"Want some water?" Devin asks.

"I was trying to help you!" Stevie jumps from his seat, too, and throws his new paper onto the floor. "He's not supposed to do that to you!"

"Everything was fine!" Deja says clenching her fists and stomping a foot. "If you hadn't told, we'd still be together at home, even Mama said."

Stevie runs from the room.

Yvette's children look at her, their eyes asking what they should do, but she takes Deja into her arms and says, "You have to go after Stevie and tell him you love him. This is not his fault, sweet girl. He did the right thing. You have to tell him."

Deja pulls away from Yvette and rushes from the room without a word.

It's late in the afternoon, and Yvette is alone in her room sitting at the table, which is covered in little paper

352

origami animals. Even Frodo Baggins is off on some adventure no doubt. She worries what their family and friends are thinking and wishes she could contact them to let them know she and her family are okay. As anxious as she is to get out and call them, she's not looking forward to leaving her children behind.

No control. So helpless. Worse than a hamster in a wheel.

She picks up one of the swans and twirls it between her fingers. She knows this is Casey's work, because the swan has been her favorite animal since she can remember. No ugly duckling, Casey nevertheless relates to the story since she sometimes feels different than the rest of the family in her slightly darker skin.

She's my sweet, sweet Casey.

Something else has been bothering Yvette, and so she gets up and walks next door to Mona's room.

"We need to talk," Yvette says when Mona opens the door.

"Come in."

They sit opposite each other at the kitchen table, which is identical to the one in Yvette's room. Each is wearing clothes provided by the shelter, and Yvette understands now why Mona's clothes never quite fit.

"Would you like a drink?" Mona asks.

"No thanks. I want to know why you haven't told Casey who you are."

Mona's face turns whiter than usual.

"Or have you, and I just don't know it."

"No. I haven't."

"Why not?"

"Is that what you want?"

"I don't know." Yvette leans her elbows on the table. "I just feel grateful to you, Mona. I know you don't particularly like me, but I want you to know how much all this has meant to me. And if you want to tell Casey, I think I'm okay with it."

I'm grateful. Like in the Stockholm syndrome.

"I don't think it's a good idea."

Yvette lifts her brows. "Why?"

"All the research I've read says it confuses children when a biological parent enters their lives after years of absence. It would have been one thing to fashion a relationship from her infancy, but to begin now, I don't know if it would be good for her."

"We have to tell her something."

Mona leans back. "I've consulted with the shelter's counselor, Mrs. Craig, on what to say. Casey may be called to speak in court, so we can't keep this from her forever. Mrs. Craig says we should be honest with Casey about her father. We don't have to provide her with all of the horrid

354

details, but we can let her know he kidnapped her biological mother and hurt other people. I don't think it's necessary to tell her *I* was that mother."

You really are one of the good guys. You poor thing. You're so far in your shell. No one can touch you.

Yvette wants to reach out and touch Mona's hand, but Mona keeps such a wall built around her that Yvette is afraid to break through. "Why don't you want her to know? This is about you, not her."

Mona's face crumples. "Can't do it. Please understand." Mona gets up and walks across the room. "Best this way. For both of us."

I won't push it. But maybe one day, she'll think differently. Poor thing. Thank God she's one of the good guys. Thank God

When Yvette stands to leave, Mona asks her to stay.

"I want to tell you the rest of my story, what happened after I left Casey with the Cardenas couple."

Chapter Twenty-Eight: Crossing the Border

From the cemetery, Fatima and I returned to the church for the priest, but the altar boy shook his head and indicated through signs the priest was no longer there, so we sat in a pew to rest. Fatima put an arm around me and patiently listened to me sob. I fought the urge to run back to the grave and reclaim my baby, telling myself she was better off, I couldn't give her what she needed. Those hours we sat and waited were the most miserable of my life. Nothing that has befallen me since has equaled or surpassed them in pain.

The light coming in through the dusty windows grew dim, and when night fell, we found ourselves sleeping once again on the hard narrow pews in the peaceful quiet of the church. On and off throughout the night, I cried for my little girl, who I thought I would never see again. When the priest came to wake us, I had just fallen asleep. It seemed I had slept for only a few seconds.

He brought us crackers and cheese and water and told us his friend would not arrive until four o'clock, but we were welcome to sit in the church. There would be two masses, one at eight and one at noon, and we could stay for both, so we did. I wept throughout both, with Fatima holding my hand, but tried not to draw attention to us, so dirty and stained were our clothes, and we reeked. But the beautiful sound of the voices singing the hymnals together gave me moments of comfort.

The priest heard the confessions of two old women and left until dusk, when he returned with three men. The men had sandwiches, which they shared with us at the priest's request. He said prayers over us, explaining in English his friend Paiso, a wiry man in his thirties with not much chin, was helping the other two find the American dream so they could send money back to their starving families. The priest prayed for a safe journey and for continued blessings for all of us.

We piled into a beat up yellow Volkswagen. Paiso drove and Chiliano, the burly one, rode up front. Fatima sat in back between Carlito, the smallest and youngest, my age, a smoker, and me. We drove for hours along the dark streets from the city, through the dirt roads of the desert, and back into a town along the Gulf of Mexico where we were taken to a safe house. Twenty other Mexicans, all about my age, waited for a guide to smuggle them across, but Paiso was not him. We were given no food, only water, by the man who ran the safe house, which was filthy and stunk and was infested with lice and roaches. Carlito smoked a cigarette, the smoke an improvement to the foul stench lingering in the air. The men spoke together in Spanish, Paiso occasionally translating bits and pieces.

"Carlito's girlfriend este muy pregnant," Paiso said. "And her father make him come to U.S. for job." Then he added, "He no say no to him, or he kill Carlito."

Chiliano and Paiso giggled, and even Carlito broke into a smile and said, "Su verdad."

Paiso laughed out loud and said, "He says it's true."

In the morning, we left, stopping only to fill gas. After several more hours we arrived in Matamoros, the border town across from Brownsville.

We were given a meal at a local church, and it seemed the best I had eaten in my life. Two women brought us hot rice and beans and steaming tortillas, and we were allowed to eat as much as we wanted. The women prayed over us before clearing the dirty dishes away and handing out blankets and pillows. We stretched out on the wooden floor, Fatima and I on one side of the church and the men on the other, and fell asleep, even though many hours of daylight remained.

Sometime in the night, Paiso woke Fatima and me and led us, on foot, out of the city into darkness. We walked for hours on long stretches of flat ranch land, climbing over barbwire, avoiding cow paddies and rattlesnakes, with very little light from the crescent moon. We had no water or food with us, no supplies to speak of, and I dreaded what would become of us if we lost our way.

At dawn we came upon a set of railroad tracks, which we followed for about a mile when a track repair train happened by and offered us a ride. The men sang joyfully as we sat on the flat bed of the rickety car, thankful to be off our feet with the wind in our hair, safe from the critters of the land. Paiso said they were singing about the American dream. The ride saved us several hours of walking and provided us much needed rest. Fatima and I leaned against one another and fell asleep to the cheerful voices of the men.

In less than two hours, we got off the train and hiked down a hill to the river to a shady place where we waited until dark with nothing to do but watch Carlito smoke another cigarette.

While the men conversed among themselves in Spanish, Fatima turned to me and said, "Thank you for bringing me with you."

She hadn't said much before, so this came as a surprise to me.

"I couldn't leave you there."

"You could. And you didn't."

I squeezed her hand. "It's been hard, hasn't it? But we'll find a better life, you and me, together."

She nodded with her eyes to the ground.

"Unless you have family," I added.

"No. There's no one."

"There's me. You have me. Okay?"

She shrugged. "We will see."

When night finally descended, the men climbed to their feet, so we followed them into the chilly river. We walked until we couldn't stand, and then we swam. I kept my head above the dark water, my teeth chattering from both cold and fear. Every so often, I flinched when something slinked against my leg. We stumbled to the bank, shivering, and, wringing out our hair and clothes, trudged across a field of grass with few trees.

We hadn't gone far when we heard a spotter plane above us. We scattered like roaches to the nearest trees, Fatima and I separated from the rest of the group. We clung to one another as the spotlight searched the trees and were relieved when it finally flew away.

We followed Paiso, running now in case the plane returned, across the field to a prearranged car hidden in a thicket on the side of the road. Paiso found the key in a magnetic box hidden under a back fender and let us all in. Fatima and I both wept when Paiso started the engine and said, "We in U.S." before he sped up the road.

Soon I recognized the road from McAllen to La Paloma, a small town not far from Brownsville. Now that I was finally back in Texas, the memory that my parents and brother had been murdered grabbed a hold of me, and my tears of joy became tears of sorrow. I had nowhere to go home to. I was afraid my house was being watched by the Taliban and that Ahmed would be notified of my return.

Paiso drove us to a church in La Paloma where we were given a meal of grilled chicken and potatoes. Although I was starving, I found I couldn't eat, so ridden was I by fear and anguish. I thanked the nuns for the food, but ate little, giving most of my plate over to Chiliano.

As I watched Fatima eat, curiosity overcame me, and I said to her, "Back in Brownsville at the university everyone thought you were a Taliban spy."

Fatima spit the food she had been chewing onto her plate and gaped at me. "Why would people believe such a thing?"

"So there's no truth to it? It's okay if there is. It doesn't matter now."

"Of course not." Her eyes were wide and round like quarters. "I despise those dirty scoundrels." Tears fell from her eyes suddenly.

"I'm sorry. I didn't know." I squeezed her clenched fist.

"We were at first happy when we heard they were coming," Fatima said. "My father had already died in the war with the Soviets, and two brothers had died at the hands of the corrupt and chaotic Mujahideen."

"I'm so sorry," I said again.

"My mother and grandmother and I thought the Taliban would bring order and peace. But when they distributed their flyers throughout Kabul with the new laws, we went home and wept. Women weren't allowed to leave their homes unaccompanied by a male relative. We had no living male relative."

"What did you do?"

"Every right women gained in the progressive cities was instantly stripped from us that day. All the schools for girls were closed. My mother, who was a teacher, lost her job." Fatima's lips began to tremble. It was the most I had ever heard her say. I thought she would say no more, but once she could speak again, she continued. "We were starving when my mother risked her life and went to an old friend of one of my brothers, Jamsheed, a tall, thin, awkward boy of nineteen, just my age. He had joined the Taliban. She tried to convince him to make me his wife, but he saw me as an infidel. This meant he could do with me as he wished. And he did."

Fatima broke down into sobs, so I patted her clenched fist. "You don't have to tell me."

"Jamsheed was ordered to go to America. He was scared to go, so he married me and took me with him. We ended up in Brownsville where we met Ahmed. We lived with him for a while. Ahmed was different then. I fell in love with him. Can you believe?"

"Yes. I can."

"When Jamsheed returned to Kabul, I stayed because I heard my mother and grandmother were dead. I knew the moment we left the country they would starve, but there was nothing I could do." Fatima covered her face with her hands and wept as I stroked her arm.

"It's okay," I said. "You don't have to go on."

"Ahmed helped me to enroll at the university. I thought, I thought…" Fatima put her head in her arms down on the table and wept.

I stroked her hair. "I will never leave you," I whispered. "You can count on that."

After the meal at the church, Paiso told us that from here, we would part ways, and he prayed with us and wished us luck, for in a few days, he would begin the journey back alone. I borrowed a phone from the nuns to call my aunt.

"Don't say anything," I said in a low voice.

"Where are you?"

"Call this number from another phone as soon as you can." I hung up.

Ten minutes later, Aunt Rachel called, relieved and anxious to see me. I told her how to find the chapel, and within two hours, she was there with Mr. Brody, engaged to my aunt, to pick up Fatima and me. When I saw her, I ran to her arms and melted into a puddle of tears. She reminded me so much of my mother—same round middle and bird-like legs and blonde hair cut in a similar bob. She cried with me, stroking my filthy hair, trying to comfort me. She took one look at Fatima and then pulled her in so the three of us made one huddle.

"You poor things," she said over and over. "You're safe now, darlings. You're safe now."

Mr. Brody drove a Suburban and offered rides to Chiliano and Carlito as well, since they wanted to go to Brownsville to find work. Before we left, my aunt gave Paiso a hefty reward for bringing me safely from Mexico.

During our ride, I told my aunt and Mr. Brody all that had happened to Fatima and me.

"You can both stay with me as long as you need," Aunt Rachel said when I had finished.

"It might not be safe," I said.

Mr. Brody took us to spend one night in a hotel in Brownsville—my aunt paid for Chiliano and Carlito to stay in one room and Fatima and me in another—and after having my first shower and clean clothes in days, I lay beside Fatima, clinging to her in the darkness. As I lay there, I recalled one night in my dorm room just after I met Bijan. I woke up that night to find Letty kneeling at my bedside looking down at me. Before I could ask her what was the matter, she bent over me and pressed her lips to mine. The kiss lasted only a moment before Letty withdrew quickly to her own bed. Neither of us spoke of it again. But during that kiss, heat moved through me with unexpected joy, and as I lay there in the hotel room with the fragile Fatima in my arms, I longed to feel that joy once more. I first kissed Fatima on the cheek, but when she turned her dark and weary eyes to me in the dim, moonlit hotel room, I saw my own longing reflected back. Like Letty had two years before, Fatima put her mouth to mine, and my tears met her tears and mingled together on our cheeks as we kissed away our pain and found solace at long last.

In the morning, Mr. Brody drove Fatima and me to Atkins to see the woman he called the Czech Widow. You know her as Bernie the clown artist. That's when I first learned of the Sunken Shelter.

Chapter Twenty-Nine: Smoke Out

"And how long was it before you were running this place yourself?" Yvette asks.

"Not long. They needed help. So many people in need, you know. And I don't really run it. Not alone, anyway."

"And you've lived here all this time?"

"Except for the year I lived behind you, yes. And that was pretty scary for me to be on the outside for so long, always on edge."

Yvette leans toward Mona, as though seeing her clearly for the first time. "What made you do it, move behind me, I mean?"

Mona slouches in her chair, her thin frame folding into itself like a paper Japanese fan. "Mr. Brody had finally tracked down Ahmed and found out about the Missing Children's Data Base. Casey's DNA could appear in it for a number of reasons—if she ever gave blood or was in an accident or lost. I couldn't risk him finding her. I had to warn you. But I couldn't just knock on your door and say, 'Guess who I am.'"

"Yeah, I guess not."

"And I couldn't say a mad man is after your daughter without you thinking I was the mad one."

"True, I guess."

"I had to start from the beginning, so you'd understand the real danger and take me seriously."

Yvette reaches a hand out to touch Mona, but instead, flattens it against the table. "Thank you for wanting to protect Casey."

"I only made things worse. You wouldn't have called the police if I had left you alone."

"But like you said, if her DNA was ever run through the data base, well, we wouldn't have seen him coming. Please don't blame yourself, Mona. You did the best you could. I'm the idiot who didn't trust you."

Yvette stands to leave, but before she reaches the door, she says, "You should be proud of what you've done for Casey. I know Casey, and I know she'd be nothing but grateful that you did what you did."

Before Yvette leaves, Mona's phone rings, and Yvette hesitates at the door, waiting for Mona to say goodbye.

"Oh no," Mona says into the phone. "Are you sure?" She ends her call and turns to Yvette. She has a desperate look on her face, mouth agape, eyes wide, eyebrows hidden beneath her frizzy hair.

What could be happening now?

"What?" Yvette asks.

Mona's face has gone pale and her bottom lip trembles. "Mr. Brody was found murdered in his home this afternoon."

This can't be happening. Yvette crosses to the table and sinks back into her chair. "What?"

"I can't believe it either."

"Oh my God. Do you think it was Ahmed?"

"I know it was."

"Poor Mr. Brody. Oh my God. What do we do now?"

Mona puts a hand to her mouth. "I need to think."

"Is there no one else tracking Ahmed?"

Mona shakes her head. "We're on our own."

God help us.

That night after a meal of microwave pizza, for the first time since they've been there, the children say they want to go home.

"I miss our house." Casey collapses onto the sofa. "When are we going home?"

Tommy sinks beside her. "I miss our trampoline and my friends."

"And Frodo never gets to go outside," Matt adds from where he sits in front of the computer. "I'm tired of changing his diaper."

Yvette and Devin decide it's time to tell the kids the truth.

This won't be easy.

"We haven't been completely honest with you," Devin says.

Matt lifts an index finger into the air. "I knew it. So what's really going on?"

Mr. Baggins joins Tommy and Casey on the sofa, and Devin and Yvette each take an arm of the chair in the corner.

Yvette folds her hands. Her stomach's tight. She doesn't want to do this. "Y'all know how Casey's adopted, right?"

The kids nod. "Yeah?"

"Well," Yvette continues. She wants to be sure she handles this right. She doesn't want Casey to feel bad about herself in any way. "We found out that her biological father was not a nice man."

Casey's eyes fill with tears.

Don't cry, Casey. All the air rushes from Yvette's body like a deflating balloon.

"Come here, sweet girl." Yvette scoots into the chair with Devin still on one arm as Casey leaves the sofa to climb onto her lap. "That doesn't mean you aren't a nice girl, okay?"

Casey nods.

"And remember," Devin says. "He's not your real father. I am. Biology only means so much."

"I know, Dad."

Yvette strokes Casey's bangs from her eyes, recalling the way Casey looked as a baby nestled against her breast with her thumb in her mouth, the other tiny fingers plucking at Yvette's blouse—the collar, or the buttons, or the bow tied at the neckline. Casey's little fingers were always feeling the textures around her, especially the tags on pillows. Between the ages of three and six, Casey would ask Yvette to turn over after her back-scratch so Casey could feel the tag on the back of Yvette's shirt.

Tears fall from Yvette's eyes as she realizes she cannot protect her little girl from all the evils of this world. She holds her close and says, "We came to this shelter when we learned that he's trying to find you. Because he's been mean to people in the past, we were afraid he might be mean to you, too, and try to take you from us."

"I don't want to go with him." Casey throws her arms around Yvette's neck.

Please God. Please don't take her away from us!

"We won't let him take you," Devin says. "That's why y'all have to stay here a little longer."

"What do mean 'y'all'?" Matt asks. "Aren't you staying, too?"

Yvette and Devin exchange glances. Yvette's heart feels as though it has stopped beating altogether. Then Yvette says, "In a few days, we have to meet before a judge to have that man's parental rights revoked. We have to present proof that he's bad."

"What proof?" Tommy asks.

"We found someone who knew him who will testify against him," Yvette says.

"Who?" Matt asks.

"Mona," Casey says. "Right? That must be why she brought us here. She knows how bad he is. And Fatima, too."

Yvette nods. "That's right."

Smart girl.

The kids let all that information soak in.

"Do y'all have any more questions for us?" Devin asks. "I know this isn't the easiest thing in the world to hear."

"How much longer do we have to stay?" Tommy asks.

"We don't know," Yvette says. "A few more weeks."

Matt puts his hands in the air. "What about school?"

"Daddy and I will work something out."

"Are we gonna have to do all the makeup work?" Tommy asks.

371

"Probably, sweet boy. But you'll get extra time."

"Any other questions?" Devin asks.

After a moment's hesitation, Casey asks, "What's his name?"

Yvette lifts Casey's chin and looks into her little brown eyes. She doesn't want to tell her, but she won't lie. "Ahmed Jaffar."

The boys ask if Casey's father has ever killed anyone, but Yvette and Devin put a stop to those types of questions. "We only know he's hurt people," Devin says. "Let's watch a little television before we go to sleep."

Please God. Please protect our family. Yvette continues to hold Casey in her arms, squeezing her close, kissing the top of her head and whispering, "It's going to be okay. Don't worry. You'll see." But it is herself that needs convincing.

It takes Yvette a moment to realize that the far-off cries aren't coming from her nightmare. She sits up in bed beside Casey and listens again.

What is that?

She hears loud voices and people moving down the hallway outside their room. Devin sits up in the other bed across from her where he's been sleeping with Tommy.

"What's going on?" he asks.

"I don't know." She climbs from the covers and goes to the door to listen. That's when she smells the smoke.

Fire? This can't be happening.

"Oh my God. Wake up the kids! Matt, get up!"

Matt sits up on the sofa that has been his bed this past week. "What's going on?"

Frodo whimpers and then stretches at the foot of the couch.

"We have to leave. Get Frodo's leash."

Yvette opens the door, and the smoke presses in, hot and thick. "Devin, bring the kids! We gotta get out of here!" Yvette knocks at Mona's door, but there's no answer. She knocks again. When a woman and her son pass by, Yvette asks where they're going.

"Emergency exits," the woman says. "Down this way in the library."

Just then, an obnoxious sound goes off, and Yvette realizes it must be the fire alarm. Mona's door flies open as water sprays from sprinklers above.

"Where's Casey?" Mona's red frizzy hair flattens with the spray.

Yvette's family has gathered behind her in the hall, coughing and sputtering. Tommy and Matt are crying. Casey is wide-eyed and clinging to Yvette's waist. Devin has Frodo tucked in his arm like a football.

I can't think. Can hardly speak. I'm an idiot on morphine.

"Hold her hand, Yvette," Mona hollers over the sound of the alarm. "Don't let her go."

"You think this is because of him?"

"I know it is. Now come on." Mona and Fatima each carry a wet cat as they follow the crowd down the smoke-filled, raining corridors.

This can't be happening.

Over a hundred people meet in the library where three wooden ladders have been yanked from the ceiling and unfolded, like the access to Yvette's attic. The smoke is thick, here, too, and most everyone is coughing and fanning the air in front of their faces and shivering with the showers, which continue to spray overhead. People are crouched low on the ground as they wait their turn to ascend. Several children are crying. Stevie and Deja kneel on the floor with their mother, praying.

A heavy-set woman in gray warm-ups is dishing out orders over a megaphone, "You will emerge in the Japanese Tea Gardens. The police and firefighters will be waiting to escort us out."

Mona is suddenly pulling books from the shelves. "Everyone save a book. Tuck it under your shirt so it doesn't get soaked. If each of us takes one, that's over a hundred books we can save."

374

Tommy and Matt help Mona distribute books to the people waiting in line to go up the ladders. Yvette picks up a few books from a case beside her and, like Sophie in *Sophie's Choice*, decides which to save. All have to do with philosophy or psychology except for one novel. She wants to save the novel but ultimately settles on Frederick Nietzsche's *The Birth of Tragedy* because she knows Mona read it while in captivity, and so it's probably important to her. She slips it under her shirt and tucks the shirt into her jeans. Her children end up with an odd assortment: *Gulliver's Travels*, *Robinson Crusoe*, and *Animal Farm*. Because the latter is a thin book, Casey sticks one more beneath her shirt.

"What is it?" Yvette asks, trying to keep the children calm.

"*The Golden Compass*," Casey answers. "I've never read it. Is it good?"

"I liked it. It's very creative. You'll have to read the whole trilogy."

I'm such a good actress. Look at Casey's smile.

Devin's not much of a reader, especially not of fantasy, so he laughs when Tommy hands him *Lord of the Rings*. "Is this really worth saving?"

He's such a good actor, too.

"Yes!" Yvette and Matt answer in unison.

As Yvette and her family wait their turn, Yvette reminds Casey to stay with her. She will have to let go of her hand to climb the ladder. They decide Yvette should go first, followed by Casey and the boys. Devin and Mr. Baggins will take up the rear.

Please help us, God. This can't be happening.

Chapter Thirty: Shuttle Trouble

Yvette climbs the ladder through the ceiling of the library and emerges beneath a sego palm. The gardens are not well lit, and the thick smoke rising from the ground further obscures the throng of people scattered and scurrying about. As soon as she's able, she finds solid ground and leans over to help Casey up from the wooden ladder. Both cough and gag against the smoke clinging to their lungs.

"Don't let go," she tells Casey as she helps first Matt and then Tommy climb to his feet.

Ahmed Jaffar could be anywhere.

As soon as Devin makes it out with Frodo Baggins, they help Mona and Fatima and then follow the traffic of people down a stone path and across a bridge that overlooks a pond surrounding them on all sides. They have surfaced from the shelter onto an island. Smoke lingers above the water like ghostly bodies waiting for direction.

Spooky and strange.

"This way," a voice says.

Firefighters point flashlights and guide the coughing, gagging people through the meandering gardens and smoke toward a stone Torii gate, which resembles a Japanese character, marking the entrance. Out front and parked alongside the curb is the fire truck with its bright lights flashing, and across St. Mary's Street are five yellow shuttle vans with people climbing into them.

"Where are we going?" Tommy clings to Yvette's arm.

Yvette kisses the top of Tommy's head. "I don't know yet."

"Probably a clinic or another shelter." Devin ushers them across the street. Mona and Fatima are behind them and Stevie and Deja are in front with their mother.

The people from the shelter are easy to distinguish from the others in the crowd. Not only are they coughing like career smokers with wet clothes sticking to their skin, but now that they are out in the open, they all have that mad look in their eyes Yvette has come to associate with Mona.

All five shuttle vans pull away from the curb loaded with other people, so the Palmers wait with the others for another ride. Casey is shivering. Yvette runs her hands up and down Casey's arms.

"What's going to happen to the shelter?" Casey asks Mona.

"I guess it's not so secret anymore," Matt says.

Mona pets Babs. "Sure it is. For all anyone knows, a group of tourists at a late event in the tea gardens was smoked out. We'll repair the damages and start it up again, won't we Fatima? Are you okay, dear?"

Fatima nods. "Reminds me of home. Always fires like this."

Poor thing. Her family is already dead, as is Mona's. Yvette wraps her arms around her children as they wait on the curb, wishing she could shield them from the pain of her own death.

Another row of yellow shuttle vans pulls in front of them. Before climbing inside, Mona glares at the driver. "Tell me your name and where you're taking us."

"Carl Napier. University Hospital."

Satisfied, she climbs inside.

The van has four rows, so Fatima, Mona, Tommy and the cats take the back row; Casey, Yvette, Matt, and Frodo Baggins take the third; Devin, Stevie, and Deja take the second; and Stevie's mother, Maria, takes the passenger seat next to Carl Napier.

"Are you all warm enough?" Carl asks. "I can turn up the heat."

"That would be nice," Yvette replies, her teeth chattering from more than the cold.

Before Carl pulls from the curb, the window beside his head explodes, his door opens, and his body is dragged from the car.

What is happening?

The van fills with screams. Yvette clutches Casey and Matt and glances back at Tommy, whose eyes are wide and terrified. When she turns forward again, Devin meets her eyes with a look of panic, undoing his belt, trying to open the van door.

Another man jumps behind the wheel and peals away, the tires screaming against the asphalt as they weave past other vehicles on the road.

"Good evening, everyone," the man says. "I am Ahmed Jaffar. And if anyone moves or speaks, I will shoot."

He glances back and gives them an eerie smile. Though ten years older, he looks exactly as Mona has described him—dark hair feathered on the sides, penetrating hazel eyes, and a confident, seductive mouth.

This can't be happening.

"Where are you taking…" Pow! Before Stevie can get out his question, Ahmed shoots him in the stomach.

Maria screams.

Yvette's mouth falls open. She floats from her body, in a supreme daze, unable to move, to think, to speak. Devin gives her a look of terror, but she gapes, numb, slow-witted, unable to process the horror unfolding before her. At last her thoughts catch up with the scene, and she remembers to pray.

Please God. Oh please protect my family. This can't be happening. I can't think.

"The next person who speaks gets the next bullet," Ahmed says calmly.

Stevie writhes in his seat. Deja sits beside him bawling, blood bathing her hands. From up front, Maria moans like a dying cat.

Ahmed meets Yvette's eyes in the rearview mirror. Time stands still as he speaks. "Good. I hate to have to follow through with my threats. Such a waste of life." He holds the steering wheel with his left hand and a revolver in his right. His right arm is bent at the elbow and the gun rests on his shoulder, hand against his neck, pointed toward Casey. He stares past Yvette in the mirror. "Hello, again Mona, my old love. I see you have taken good care of Fatima. I give you both permission to say hello to me."

"Hello, Ahmed," Mona says.

When Fatima makes no reply, he asks, "Fatima has nothing to say to me? Surely after all these years you wonder how I am."

Fatima squeaks, "I have plenty to say to you."

Brave girl. It might get you killed.

Ahmed laughs. "I see your sense of humor has been restored. That's wonderful to hear. I wonder why you have not yet committed suicide. Perhaps I cured you."

"She has found a higher purpose," Mona says. "Like you, we are in the business of helping people."

Yvette becomes more aware of her surroundings. Frodo Baggins is frozen on Matt's lap like a squirrel in the street. Casey and Matt tremble and pant beside her. Deja and

Devin, helpless, gaping, and wide-eyed, lean over Stevie writhing in the seat in front of her. Maria moans in a low, guttural wail that doesn't sound human. The seat behind Yvette is perfectly silent. Yvette wishes she could see Tommy.

"Ah, yes. Your little shelter. If you hadn't hired that Irish Setter, Jonathan Brody, to check up on me, I might not have discovered your secret."

Where are the police? Surely they've noticed the body of poor Carl Napier.

Yvette squeezes Casey's hand and then Matt's. She wishes she could tell them all will be okay, but she has accepted their imminent death. Yvette grits her teeth at the thought of what Casey's future may hold if Ahmed takes her. She wishes their last moments together could be sweet and reassuring—not this brutal attack on their senses, this assault on love and life. Unspoken words for her husband and children burden her heart as the tears flood her eyes. She longs to return to her ordinary life with her ordinary family, leading the Webelos and the Girl Scout meetings, answering Matt's homework questions about ancient China, taking Frodo Baggins for long walks, watering her vines, and making sweet, sweet love to her husband.

But there was one thing she'd do differently: she would live her life with the utmost gratitude. No more self-pity at her hamster-wheel analogies. She loved her family and her life and now that she is losing both, she's so sorry she was ever anything but grateful. It sounded trite and cliché even as she thought it, but she would give anything to go back exactly where she was before Mona walked into her life.

"I'm sure you all know why I am here." Ahmed seeks Casey's eyes in the mirror. "Do you know who I am to you, Casey?"

Casey nods.

Yvette squeezes her hand again.

Watch what you say to my little girl, you bastard.

Ahmed turns onto the highway. "You are a beautiful child. You remind me of my mother."

"Thank you." Casey's voice sounds small and full of tremors.

A lump lodges in Yvette's throat.

This can't be happening.

"I have been searching for you for years. I could hardly believe my good fortune when I was notified of your whereabouts. You can imagine my disappointment when I arrived at your home to find you gone."

Yvette's stomach is queasy, and she presses her hand into it, hoping not to vomit. Her hand hits against the book, and she takes it from her shirt, giving her an idea. A crazy idea. But what has she got to lose? She can't afford to be spineless now. What would her mother do? Her mother would fight to the death, in fact, did fight to the death, first as a girl who'd been horribly abused and then later as a single parent mourning the early loss of her husband. Yvette must, too, fight to the death for the sake of her family.

If she can distract Ahmed long enough for Devin to disarm him, they might have a chance.

Ahmed continues to address Casey. "I have been hoping to find you so that I may teach you what I have learned and pass on my legacy to you. My work is very important. One day, it will save thousands of lives."

Fatima whimpers, but Yvette is too afraid to look behind her.

You have to act, Yvette. It's now or never. You have to do something or see your family destroyed.

"You know I only came for one of you," Ahmed says. "But because I hate to waste life, I may decide to use the rest of you as subjects in my ongoing experiment. Would you like that, Fatima? Just like the good old days, yes? I am very close to finding the cure to suicide."

It's now or never, Yvette!

Yvette takes a deep breath and lifts her book for Casey and Matt to see. She motions for them to take theirs from beneath their shirts.

"What's that you have there?" Ahmed says, staring at her in the rearview mirror.

Yvette freezes. *Oh shit oh shit oh shit.*

"That, in your hand. Is it a book? Answer me!"

"Yes. It's a book," Yvette says in a shaky voice. "Nietzsche's *Birth of a Tragedy*. Have you read it?"

"Of course I have. And so has Mona, remember old love? If I recall, you weren't a fan."

Stevie has stopped gasping for air and lies quietly with his head to the side. Yvette can no longer tell if he's breathing.

"You remember correctly, Ahmed. I miss those days."

"Liar! Do you think I've forgotten how you betrayed me? Do you think I've forgotten what a good little actress you can be? I should shoot you now!"

"But we did have some good times," Mona says with an attempt to sound calm. "I wanted my freedom more than anything, but there were times I did love you, Ahmed. Even now. Why don't you let these others go, and you and I can reunite and live as we once did."

Ahmed pulls the trigger and a bullet flies past Yvette's ear.

Fatima screams, and a gasp escapes Yvette's lips. She turns back and is relieved to see Tommy isn't hurt, but poor Mona is bleeding from her abdomen.

Think! Clear your mind. It's now or never! Think, Yvette!

Yvette's heart skips a beat as she takes the book and flings it at the windshield, in front of Ahmed's view. Immediately after, Matt throws his. Then Yvette takes Casey's books and lands them, one after the other, in the same spot. Deja and Devin and Tommy all follow suit.

As Ahmed hollers at them and bats against the barrage of books that fly into his face, one after another, Devin leaps from his seat and grabs the hand holding the gun, which is going off, bullets ricocheting through the van. One lodges into Matt's shoulder, and he cries out.

Matt!

Ahmed loses control of the steering wheel, causing the van to swerve left and right. The kids scream when another vehicle brushes against them on the driver's side.

God help us. This is really happening.

Maria grabs the wheel and pulls it toward her, but Ahmed head-butts her and she falls back against the passenger door. Deja bites into Ahmed's arm like a wild dog until Devin at last holds the gun and puts it to Ahmed's head.

"Pull over!"

"No way, man! You just insured the death of everyone on board. I'm taking every last one of you with me!"

Ahmed fights Maria for the wheel and points it in the direction of a concrete wall approaching a half mile ahead on the side of the highway. Devin pulls the trigger and shoots a bullet into Ahmed's head. Blood flies everywhere, including the windshield, making it difficult to see.

The van swerves dangerously and then screeches against a guardrail. Like a lioness, Yvette leaps from her seat and climbs in front of Deja, just behind Ahmed. She reaches over his bouncing, bloody head and finds the wheel, pulling them toward an exit. The van grazes another car on the access road as she turns into a gas station.

"Hit the brake, Maria!" Yvette screams.

"Mis Dios, I can't reach it!" Maria reaches first with her foot and then with her hands. The van crashes into a convenience store and Yvette realizes their fate now rests with God as she issues her silent prayer.

Please let us live.

She falls forward into the bloody front seat as the airbags hiss to life. Yvette's throat hurts from the loud screams ripping through her mouth.

Chapter Thirty-One: Goodbye

Yvette sits beside Casey and Tommy in the waiting room of University Hospital across from Maria and Deja. The five of them were seen by a doctor hours ago and given warm blankets to wrap around their still-wet clothes. Yvette has been to see Devin and Matt, who are recovering down the hall, Devin from a broken collarbone and Matt from a gunshot wound to his shoulder. Heidi and Gloria have come to see them and have taken Frodo Baggins and the two cats and offered to take Casey and Tommy, but they refused to go. Maria and Deja cling to one another. Stevie is in surgery. Apparently the hard back edition of *Harry Potter and the Deathly Hallows* slowed down the bullet's entry into his body, causing less damage to his internal organs. The doctor who came to give an update an hour ago seemed hopeful.

Please God.

Fatima is undergoing a psych evaluation on the third floor, and Mona is in critical condition in ICU just across the hall from them. Yvette worries Fatima will be deported and Mona will die. Her stomach is churning as she waits to hear news from Mona's doctor.

"You're sure he's dead?" Tommy asks again. "The police confirmed it, right?"

"Yes. Ahmed Jaffar is dead."

Casey shudders, and Yvette wraps her arm more tightly around her daughter.

"I want to see his dead body," Tommy says. "I want to know for sure he's dead."

"Quit talking about it, Tommy," Casey says. "Look at Deja."

"I'm okay." Deja wipes her eyes with the back of her hand. "Or I will be, anyway. It's Stevie I'm worried about."

"What a hard life that little boy has had." Maria blows her nose and clears her throat. "My poor, sweet boy."

Yvette wants to say something to Maria, but no words seem good enough. Her mind is consumed by fear and worry, and she wishes she could vomit to relieve her queasy stomach, made sick by her own gratitude that her immediate family members are safe. She's glad it was Stevie and Mona and not one of her own, and this makes her despise herself.

I am happy my family's alive.

Mona's doctor enters the waiting area and crosses over to Yvette. "She doesn't have much time. You might want to come and say your goodbyes."

"Oh my God."

Yvette and the kids stand up and follow the doctor across the hall through the ICU to Mona's bed where she lies pale and rasping for air, a light blue curtain the only divider between her and patients on either side of her. When Yvette touches her hand, Mona opens her eyes.

She's a ghost. Was always a ghost.

Mona searches their faces. "Fatima?"

"She's with a doctor."

In a scratchy, tired voice, she says, "Don't let them deport her, Yvette. Please make sure of that."

"I promise." Yvette can no longer hold back the sobs as they overtake her and cause her to shudder. She backs into the edge of the curtain and catches a glimpse of the heavy-set man in the adjacent bed. His eyes flick open, look at her blankly as though his soul has already left him, and fall closed. Yvette pulls the curtain around her and turns back to Mona.

Casey moves closer to the bed. "I know who you are."

Mona's beady eyes widen with fear, as though Casey is the angel of death come to take her away.

Yvette hasn't spoken to Casey about this, so she can only guess that her daughter figured it out on her own.

"Thank you." Casey takes Mona's frail white hand in her own shaking bronze one. "You saved my life. Twice." Tears stream down Casey's cheeks. "I will always love you for that."

Such a good girl.

Mona's face twists and curls, and her lips tremble as she nods her head. When she can, she says, "Thank you, Casey. I love you, too. Though, to me, you are my Anna."

"I like that name," Casey says.

Yvette can finally break through the invisible wall Mona has had around her, like quills on a porcupine all released and gone. She strokes Mona's wild red hair and caresses her pale cheek. "Thank you, Mona. Thank you for saving my family. I promise to watch over Fatima and the cats. I promise, okay? I won't let you down. We'll help her rebuild the shelter. I'll make sure it's up and running again, and my family will continue to help others as you have. I promise, Mona. Okay?"

"Don't let them deport her."

"After all she's done for so many American victims, they wouldn't. I'll see to it. I promise."

Mona struggles to speak. "Can you bring her to me? Where is she?"

Yvette turns. The doctor has moved to the next bed, not the soulless heavy man to their left, but a teenager with half his face scraped off. Yvette pulls the curtain aside. "Doctor? Is there time to bring Fatima? She's Mona's dearest friend. Her partner."

"Is she the patient undergoing the psych evaluation?"

"Yes."

"Then I'm afraid there's no time. The evaluation will take at least an hour."

The old Yvette would have accepted the doctor's reply, but after climbing fences in the dark of night, dressing up as clowns to go into hiding, being smoked out of a shelter, and enduring the most frightening ride of her life, Yvette refuses to back down. "Surely we can interrupt the evaluation for two loved ones to say goodbye."

The doctor furls his brow. "I'm not sure what room she's in, or who's conducting the evaluation."

Yvette's lips press into a straight line. She puts her hands on her hips. "I bet the nurses can tell you where Fatima is. Please, doctor."

"This may not be good for the psych patient."

Yvette speaks in a firm voice. "Fatima has a lifetime to recover and has been through worse. Mona needs this, doctor. I insist."

"I have another patient waiting. I'm sorry I can't help you more." He moves past her to the next bed, leaving Yvette with her mouth agape. Apparently, growing a backbone doesn't necessarily mean getting your way. She slumps her shoulders as sobs choke her, returning to Mona's side a failure.

Mona reaches out for Casey's hand, and more tears slip from her eyes at the touch. "Casey, I'm thankful you ended up with your mother and father and grateful you've had a happy life. I wish it could have been me, but since it wasn't meant to be, I'm glad it was with Yvette and Devin and Matt and Tommy."

"I wish I could have met you sooner," Casey says, frowning as tears slip down her cheeks.

Mona's lips twitch up into a smile as she fights to breathe. "Me, too. Me, too."

Casey lays the back of Mona's hand against her cheek, where her tears sink into Mona's dry, trembling hand. "Please don't go. I want more time to get to know you."

"I'm not leaving you, dearest darling," Mona rasps. "I'll be in your heart forever. I will always be a part of you, okay? Do you understand?"

Casey nods.

Yvette is transported to her own mother's death, and a longing stirs deep within her. She's overcome with sobs as she squeezes Casey's other hand.

Yvette looks at Tommy's sad face, just on the verge of tears, his jaw clenched and brows bent. Casey sobs openly, but Tommy is at that age where he thinks he's not supposed to cry. "Can you two wait here with Mona while I go look for Fatima? Do you think you can handle that?" She's afraid to leave them. Mona could die before she returns, and her children have never witnessed death. It would be too much. But if there's a chance she can make it back with Fatima, well, she has to try. And she doesn't want to leave Mona all alone to die.

The kids nod. Yvette can see they're frightened. "Would you rather come with me?"

"No, it's okay," Casey says bravely.

Yvette kisses Casey's hair, then Tommy's, and hastens from the bedside, through the ICU, and to the hallway and the nurses' station. The two nurses behind the desk don't look up at her, and she stands there, uncertain. One woman sits at a computer screen with the tip of her tongue pressed through lip-sheathed teeth. The other stands behind the seated one with her back to Yvette looking over papers on a clipboard. Mona's life hangs in the balance.

"Excuse me," Yvette says softly. When neither reacts, she says loudly, "Excuse me. I need to find a patient. Her lifelong partner is dying."

Both women look at her.

The one with the clipboard asks, "The patient's name?"

"Fatima. I don't know her last name. She's undergoing a psych evaluation."

The one at the computer says, "I need a last name."

"I don't have one." *Think, Yvette.* "Can you tell me where the psych ward is?"

The one with the clipboard takes a few steps around the desk so that she is standing beside Yvette. "Take that elevator up to the third floor. Make a left and keep going. Follow the signs and you'll find it. I'm sorry we couldn't help you."

.

Many more minutes pass with Casey holding Mona's hand. Then the door opens and Fatima is brought into the room in a wheel chair by a nurse. "Mona!"

Yvette backs away to make room.

"Come here, my dear," Mona says. "I want to see your beautiful face."

"You saved my life. I wish I could save yours. What will I do without you?"

"Thank you for bringing me years of happiness when I didn't think it possible. Our work together has been so satisfying. You keep it going, okay?"

"Without you?" Fatima is sobbing as she strokes Mona's hair.

"Yvette will help you, right Yvette?"

"I promise," she says in between sobs.

Mona erupts into a fit of coughing.

The nurse says, "Fatima, we need to get you back to the doctor."

"Goodbye, my dear," Mona manages to say. "You've been everything to me."

"No. Don't go. Stay with me, Mona. You're all I have left."

"I'm not leaving you, my love. I'm part of you. And you have Casey, who is part of me."

Fatima turns to Casey and a glimmer of hope enters her eyes.

"I'm so sorry, Fatima," Yvette says. She leans down and squeezes her hand as the nurse wheels her away.

Mona's nurse steps forward and says, "I need a few minutes alone with the patient."

But when Yvette looks back at Mona, she can see for herself that Mona has already gone.

No.

Yvette drops to her knees and lays her head on Mona's fragile body, its defenses finally withdrawn with complete abandon.

Tommy and Casey throw their arms around Yvette and the three of them weep together over Mona's lifeless body. Yvette weeps for Casey's loss, for Mona's hard life, for Fatima's grief, and for her own mother and father and the years she's lived without them. She weeps for all human pain and suffering, but also for hope and peace, and determines more than ever to live more purposefully and thoughtfully and to be grateful for what she has. She clutches her children to her and wipes her face with each shoulder. Then she climbs to her feet and ushers her children from the room.

Chapter Thirty-Two: Mystery Boxes

Yvette tucks in the card with the right address and seals the UPS box with packing tape. Then she adds it to the stack in her living room. Four loved ones of the Rodriguez family will be notified tomorrow of Deja, Stevie, and Maria's new location. Stevie was released from the hospital a week ago. Everyone credits J.K. Rowling.

But I thank God.

"Hey, mom. What do you think of this one?" Casey holds up her most recent drawing of Babs and Boots, which she has colored with map pencils.

"That's so good, sweetie pie! Fatima's gonna love it!"

"Can I take it over to her now?"

"If Tommy or Matt goes with you. Why don't y'all take Mr. Baggins for a walk? He misses the cats, don't you boy?" Yvette laughs. She never would have believed Frodo Baggins would grow fond of Babs and Boots. "Make sure to talk to the new kids, too. They like Frodo."

Fatima is living with the cats in the house she and Mona rented once before, the one that shares Yvette's back fence. With help from the shelter, Yvette and Devin bought the house and use it as another location for victims of abuse until the sunken shelter is restored. Now that school is out for the summer and Devin and Matt have fully healed, all five of them have been spending time with other volunteers beneath the Japanese Tea Gardens bringing the Sunken Shelter back to life.

Just as I promised.

The library has been Yvette's special project. She was able to recover many of the books taken out that horrible night. She was also able to salvage some left behind. In addition, she has managed to find colleagues and students through her online teaching to donate books for readers of all ages. When the shelter reopens, Yvette will host a private dedication ceremony during which the library will be named the Mona Smith Memorial Library.

She and I are both free from our cages.

Yvette has come to realize that if she was ever in a cage, it had been self-imposed. The purpose she longed to seek has always been inside of her, not outside, not far away where only pilgrims attained and understood it. She had only to create it and live it, fully aware and grateful.

The doorbell rings, and it is UPS come to pick up Yvette's mystery boxes. Devin is in the front watering the live oak, which will make it after all. Yvette signs for the order and helps carry the boxes to the truck and then joins Devin by the tree. All three kids explode through the front door with Mr. Baggins in the lead.

"We're going to Fatima's now," Tommy says. "Be right back."

Yvette and Devin wave.

Once the kids turn the corner and are out of sight, Yvette says slyly, "We might have time for a quickie."

Devin looks at her with a twinkle in his eyes. "Let's go." Before he turns off the hose, he teases Yvette with a light spray.

Ohhh, cold! Delightfully cold!

She runs to the door, giggling, the cold water exhilarating "You better watch it!"

"Believe me, I'm watching it, and I like what I see." He follows her into the house.

This is really happening. Thank you, God.

THE END

Eva Pohler is a *USA Today* bestselling author of over twenty novels for teens and adults.

To learn more about Eva and her books, please visit her website at http://www.evapohler.com.

Books by Eva Pohler

The Gatekeeper's Sons (#1)

The Gatekeeper's Challenge (#2)

The Gatekeeper's Daughter (#3)

The Gatekeeper's House (#4)

The Gatekeeper's Secret (#5)

The Gatekeeper's Promise (#6)

The Gatekeeper's Bride (#0)

Hypnos: A Gatekeeper's Spin-Off Series (#1)

Hunting Prometheus: A Gatekeeper's Spin-Off Series (#2)

Storming Olympus: A Gatekeeper's Spin-Off Series: (#3)

Charon's Quest: A Gatekeeper's Novel

Vampire Addiction: The Vampires of Athens Series (#1)

Vampire Affliction: The Vampires of Athens Series (#2)

Vampire Ascension: The Vampires of Athens Series (#3)

The Purgatorium: The Purgatorium (#1)

Gray's Domain: The Purgatorium (#2)

The Calibans: The Purgatorium (#3)

The Mystery Box: A Soccer Mom's Nightmare

The Mystery Tomb: An Archaeologist's Nightmare

The Mystery Man: A College Student's Nightmare

The Mystery House: San Antonio

The Mystery House 2: Tulsa

CPSIA information can be obtained
at www.ICGtesting.com
Printed in the USA
FSHW022051221218
54647FS